# PANDORA'S ARK

*Book 4 of the Vatican Knights Series*

By
Rick Jones

# Table of Contents

# PROLOGUE

*Jerusalem, 956 B.C.*

At the precise moment of dawn when Jerusalem became capped with a blood-red sky, the old priest stood along the edge of the parapet that surrounded the city and measured the vast numbers of Shishak's army that stretched endlessly across the desert landscape.

Days earlier, runners brought forth news that Shishak's ranks had taken the city of Judah in the north and planned to march on Jerusalem for treasures of gold and coin to proffer to their false gods.

To the Hebrews, he was known as Shishak. To the Egyptians, Sheshong I, the warrior king of Egypt's 22$^{nd}$ Dynasty, and had no boundaries when it came to war. With a league of 1200 chariots and 60,000 horsemen made up of Libyans, Sukkites and Cushites packed so close together, not a foot of land could be seen between them.

As the old man stood there in examination a warm breeze began to stir, causing his triangular-shaped beard to flag over his shoulder as an undeniable sadness filled him with a horrible reality. Even with the heat of the desert sun as an ally and towering walls to stop an approach, they were not enough to counter the pharaoh's army.

Jerusalem was about to fall.

High within the sentry towers horns blared in warning, a harsh and caustic sound that galvanized the masses to frenzy. The wealthy instinctively grabbed as many coins as they could, while those in lower castes took arms to help bolster troops along the walls. Those who saw the futility of challenging Shishak's ranks, however, took flight through the southern gates where they were met by the Sukkites, who cut them down with the savageness of intoxicated hunters.

With the priest's face bearing the weight and looseness of a rubber mask, as his eyes watched the bone-cutting slaughter by the wielding swords of Shishak's army, he began to regard the treasures within the Holy Temple. Physically challenged by age and infirmity within the joints of his limbs, Abraham took to the ladder with the slowness of a bad dream and began to descend the rungs, asking the Lord in silent prayer to give him enough time to save the greatest of His gifts from Shishak's authority.

Getting a foothold on Jerusalem's soil with tiny plumes of dust taking flight from the impact of his sandals touching down, the priest fought his way through panicking masses to get to the Holy Temple.

The ornate columns, grand doorways, and golden dome of the temple appeared like something unattainable sitting at the very edge of an endless road, the temple always too distant no matter how hard the old man tried to close the gap between them, his glacial strides caused by his constant struggle of wading through hordes of people who ran the streets with abandon.

When he finally reached the gateway, he allowed his eyes to gaze upon the horizon where he noted the colorful preface of a new day, the moment of dawn when the warmth of the rose-colored light began to alight upon his face. And for as long as he could the priest relished the moment, knowing that this was going to be the last sunrise he would ever see again.

**With detailed examination** Shishak studied the city of Jerusalem from a distant rise with eyes so dark they seemed without pupils. Yet as cruel as they appeared, they also possessed great intelligence and the weight of supreme confidence.

To the Jews, he was known as Shishak. To the Egyptians, Sheshong I, the warrior king of Egypt's 22$^{nd}$ Dynasty who knew no boundaries when it came to the atrocities of war.

Mounted on a white steed that possessed a mane as blond as corn silk, Shishak sat as still as a Grecian statue overlooking his troops. He was tall and lean, with skin the color of tanned leather. His head was shaved, his physique strong, with a firm jawline that was framed by rawboned features. In totality, with every cord and sinew of muscle showcased beneath an ornamental collar of jeweled gold, Shishak looked his part as the 'Warrior King.'

Beside him was Darius, his most celebrated lieutenant, whose skin was so dark that it resembled the color and sheen of eggplant. The wide breadth of his shoulders, the large expanse of chest, and the thickness of his arms had all been borne from years of wielding a weighted sword and shield.

For the moment, the lieutenant was having a problem maintaining control of his horse, the mare whinnying, then rearing, its front legs pawing the open air before settling under Darius's control with a pull of his reins.

"My king," he said, gaining control, "the sky. The color of blood is never a good omen. Even my steed senses ill forebodings."

"Your steed," he told Darius, before giving him a sidelong glance, "does not bear the foresight of an oracle. The dark omen you see is an omen issued from your own heart." He turned back to view Jerusalem with passive repose. "Whereas you see menace," he said evenly, "I see a sign from Ra that the blood of our enemies will cover the ground and become one with the sky." He nodded as if to confirm his thoughts. "Like those in Judah," he added, "their blood will serve as a testament of our victory rather than the dark prophecy you see it to be. Today the color red is a good color. And before the day is through, Darius, the hooves of my stallion will leave imprints in the sand that will be thick with the blood of our enemies."

Shishak prodded his horse forward and surveyed his army. The sheer number alone was incomprehensible. The terrain was laden with soldiers as far as his eyes could see.

Pleased, he returned to Darius's side. "Alert the battalions," he told him. "And prepare them for victory."

"Aye, my King." Darius then signaled to his field commands to prepare for battle by raising his sword high, its blade silhouetted against the blood-red sky, then rode along the front-line shouting rants to fuel the blood lust of 60,000 men.

When Darius returned to his position beside the pharaoh, he sheathed his sword. Around them Shishak's warriors thrust their pikes and swords in the air, chanting victory in the name of Ra.

"They're at your command, my Lord."

Shishak slid his sword from his jeweled scabbard and raised it high, the cries of his army escalating, the anticipation of battle now at fever pitch. He then turned to Darius with his eyes burning with the eagerness to fight and thrust and kill. He would not sit back as a spectator perched from afar but engage in a bloodletting until the air smelled ripe with copper. "I want all the riches within the Holy

Temple," he told him. "Everything is to be proffered to the Temple of Ra, as an homage to our victories."

"Aye, my King."

"But we have to get there before the priests do," he added.

"The Sukkites are cutting a path through the city from the north as we speak, my King."

Shishak raised the point of his sword to its highest point. "Then advance the others," he ordered. "I want the *one* thing they covet most."

"Our sources say that the holiest of treasures sits in the Chamber's center surrounded by mounds of gold."

"Then let us claim what rightfully belongs to Ra," he said. And with that, he pointed his sword in the direction of Jerusalem, which incited cries from his forces, and watched his army charge the city walls with the intent to leave no one left alive.


**In Jerusalem, he** is called Abraham, a high-ranking priest who is coveted by the masses and wise beyond his years. Yet in his seventy-plus years of living, he had grown so aged and weary that his flesh looked like the tallow of melted wax, giving off the impression that he was as ancient as the sands that surrounded the city. Though driven by conviction despite the burning sensation in his lungs and growing heaviness in his legs, Abraham hurried along darkened corridors toward the Sacred Vault with markedly forced strides.

Before he reached the Chamber door, he came upon three young men adorning the cowled robes of priests. They were not quite men of stature, but boys on the cusp of growing their first beards that would eventually identify their positions within the sacred hierarchy.

The moment they saw Abraham, a priest held his hand out for the old man to grab in purchase to better steady him. With lungs wheezing and his face taking on the pallor as pale as the underbelly of a fish, Abraham was eased against a wall to calm him.

"You must find others," he told the priests between hitches of breath. "When you do . . . then send them to the Sacred Chamber . . . where I will meet them."

"Is it Shishak?" a priest asked. "Is he moving on Jerusalem?"

The old man offered a hasty nod, then: "Hurry! We haven't much time!"

"What about you?"

Abraham waved his hand in dismissal. "I'll be fine," he said. "Go!"

Without further questioning the priests moved with urgency, leaving Abraham to gather enough strength to press on. With the alacrity of an aged man in faltering condition, he made his way through the hallways on legs that were going boneless. But his priestly convictions to save the Lord's treasure drove him forward by reserve alone.

As the old man descended the stairway the atmosphere became sepulchral and dead, the air unmoving. On neighboring walls, his shadow danced with macabre twists as flames from the heads of wall torches lapped the air. And in servitude to his Lord, he begged for added strength, his words no longer coming in whispers.

"Please, God! Give me the power to serve You in this time of need. Give me the power to see this through."

As the last word left his lips, Abraham reached the landing of the Chamber's floor.

Not less than twenty meters away stood the bullet-shaped archway that led to the Sacred Vault.

After opening the thick wooden doors that were held together by black steel bands and rivets, the sight of the treasure never failing to steal away the old man's breath.

Along the walls, several torches burned. The light of their flames danced in play over every piece of gold, casting a spectacular aura even from the smallest coin.

The Chamber was perfectly circular with pyramidal mounds of gold and rubies and sapphires lying everywhere, some piles as high as a man is tall. Against the wall opposite the Chamber doors sat the Gold Shields of Solomon, nearly three hundred in total, each glittering spangles of gold as the light of the nearby torches reflected off their surfaces. But in the center of the Chamber was the most coveted item of all, something that carried brightness beyond what gold alone should have given it. Casting a perfect nimbus in ethereal shades of yellow and white, sat the Ark of the Covenant.

The high priest moved cautiously within its spectacular golden glow—into a light that appeared to be alive—and with his hands held out so that his palms faced ceiling-ward, he began to pray.

The Ark was brilliantly crafted, having been made from the wood of the acacia tree and covered with the purest gold. It was a cubit-and-a-half broad, a cubit-and-a-half high, and two cubits long with the upper lid, the mercy seat, surrounded by a rim of gold. On each of the two sides were two gold rings where two wooden poles are placed, so that the Ark could be carried. Situated on top of the Ark were two cherubim figures that faced each other with the tips of their outspread wings touching the others, forming what was considered to be the throne of God while the Ark itself was judged to be His footstool.

With Shishak getting closer, Abraham prayed for divine guidance, his answer coming in the form of eight men wearing hooded robes with knotted ropes that cinched their waistlines.

"The poles," said Abraham, pointing to the long dowels covered with the decorative sheathing of gold. "We haven't much time!"

Once the poles were inserted through the golden loops and fixed, Abraham grabbed one of the torches and beckoned the priests to follow.

Even with eight men The Ark of the Covenant was quite heavy as each man labored to carry it across the Chamber floor.

With Abraham leading the way, the light of his torch illuminated an opening against the far wall. The access, however, was lost in shadows so deep that the light of his torch barely penetrated the darkness until he was right upon it.

"This way," he said.

The Covenant was led down a corridor, the surrounding walls rough and poorly bored, the surface which they walked upon often descending, then ascending, like the caps of rolling hills, a difficult terrain to manage with such a burdensome weight to transport. The ceiling was also uneven, often rising and lowering in spaces that barely gave the Ark enough clearance. But at the corridor's end lay a magnificent chamber, a second chamber, one that was capped by a hand-smoothed dome that transitioned downward into walls that were without blemish. In the center of the room lay an elevated block of stone on which to rest the Ark upon.

After the priests settled the Ark upon the platform, Abraham went along the chamber walls lighting one torch after the other, the light reaching the Ark from all sides. As it did the Ark seemed to come alive with something tangible and intangible at the same time, a spiritual force of unbridled warmth that prompted the priests to take to a bended knee.

Abraham, however, stayed on his feet and moved with urgency.

Next to the last torch was a circular recess—a hole—that was large enough for a man to reach deep inside to his shoulder. Reaching inside, Abraham grabbed a steel ring and turned it counterclockwise. And then the earth came alive. There was a grinding noise as mammoth stones rubbed against each other, the ground beneath them trembling, shaking, the entire chamber floor threatening to open into a chasm.

While the priests continued to kneel by the Ark, dust cascaded from the ceiling, showering them until their cloaks became the color of sand. And then with a final shudder, the entrance collapsed with tons of falling rock blocking the way, the corridor imploding as thick, cloying dust raced into the chamber in a plume.

And then with a final shudder the shaking stopped, the chamber now a dust-laden cavern with no way in or out. A horrible silence fell over them.

One of the priests got to his feet, a fledging. The look on his face was incredulous with the realization that the fate of his life had been determined by the twist of an old man's hand. "But why?" he asked him.

The old man placed the torch within its holder and then ventured closer to the priests who were now standing. "Please forgive me," he said. "I couldn't allow Shishak the right to bear the Ark."

"But there are the Shields of Solomon and the other treasures?"

"This is the *only* treasure," he countered.

"And what about our lives?" asked another. "You didn't even grant us the opportunity to save ourselves."

"I couldn't afford to," said Abraham. His tone was truly sorrowful, but not repentant. "If Shishak got hold of any of you, then he would have stripped the flesh from your bones to obtain the whereabouts of the Ark."

The old priest closed his eyes with his palms held ceilingward, and then he turned toward the Ark of the Covenant. "This is bigger than all of us," he told them. "Is it not better to die in the presence of God than by the hands of the Pharaoh Shishak?"

The other priests bowed their heads, one by one, with each man coming to terms that the elder priest was right. Dying in the presence of God was Glory compared to the tortuous blades of Shishak.

In unison, the Keepers of the Ark began to pray.

**Jerusalem had fallen**, the bodies of its citizens lying in waste in city streets, their blood running and becoming one with the blood-red sky as Shishak ordained. In the end, it was not an omen of ill fate as thought by Darius, but an oracle of glory sent by Ra. This Shishak was sure of.

As the Egyptian king led his league of soldiers toward the Temple, the color of the morning sky was no longer red, but blue, with towering pillars of black smoke reaching skyward toward the emerging new-day sun. Jerusalem was burning.

The Temple Mount was exquisite, even by Shishak's standards who ultimately respected Egyptian architecture. The Temple itself was a massive complex of stone arches and monumental columns. The towering walkways and wide staircases that took worshippers to grand hallways that seemed endless mesmerized Shishak to the point where he felt somewhat remorseful in defeating a city so rich in the complexity of its structure and beauty. At one point he even considered imbibing this architectural culture into his. But then he quickly dismissed the notion, sensing that this culture would only tend to belittle Egyptian sophistication.

Once at the Holy Temple, Shishak remained upon his horse for a long moment before getting off his steed, placed his hands against the door as if to learn the secrets within through osmosis, then gestured for his troops to knock it down.

It took nearly an hour, but the door was destroyed, the wood lying in splintered pieces, the opening giving way to a dark passageway that led to the depths beneath the Temple Mount.

With his torch ablaze, Darius moved toward the darkness with his light piercing little of the descending stairway. "The Chamber lies deep," he told Shishak. "We'll need many to carry the treasures, especially the Ark."

"The Ark is first and foremost," he said. "Make sure great caution is taken."

"Aye."

They descended slowly with several torches lighting the way, the stairs well maintained. Once at the bottom they noticed the dust-laden floor, which seemed odd when the rest of the complex was immaculate, especially for a place of great worship. As they entered the Chamber they were awed by the vastness of wealth, which was far more considerable than they originally thought. Lined against the walls were the Shields of Solomon, a pillager's dream. And throughout lay conical-shaped mounds of gold coins as well as gems of every size, of every color and shape. Yet they did not appear opulent or bright. The color of gold was instead muted, the shine hindered by heavy dust that continued to eddy in the air.

Shishak moved to the center of the room. The space was empty. "Where is the Ark, Darius? You said it would be in the room's center."

Darius made his way beside him. "They moved it," he said. "There isn't an open spot within this whole Chamber, except for this area."

"If that was so," said Shishak, "then there would be evidence that something was recently moved, yet the floor remains heavy with dust without a hint that something was ever here at all." Shishak took a few steps to his left and lifted a golden pot of manna. The ground beneath it was clear of dust, the evidence that the pot was there while dust gathered around its base prominent, his point made. He tossed the pot aside. "It was never here," he finally said. "Grab everything and make it ready for transport. These treasures should be residing in a temple of a true god."

"Aye."

"And, Darius?"

"Aye."

"If one soldier steals a single coin, I want you to execute him on the spot and make an example of him to the others. And especially watch the Sukkites. Mercenaries seem to have a weakness for profit that is not their own."

"Aye."

As the treasures were being gathered, Shishak wondered what happened to the Ark, never realizing that it was less than one hundred meters from where he stood.

# CHAPTER ONE

*Near the Temple Mount, Jerusalem, Present Day*

Adham al-Ghazi had been searching for the Ark of the Covenant for several years, reading every written piece of work regarding its whereabouts and exploring the true possibility of its existence. He had gone to the Sanctuary Chapel in Saint Mary of Zion's Church in Axum, Ethiopia, only to find the Ark to be a duplicate. He also traveled to Elephantine, Egypt, as well as to other locations throughout the Arab world only to uncover replicas ranging from the poorly fabricated to adequate imitations.

The last remaining location to excavate lay beneath the Temple Mount in Jerusalem, which had been declared by Israeli and Arab factions as *their* sovereign territory. But in reality, it remained a region in limbo since the United States refused to acknowledge the land as strictly Israel's, even though it remained under their control.

For over a year al-Ghazi had quietly worked his way beneath Jerusalem by stitch-boring a lengthy tunnel. And though the process was quiet, it was still vulnerable to detection. With acquired and detailed notes and possible GPS coordinates acquired from Iranian intelligence, he spent many long nights calculating within certainty the Chamber's precise location.

Once they had drilled to within one hundred yards of the location, and in fear of alerting the Israelis by the vibrations meted out by the drills, they labored tediously with pickaxes and shovels from that point on, the momentum becoming glacially slow.

However, al-Ghazi's patience would soon prove to be fruitful.

Day after day and night after night the pickaxes swung. And al-Ghazi watched as his hands never touched an instrument of labor. After all, he was a high-ranking lieutenant with al-Qaeda.

He had been involved with planning several attacks against Israeli and American objectives, as well as anyone associated with either faction. Prior to Bin Laden's assassination in Pakistan, he had been asked by the former leader to plan out and head the excavation for the Ark. For what reason he didn't know, nor did he dare ask questions.

The man was tall and lean, wearing clothes that were always immaculately clean and pressed, even within the tunnels where dirt seemed to constantly flow through the air, but somehow repelled by the man who never seemed to get dirty or sweat. His face was thin, his beard meticulously shaped, and his eyes appeared dark and moody and filled with a quiet intensity. However, he was patient to the core, which was a deadly concoction when mixed with a black desire to kill for a cause.

Standing over a table bearing maps and compasses, the air around him cloyingly thick and hot, the chamber beneath the ground in which he stood lit only by a string of bulbs that offered feeble lighting at best, he seemed unaffected as he studied the details of the mapped progress. Lines had been drawn in red, noting that they were nearing the Temple Mount. With the progress using pickaxes, he considered at best another two to three months if they worked around the clock.

The man clenched his jaw, the muscles working. It was the only sign of his impatience, thus far.

A worker, skinny and dirty with the grime of earth, entered the chamber with a pickaxe in hand, his breathing labored. From his point of view, al-Ghazi seemed more like a shadow in the dim light. "Commander, we broke through."

Al-Ghazi raised a brow in skepticism. "Impossible," he said. "We have thirty meters to go."

The man nodded. "We found *a* chamber."

Al-Ghazi ran a finger over the charts and numbers. There was no way his configuration was incorrect. If there was an adjoining chamber, then it was not within the schematics provided.

"Have you looked inside?" he finally asked.

The laborer nodded. "The light would only penetrate so deep. But the area appears large." The man bowed his head in homage to al-Ghazi. "We thought it would be better if you entered first since the glory of the discovery is yours."

When al-Ghazi passed the man, he patted him upon the shoulder. "You considered well, my friend."

The tunnel leading to the opening in the wall was well bored, the walls rough, but enough space to move freely about without bending at the waist. Once at the passageway, the other laborers gave him a wide berth.

A laborer then handed him a heavy-duty flashlight that had the advertised capacity of lighting an area with the same power as 10,000 candles. Yet it was incapable of penetrating deep into the cavern.

"It's a hollow chamber," he said. "But it's not *the* Chamber."

With guarded care, al-Ghazi entered the room with his flashlight scoping the area and the immediate ground in front of him.

Pressing on he noted a glint of light—a spangle of gold—from the corner of his eye before it winked out and disappeared. Adjusting the flashlight to the source of the glitter it cast upon something not quite decipherable in the darkness. Whatever it was lay just beyond the light's fringe, but a form, nonetheless.

As he moved closer the flashlight began to give the artifact shape, contour, and clarity. And in an instant, he knew he had finally found the true Ark of the Covenant.

He had read all the ancient tablets, texts, and scrolls regarding the whereabouts of the Ark, as well as the Bible and Quran only to find the locations documented by witnesses who had most likely seen replicas and duplicates. But never was there any mention of a room connected to the main chamber beneath the Temple Mount. And since the room did not exist by historical reference, al-Ghazi concluded that the true Ark was never meant to be found. By the luck of Allah, he found it by serendipity.

The Arab moved closer, the Ark dulled by years of collecting dust, but pure. With his flashlight he moved its beam over the Ark and along its base, noting the skeletal remains of the Ark's Keepers. For 3000 years the cloth of their robes degenerated, leaving nothing but swatches of fabric awkwardly entwined around the bone. And for 3000 years their secret was safe.

*Until now*, he thought.

Lifting a hand to the Ark, he let his fingers graze softly over the wings of the cherubim figures and smiled. To touch the Ark was certain death, which was chronicled in just about every written piece of document in existence. But here he was, a hand gliding over the actual Ark of the Covenant sensing no heat, no cold, nor a static charge of electricity. It was simply gold and nothing more than a vintage scarecrow that kept the masses in line and their blind faith intact. Or so he believed. Nevertheless, such a treasure would harbor more than just faith and hope. It would soon hold death and darkness.

"Remove the cap," he ordered.

Four men that looked as if they had mined for days without bathing, their bodies shining with sweat and grime, carefully pushed the cap to one side, then lifted it and gingerly placed the lid on the ground between the skeletal remains of two Keepers.

Inside the Ark lay more treasures.

Lying untouched for three millennia were four items: a gold pot filled with the dust of something having perished over time; the staff belonging to Aaron, the brother of Moses; and two stone tablets written in the language of Adam, the Ten Commandments.

Even though he was a non-believer, al-Ghazi seemed awed by the discovery in what appeared to be reverence.

With a great measure of prudence, al-Ghazi lifted one of the tablets, the writing well preserved, and traced his fingers over the engraved words.

"Written by the fingers of God," he commented softly to no one in particular. And then he returned the tablet to the Ark with the same care of laying a baby within its crib. "We'll take the tablets," he added. "But leave the staff and the golden pot as proof to the Israelis that the Ark has been discovered and that have it. And be careful transporting it!"

Bowing their heads in acknowledgment, the miners removed the original poles, which had become brittle and flaked when touched, and replaced them with metal rods.

Within the hour the Ark was removed from the chamber with the staff of Aaron and the golden pot left behind and loaded onto the back of a canvassed truck more than a mile beyond the Temple Mount.

As the truck carried away the item fully covered in cloth, al-Ghazi got on an untraceable satellite phone and dialed a number locked into its memory. Within three chimes al-Zawahiri answered, once a conduit to Bin Laden, who asked al-Ghazi if Allah smiled down upon him on this day.

Al-Ghazi was as giddy as a child who could hardly contain himself but forced the issue that he was a soldier and needed to act accordingly, which meant stoically. "By the graces of Allah, we have found the Ark," he said.

"But is it the true Ark?"

"No doubt," he returned. "It was right under the noses of the Israelis all the time in an uncharted chamber. By the will of Allah, it was meant to fall into our hands."

"Good job, Adham. The principals will be pleased now that our efforts have paid off and our patience soon to be rewarded."

"Just to let you know, my friend, we're returning to the base with the cargo."

Al-Zawahiri seemed pleased. "Then I'll notify the rest of our constituencies and inform them of your success," he said. "And continue with the next stage."

Al-Ghazi took in a breath of the hot desert air and relished it, like something intoxicating, then released it as a long and soothing sigh. Closing his eyes, he bid al-Zawahiri the blessings of Allah and terminated the call.

# CHAPTER TWO

*Jerusalem, Beneath the Temple Mount.*

Yitzhak Paled was the head of Mossad's Lohamah Psichlogit, which was the unit responsible for psychological warfare, propaganda, and deception operations within the Agency. Although a slight man who was thinly built, he was still lean and firm and without any mannerisms other than what he relayed to others: and that he was not to be challenged in any way.

Standing in the second chamber beneath the Temple Mount, several lights erected on poles and cables lit the area brilliantly. Surrounding the center platform where the staff of Aaron and the gold pot lay, were the nine Keepers of the Ark, their bones brown with the coffee-like stains of aged calcium.

Standing next to the platform, while others worked around him, Paled stood with a hand to his chin in deep thought.

There was no doubt in his mind that the Ark in question was the *true* Ark for the simple fact that neither he nor the Israeli government, knew of this chamber. Nor had it been recorded in any text.

In fact, the Ark of the Covenant had been beneath them all this time. The Keepers testament to that since the other arks throughout northern Africa had already been established as fakes, phonies, or duplicates.

How the Arabs intercepted it was beyond him. More so, Paled was livid that Mossad Intelligence was handed a direct message from the Arabs stating that they had custody of the Ark and that the proof lies at the Israeli's feet. He took it as a slap in the face, a one-up-on-you type of gesture on the part of the Arab world.

*But why would the Arab state go so far to secure the Ark in the manner that they did? How could they have possibly known its location?*

As the staff of Aaron lay on the platform, there was no doubt in Paled's mind that Carbon-14 testing on the rod and the bones would prove to be at least 3000 years old, if not older.

Once more he asked: *Why?*

Contemplating, Paled appeared lost, wondering what the Arabs had in mind. Obviously, they had taken the Ark for a specific purpose. But the reason eluded him.

*Could it have been for money?* he considered. *Or perhaps ransom to fund terrorist groups or activities?*

Of course, these were the logical ideas that immediately came to mind.

And there was another consideration. The Ark could be used to turn any situation into a hot-button issue between religious denominations who felt entitled to its possession, which would cause tempers to flare if they were so denied.

The Jews, the Catholics, the Muslims—they all had a rightful stake.

Paled continued to rub his chin while the bones of the Keepers were carefully gathered by Company men. No matter how careful the workers were, a femur or rib snapped due to the severity of their brittleness. And then in reverence, the staff of Aaron was taken and placed into a metal lockbox and sealed. It was, without a doubt, a truly magnificent treasure.

But the biggest treasure was the Ark and the tablets within.

"We're almost done," said Jacob, a minor player in the Lohamah Psichlogit.

Paled tried to make a logical determination for the theft before turning to Jacob with a questioning look. "Why take the Ark and leave behind the staff?"

Jacob shrugged. "For ransom?"

Paled shook his head. "It goes beyond that," he said. "I believe they have something else in mind."

Jacob took a step forward and noted the bare spots where the legs of the Ark sat on the platform, where the dust gathered around them for 3000 years. "Primary guesses?"

"Some," he answered. "But as a member of the Lohamah Psichlogit who sees things in a perspective where psychological warfare, propaganda, and operations of deception are a function, I believe they'll use the Ark as a weapon of some kind, psychological or otherwise." He took a step closer to the platform. "Tell me, Jacob . . . What do you see?"

Jacob hesitated, musing. "I see the Arabs using our own game against us," he said.

Paled nodded. "And should they play the game well enough . . ." he said, his words trailing off. *Then they could incite a war like no other . . .*

*. . . and destroy us all.*

# CHAPTER THREE

*Vatican City, Very Early Morning*

Pope Gregory XVII thought he had seen a fleeting shadow dart across the Papal Chamber from the corner of his eye.

The room was dark, the corners and recesses even darker with scant lighting from the moon coming in through the open doors that led to the balcony. A marginal breeze blew in from the west, causing the hemlines of the scalloped drapery to wave in poetic motion that was slow and balanced as if the entire moment was caught up in a dream. And though he could feel a cool and gentle breeze sweeping into the room and touch his flesh, his mind remained fevered and hot, perhaps the illness drawing the illusion that somebody else was in the room with him.

Nevertheless, the pontiff called out, his voice cracked and feeble: "Is somebody there?"

Silence.

Pope Gregory tossed the cover of the comforter back and sat up, swinging his legs over the edge until the soles of his feet touched down against marble flooring.

With the passing of Pope Pius XIII, Gregory had succeeded him, serving six months at the Papal Throne. Under his leadership conservatism reigned, pulling away from Pius's more liberal stance to bend to the will of the masses for reform in an ever-changing world. But Gregory believed that the people should bend to the will of God rather than God bending to the will of men. So, the pendulum began to swing back to a more conservative position, once again raising the ire within the Catholic citizenry.

Although he had drawn criticism from within the ranks, he was also lauded by those within the College as one not to back away from adversity, no matter how loud the voices may cry.

Getting to his feet, Pope Gregory's world shifted, the shadows elongating and coming alive, reaching out and then pulling back, the products of a sick mind. At first, he wobbled, took time to correct himself, then made his way toward the veranda with a buffeting wind blowing the hairs back from his scalp like the whipping mane of a horse.

A few hours ago, he was as robust as Atlas who carried the religious world upon his squared shoulders. But now he was amazingly weak with barely enough strength to lift a hand.

His stomach also burned like magma, hot and uncomfortable. And then his entire body became a tabernacle of pain as he hitched in his stride and tumbled toward a column by the veranda door, using it as a crutch, and looked out into the night.

Beneath the light of the gibbous moon with the obelisk and the Colonnade standing sentinel beneath its gaze, with nothing but cold, blue shadows stretching out across the bricks of the plaza below, Pope Gregory marveled at the beauty of the country he had come to reign.

As he stood there his pain intensified as if something serpentine wended its way through his guts the moment he started toward the edge of the veranda in a stumbling gait with a hand across his abdomen, and the other stretched out for the guardrail.

With breaths coming in short gasps and his lungs laboring to pull in enough oxygen to keep him conscious, Gregory continued to admire the land that his papacy brought him. For six months he ruled as best he could under the servitude of God. And for six months he believed that such servitude should have been rewarded with an exceptionally long time to rule the Papal Throne. Six months was not even a blink of time within the cosmic eye, he considered.

"I know you're there," he said, his breaths coming with far greater difficulty.

But there was neither answer nor moving shadows. Nor was there the sound of a pin dropping or the hint of a possible footfall.

"In the eyes of God, do you truly believe that He will condone what you are about to do?"

The slight rush of a breeze passed through his ears, a sweet melody to calm and soothe. And he closed his eyes, waiting.

"God will not favor you," he said. "No matter what you do as a member of the Church, He will only favor you in the end with the fiery lakes of Hell."

The pontiff stood at the edge of the veranda with a hand against the rail and a forearm across his stomach, and then he began to teeter back and forth threatening to spill over to the pavement below.

"With the fiery lakes of Hell," he whispered. And then his eyes flared the moment he felt a hand on his back and a push hard enough to send him over the edge. The old man began to pinwheel his arms while turning to face his executor, his feet losing purchase and going airborne as he slipped over the railing, the pavement hurling up at him at an impossible speed, the edge of the veranda dwindling and becoming smaller. The moon was spinning, its face becoming a sad memorial denoting the end of the old man's life.

And then he struck the bricks, hard, the impact sounding like a melon striking the pavement during a moment of dead silence.

Yet the pontiff survived with the smell of copper permeating the air and blood fanning out in all directions.

Coughing, with blood spraying out from broken lungs, with his eyes skyward, he thought he saw the shadow of someone staring down at him from the veranda. He was unmoving and seemed to be wearing vestments. And then he pulled away, gone, leaving as silently as he entered.

As the pontiff focused on the point of the veranda, as his life slowly leeched away from his body, his vision began to implode at the edges with his sight turning black, then purple, and then the subsequent flashes of sunburst light leading to Ethereal Illumination.

With a broken hand twisted by the impact, the pontiff raised it to the Glory of the Light only he could see, smiled, and allowed himself to pass.

*Boston, Massachusetts, The Archdiocese of Boston*

For the past six months Cardinal Bonasero Vessucci served the Diocese of Boston after his loss for the papal selection, having been criticized, then subsequently ostracized, for sitting in as lead counsel of a clandestine group of cardinal's known as the Society of Seven. They, along with Pope Pius, recognized the fact that times had become volatile and the Church, having diplomatic ties with ninety percent of the countries worldwide, had become a viable target. And to protect its sovereignty, its interest, and the welfare of its citizenry, Cardinal

Vessucci spearheaded a covert group of elite commandos known as the Vatican Knights.

Their missions were normally in hotspots around the world, using tactics and methods to achieve the means—techniques that were often brutal when there were no other options available. In the course of their duties people died, but many more lived, usually the innocent or those who could not protect themselves.

But Pope Gregory refused to see their necessity in a world growing cancerous every day and quickly disbanded the Knights. His subsequent move was to scatter the members of the Society of Seven to every corner of the globe with Vessucci ending up in the United States.

And though he loved the Church, he missed his soldiers just as much, knowing every day for the past six months that the Church had been left open and naked. *How many people lost their lives when they could have been saved?* he wondered. And he asked himself this question just before he recited his ritual prayers to start the day, wondering if the Knights had been forced to leave their calling.

Just as he was about to get into bed there was a knock on his door, a soft tapping.

"Just a moment."

When he opened the door, a bishop was standing there, his face grim.

"Yes, Bishop."

"I'm afraid I've received some rather terrible news that I must pass on to you."

The cardinal opened the door wider as a gesture to allow the bishop to enter, but the man remained standing at the threshold. "We've just received word that the pope has passed."

Vessucci's jaw dropped.

"It appears that he met with a horrible accident and fell off the balcony. He was pronounced dead prior to being sent to Gemelli."

Vessucci was genuinely stunned. The pontiff had only been in office for six months. More so, he was so physically fit that he was set to rule for at least two more decades, perhaps longer. "When?"

"About two hours ago," he said. "It's about to be announced to the world. But before it is," he handed Vessucci a piece of paper, "your presence is required at the Vatican."

Vessucci stared at the paper for a long moment, before lifting his hand to receive it. "Thank you," he whispered, then closed the door softly. Without looking at the paper he knew what it was: a request to band with the College of Cardinals and prepare for another Conclave. He didn't even look at the writing. He gingerly placed the paper on the nightstand and stared out into space.

He had come close to winning the seat six months ago, having a strong camp but not enough to defeat the two camps that joined together to trump his. This time around, however, his chance for the Papal Throne was well within his reach.

Slowly, he rose to his feet, gathered his wits, and began to pack his bags for Vatican City.

# CHAPTER FOUR

*Las Vegas, Nevada, Downtown Area*

Six months ago, when the Vatican Knights were disbanded, Kimball Hayden became a wayward son in a society he rejected long ago. From the onset as a young man trying to make a name for himself in the power halls of the White House, he became a political assassin leading a CIA wetwork team tagged by the brass as the "man without a conscience," since killing had become a polished skill possessed by few others on this planet.

For years he reveled in his ego, each killing becoming a building block to his monumental legend that grew every time he drew a blade across the throat of an insurgent or put a bullet in a man's brain. When it came to killing, there was no one more consistent or dependable than Kimball Hayden.

Until one day while on a mission in the Middle East where he had an epiphany after being forced to kill two shepherd boys who threatened to compromise his position. After burying them beneath the desert sand, he laid there the entire night staring up at the sky, at the sparkling pinprick lights that made up the constellations and wondered if there truly was a God.

On the following morning, as the sun rose, he made a conscious decision to abscond from American service and disappeared, the Pentagon believing he had been killed in action, and posthumously awarded him the accustomed accolades as an empty coffin was buried at Arlington as a symbol of the warrior's testament to duty.

But regardless of how courageously symbolic he was to others, should American forces ever discover that he was still alive, especially knowing the black secrets he possessed regarding past administrations, which included the sanctioned killing of a United States senator, then his accolades would have no meaning, and he would be targeted with extreme prejudice to ensure that all past misjudgments on the part of the political body would remain secret.

And this is why he never returned.

But then his life took another turn.

During the moment his coffin was being laid to rest in D.C., he was sitting in a small bar in Venice, Italy, watching the images on TV play out as American forces and their allies moved in on Saddam Hussein to free Kuwait. It was here that a cardinal of the Church took a seat in a booth opposite him without permission and offered him a chance at redemption by serving as a Vatican Knight.

When Kimball questioned him about this knighthood, Cardinal Bonasero Vessucci stated that only a man of true integrity who can hold loyalty above all else, except honor; a man who truly believes in the sovereignty of the Vatican and holds to protect its interests and the welfare of its citizenry; and a man who is truly repentant for past actions of a dark nature, is a man who could be made whole in the eyes of God.

Kimball had finally found his home within the auspices of the Church.

And for years he plied his very particular set of skills to save lives across the globe with a team of the world's best warriors, the Vatican Knights.

But the passing of Pope Pius gave rise to Pope Gregory, who in turn disbanded the group as an affront to God.

Not only was Kimball without a country, but he was now without a church. And there wasn't much call for a man with his skillset except for mercenary work, which he wanted nothing to do with. So, he returned to the states under a different name, someone who had a simple dream of working an honest job.

The man who used to be Kimball Hayden was now James Joseph Doetsch, better known as J.J. Doetsch. With a new identity to keep him under the radar, Kimball Hayden was now a porter picking up trash off casino floors. Since it was an honest job, then he was fine.

Over the months he maintained his incredible physique and exercised at every opportunity. He also practiced religiously with his knives, going through a set routine similar to Tai Chi. If nothing else, Kimball Hayden remained very deadly.

"Yo, J.J."

Kimball, pulling a trash bag from a barrel on the casino floor, his hands wrapped in latex gloves, stopped and looked at the floor manager who was beckoning him with a bird-like hand.

"Yeah, boss?"

"Come here. Got something I want to pass along."

Kimball moved beside him; the height difference amazing as the little man with the doughy face looked up at Kimball the same way a small child looks up at his father.

"Remember when I told you about the gig that my brothers-in-law was involved with? You know, the cage fighting thing?"

"Look, Louie—"

The smaller man raised his hands and began to pat the air. "Just hear me out," he said.

Kimball did, but his body language, the grim twist of his mouth and arms crossed defensively across his chest, told the man he wasn't going to be too receptive.

"Just hear me out," he repeated. "That's all I ask for, for chrissakes."

"I'm listening."

"You can get in a cage for five minutes—just five—and make yourself five grand tops." He then stood back to appraise Kimball; his arms held out as if to showcase the large man to others. "Look at you. You're a monster. Why in the hell are you wasting your time here for just over minimum when you can work the circuit for so much more?"

"And I suppose you'd get a percentage of my take?"

Louie smiled. "Of course. As your manager, how does fifteen percent sound?"

Kimball shook his head and turned away.

"All right then. How about ten?"

"I'm not hearing you, Louie."

The pudgy man moved beside him. "You're wasting your talents, J.J. You always said the only thing you ever wanted was an honest job. Well, here it is, sitting in our lap. It's legit; the circuit has top-notch billing and everything you could ever ask for. And the bottom line, J.J., is that I see six, maybe seven figures a year once you hit the top."

"Not interested."

"You'd rather pull trash for the rest of your life?"

"Just temporary duty, that's all."

"I don't get it. Why won't you fight?"

Kimball looked him squarely in the eyes. "If I'm going to fight, Louie, there has to be a cause behind it."

"Money ain't cause enough?"

"For me? No." He went back to emptying the cans, placing the bags in a rolling trash cart.

"Will you at least think about it?"

"Yeah. Sure. Whatever." he said. "I'll think about it along with other things."

Louie smiled; his emotions uplifted with slight hope. "That's great," he said, his smile blossoming. "That's great! You just tell me when."

*How about never?* Kimball returned the smile and kept his mouth shut.

"Got a gig coming up in two weeks," he added. "You just let me know, J.J. You just let me know. I hate to stand by and see a man like you waste your life away, that's all."

Kimball's smile slowly melted away.

Louie turned and began to walk away. And then, while calling out over his shoulder, he said, "Everyone has a purpose in life, J.J. So, I'm telling you that fighting is yours. I can see it in your eyes. You're a warrior. Think about it."

Kimball roughly tossed the trash in the bin and watched Louie disappear behind a bank of slot machines. He seemed to have prophetically hit the nail on the head. Was he fated to fight and do nothing more with his life? In a moment of self-defeat, Kimball sighed. No matter how fast or how far he tried to run, Fate was always standing at every corner waiting to hand him the scepter of war.

He looked at his watch. Ninety minutes to quitting time.

He went back to work.


**After clocking out** Kimball took leisure and headed off to one of the neighboring casinos that offered a parfait glass of shrimp for $1.99, then he ate beneath the lighted canopy of the Freemont Street Experience. Music blared to the beat of the Rolling Stones and The Doors, as cartoon images played overhead. When the show was over, he placed the glass aside and headed east on Freemont where the neighborhood was severely depressed with motels in disrepair and meth whores working for fixes. Homeless people gathered in small groups with shopping carts filled with treasures when people of comfort often considered them trash. Further east towards Boulder Highway, where the motels were sitting on the fulcrum point of becoming condemned but not quite there, was Kimball's apartment. It was the only place he could afford on his wage without applying for government aid and possibly draw attention.

It was night, the air hot and dry. It was always hot. And the smell of the city was all around him. The sweat, the ozone, the smoke from tailpipes, and the smog of big-city air all twisted into a terrible cocktail.

But it was home.

As he turned down an alleyway, he noted a figure of a small man, perhaps a teenager, standing next to a Dumpster. The closer Kimball got to the shape; it would counter with steps to confront Kimball in the middle of the alleyway, ultimately coming face to face by the time their paths crossed.

"Something I can do for you?" Kimball's sixth sense kicked in, meaning that they were not alone.

"Got any smokes, man?"

"Sorry. Don't smoke." When Kimball tried to sidestep him, the man stepped in front of him, blocking him. Kimball could see that he was neither a teenager nor a man, but on the cusp, perhaps twenty and wasting away.

"What about money? You got money, don't you?"

"How about you get out of my way? That way you and your friends won't get hurt."

From the shadows came movement. Three others, all in the same condition of being wasted and thinning on drugs, were positioning themselves so that Kimball was flanked on both sides with another behind and the punk in front.

"You don't want to do this," he told the kid. "Trust me. You really don't."

There was a snicker as a blade shot out from a stiletto in the punk's hand. Another three followed in concert: ...*Chic! . . . Chic! . . . Chic! . . .*

In Kimball's mind, it was an easy estimation of four knives total.

"Give me your wallet, dude."

"The only way you're getting my wallet," he told him, "is if you come and take it."

"Are you kidding me? There're four of us."

"I see that," he said. "Unfortunately for you, the odds favor me quite a bit."

The punk cocked his head and gave a questioning look.

"Last chance," Kimball said sternly. "Get out of my way."

The punk did not hesitate, but came at Kimball with unskilled and reckless abandon, the point of the blade going in as a straight jab.

Kimball pivoted and sidestepped the punk, the blade missing its mark and going wide, the punk tripping and sprawling to the ground in the face-first approach as his chops hit the pavement hard, his teeth fracturing and breaking.

Kimball took a step back to access the situation, barely able to choke back the laugh which irritated the punks to no end.

The attacking punk gained his feet and put a hand to his bloody mouth. "You think that was funny?"

"Are you kidding me? That was friggin' hilarious."

The punk attacked in rage, swinging wildly, the blade cutting the air in diagonal Xs, back and forth, side to side, Kimball falling back, waiting.

And then the former Vatican Knight struck.

Kimball lashed out with his left hand, caught the punk by the wrist, and twisted, snapping the bone and causing the knife to fall. He then brought up his right leg and kicked the punk with such force that the young man went airborne and carried across the alley in what appeared to be an impossibly long distance, the kid landing on a pile of trash bags where he remained unmoving.

Keeping his eyes on the other three, he slowly picked up the knife.

They faced him. And it was obvious to Kimball that they were determining if attacking him would be the wrong thing to do. To help them with their decision, Kimball began to play the knife across and over his fingers like a majorette twirling a baton. The motion was poetic and effortless, the skill taking years to achieve with his ability unlike anything the punks had ever seen before.

"Your choice," he said.

The punks backed away, two of them withdrawing their blades and pocketing their knives. The third wasn't so sure, keeping his knife ready.

"We just want to take our friend and go," said the skinny punk with the knife.

"Do what you want. I'll give you thirty seconds."

The punks hustled, stirring their friend who was half-conscious and murmuring nonsensical syllables. When they gathered the punk to his feet he cried out in agony as the pain in his wrist suddenly became white-hot.

One of the punks came forward. "Can we have his knife back?" He held out his hand as a gesture to receive.

Kimball nodded. "Nah, I think I'll keep it for posterity."

The punk fell back with his group, and then they headed for the opposite end of the alley.

Kimball pocketed the knife, watching. When they rounded the bend, he hastened his pace. Regardless, there were always vultures out there waiting in the shadows ready to close in on what they think may be carrion to feed on. This was not a good area to take things lightly or remain complacent.

When he reached his apartment, he finally felt at ease, knowing he was safe because his apartment was rigged to deal with any unwanted visitors.

The interior was small, hot, and closed in, with the kitchen nothing but a single-basin sink and a microwave oven. The bedroom was equally small and allowed nothing larger than a super-single-sized bed and a neighboring nightstand. Across the way was a small dresser with a 13" flat-screen TV. Next to that was a bathroom, small, with walls that were stained with patches of black mold that he had to wash away with a sponge weekly.

But it didn't matter to him. It was just a place to lay his hat.

Removing the knife from his pocket, he depressed the button and watched the blade slide out. The metal was clean and shined with a mirror polish. But it wasn't a well-made knife. More like something that was made in Tijuana and brought across the border.

He tossed the knife onto the dresser, took a quick shower, and felt fresh and new as he got into bed. Most nights he would lay there and watch the news, often using the remote to switch channels by the second—going from channel to channel until settling on a station.

But tonight, he just wanted to lay in the dark and think about what Louie had to say about how he saw the fight in Kimball's eyes, which caused him to wonder if his destiny was truly set. The skirmish in the alley was testimony to that, the "fight" always seemed to be within arm's length no matter how hard he tried to avoid it.

With Louie's words and the images of the brawl in the alley playing out in his mind, and if he wasn't so consumed with the sequence of the day's events, then he would have been watching TV. And if he had, then he would have learned that Pope Gregory had died of an apparent accident by falling off the Papal Balcony.

What a day.

# CHAPTER FIVE

*Moscow, Russia*

The man was in his late sixties but moved with the alacrity of somebody much older. With a cane in one hand and a small bundle of bread and eggs in the other, the old man walked along the cold streets of Moscow. Above him the sky was gray; the sky was always gray as the man shuffled along in a laboring gait to his apartment on the third level of the complex. Every day the journey of climbing the stairs was beginning to prove too much for his increasingly feeble legs.

Someday, he considered when his legs finally gave, so would he.

He would sit by the window with a bottle of vodka and drink himself into a stupor with the last thought on his mind of the Cold War when he was someone of purpose. Now that the walls have crumbled and communism nothing but an afterthought, the old man had become a societal burden surviving on a meager stipend equal to four hundred American dollars per month. Often, he would go days without heat during a Russian winter because he didn't have enough rubles to pay the bill.

Yet the old man eventually adapted, finding warmth with booze and aged memories.

Climbing the stairway only to take a time-out on every fourth or fifth step to catch his breath, the old man worked his way to his apartment that was approximately 350 square feet of living space.

Once inside he placed the eggs in the refrigerator and the bread on the counter, then leaned against the badly stained kitchen sink to regain his strength.

"You're getting old, Leonid," he told himself. "It's getting close to putting this old dog down."

The old man removed his scarf, his jacket, and draped them over the kitchen table that wobbled on weak legs. And then he made his way to a time-worn lounge chair situated before a small casement window that gave him a view of Red Square. This was his comfort zone. Just him, his memories, and the cheapest bottle of vodka he could afford.

Yet the chair was moved away from the window and the drapes were drawn, pinching out the drab light of an overcast day.

The old man stopped, his heart fluttering irregularly in his chest. "Who's in here?"

From the depths of the shadows, a man sat in the old man's chair, which to the old man was sacred property. He was cast in obscurity as a silhouette bearing no contour or shape, just a mass of darkness.

"I've come to give you back your respect," the shadow simply stated. "To give you back all those years of glory and achievement."

The old man recognized the voice immediately, clicked his tongue in disgust, and waved his hand dismissively. The Middle East accent and the steady lilt in the man's voice told Leonid that it was Adham al-Ghazi, not a man he expected or wanted to see under any circumstances.

"You come into my home unannounced and scare an old man half to death! What's the matter with you?"

Al-Ghazi said nothing.

"Say what you have to say, and then leave."

Al-Ghazi sat unmoving, a shade of deep black. And then, "My bathroom in Iran is bigger than this place," he said. "And it smells better, too. It's a shame that a man of your talent is forced to live in such conditions."

"If you've come all this way to tell me that your crap doesn't stink, then you're wasting your time."

"Still a spitfire, I see. That's good."

"What do you want, Ghazi?"

The Arab stood and moved into the light. He was impeccably dressed in an expensive suit bearing pinstripes and a matching silk tie. His beard was perfectly trimmed, not a single hair was misplaced or out of proportion from any other hair on his chin. To Leonid, it appeared perfectly sculptured.

"I want to give you back your glory days," he said, placing his hands behind the small of his back. "I can give you back what Russia cannot."

The old man waved his hand dismissively for a second time. "Impossible," he said. "That ship has already sailed, and Mother Russia is gone."

"Perhaps. But a new ship has arrived." Al-Ghazi reached into his jacket pocket, produced a thick envelope, and placed it on the kitchen counter. Leonid Sakharov didn't have to be told of its contents. "That's just a beginning, my friend. When you're finished, then you'll be able to live out your life in luxury. I guarantee it."

Leonid Sakharov stared at the envelope, refusing to make any type of commitment by picking it up.

"Whereas Russia has turned a blind eye to you," added al-Ghazi, "my people have not."

"Your people are al-Qaeda."

"My people, Leonid, can make you whole again. No more pining away in that rat trap of a chair of yours looking over Red Square and reminiscing of old times while drinking rotgut. Unless, of course, that's the way you want to go out. As a seething old drunk who has nothing to look forward to besides a cheap bottle of vodka every morning."

"And what's it to you? Maybe I like being 'a seething old drunk who has nothing to look forward to besides a cheap bottle of vodka every morning,'" he mimicked.

Al-Ghazi smiled. "You're so much better than that," he told him. "In fact, Leonid, I know you don't believe that yourself. Or you wouldn't get up every day just to reminisce about times that used to be. You want to be there again, don't you? To ply your trade and be someone who is needed."

The old man cast his eyes to the floor. Al-Ghazi hit the head of the nail straight on. A tired Old Man he may be, but al-Ghazi was correct to presume that he lived every day in a drunken haze just to make his world more bearable. "What is it that you want?" he finally asked.

"Your services, of course."

"It's been more than ten years," he said.

"I'm sure it's like riding a bicycle."

The old man hobbled his way to a stained sofa, the foam of the cushions bleeding out through tears in the fabric and, fell into the seat. "Why?"

Al-Ghazi's smile never wavered. "Do you know what truly resides within the Ark of the Covenant?" he asked.

"I couldn't give a rat's ass."

"Not a religious man, I see."

"Not too many people in Russia are," he said curtly. "It kind of went to the wayside when Stalin came aboard."

"Yes, of course."

"So again: Why?"

"The Ark," he began, "is said to contain five items: the two tablets of the Ten Commandments, a pot of gold Manna, the rod of Aaron, and one other item that cannot be seen or heard until it's too late."

There was a lapse of time as the two men stared at each other.

And then: "If you haven't noticed," said Leonid, "I'm an old man who doesn't have much time. So get on with it!"

"It is said that once the lid of the Ark is opened, then those who are not selected by the God of the Covenant will die by the demons who reside within."

Sakharov sighed. And al-Ghazi could see that the old man was becoming taxed.

"All I want you to do, Leonid, is to do what you do best."

"Right now, it's getting drunk."

"You know what I'm talking about."

"Actually, I don't."

Al-Ghazi leaned forward. "A few days ago, my group came in possession of the Ark of the Covenant, and the lid was opened."

"You're saying you found the Ark?"

"The true Ark, yes."

"And let me guess. There were no demons, right?"

"No demons," he confirmed. "Another fallacy, I believe."

"And what do you propose to do?" he asked. "Sell it to the highest bidder? Maybe to the Catholics or the Jews or the Muslims, whoever has the deepest pockets so that you can go on and continue to fund your terrorist campaigns?"

Al-Ghazi's smile diminished. The old man was starting to get to him. "Nothing of the sort," he answered tautly. "I have another purpose for it."

"And that would be?"

"To fulfill a biblical prophecy that so many richly believe in," he said.

"And what would that be? Not that I care, mind you."

"Their prophecy states that the Ark of the Covenant serves as a preamble to World War Three. That the religious factions are willing to war over this box made of acacia wood and gold, simply for the history it possesses."

"Doesn't it bear the same historical nostalgia for you? You're Muslim?"

"What Allah wants first and foremost is for the infidels to be annihilated. This Ark can serve as the catalyst to get this done."

Leonid cocked his head and squinted. "You want to start a war?"

"Maybe not a war," he said, "but a means to destroy all those who do not support the teachings of Allah. If a war starts, then it would be by Allah's will."

The old man reared his head back, just a little. "You're friggin' nuts," he finally said.

"Religion is a hot-button issue," al-Ghazi returned. "People are so devoted to the concept of *their* god that when someone dares to speak against their god or religion, they then become easily angered. But what would it be like, Leonid, if they cannot attain what they believe belongs to them rightfully? Animosities rise, tempers flare, and battles begin. And for what? A golden box?" Al-Ghazi studied the old man momentarily before speaking again. "People die every day in the name of religion," he added. "And for a lot less."

In fluid motion al-Ghazi parted the drapes, giving the old man a view of Moscow.

Leonid nibbled softly on his lower lip, and then looked out at Red Square and at the domes of St. Basil's Cathedral. He missed his life— missed what he had. And al-Ghazi picked up on this.

"Come with me," he goaded. "Take back what Russia took away. Be someone who can make a difference."

*Make a difference.* This simple statement affected the old man greatly, the words playing continuously in his mind the entire time he remained silent, though he was still self-debating.

And then, after looking at al-Ghazi with a sidelong glance, he asked, "What is it that you want me to do?"

Al-Ghazi's smile flourished as he leaned forward to draw Leonid into close counsel. "What I want from you, Leonid, is one thing."

"And what would that be?"

"I want you to put the demons back inside the box."

The old man knew exactly what he was talking about.

40

# CHAPTER SIX

*Somewhere Over the Atlantic Ocean*

Cardinal Bonasero Vessucci sat in the Economy class looking out the window at the ocean below. Whitecaps broke against waves that matched the color of an overcast sky, that of battleship gray. And the rain began to dapple against the window as the plane rode the leading edge of a turbulent wind.

For the past few hours, he considered many things, especially the moments on the papal veranda standing alongside Pope Pius holding counsel on many subjects, usually on splendid days where the sun was high in a cerulean blue sky. But he kept thinking about one thing: the stone guardrail that encompassed the landing.

It was beautifully crafted, the stonework bearing the images of angels and cherubs, and stood nearly five-foot-high, which was taller than most rails since it acted as a safety feature to keep those from toppling to the cobblestones below.

What was the reason for Pope Gregory to lean over the rail to such a degree that he would lose his balance and fall, especially at such an early hour when the shadows were at their darkest? Had he seen something below?

He rubbed his chin at the thought. Possibly, he considered. But there were other considerations as well. The man could have hoisted himself along the railing, and as an abomination to God cast himself over its edge to the street below, which Bonasero immediately disputed with incredulity. Or he could have been pushed. But this, too, was disputed with incredulity since it would infer that Gregory was murdered.

Still, something nagged at him, something that went beyond the surface since the quick answer by investigating authorities was that it was nothing more than a horrible accident; therefore, any other alternatives were summarily dismissed with no need for further examination.

So, the final report would read like this: Pope Gregory had died from the consequences of the fall. And that may be true, he thought, at least to a certain degree. But what precipitated the fall, to begin with, still bothered him.

The cardinal closed his eyes, settled back in his seat, and waited for the plane to touchdown in Rome with a single thought on his mind: The pope's death was not as simple or as clear cut as it seemed.

This he was sure of.

# CHAPTER SEVEN

*Moscow, Russia*

It was night, and the old man sat alone in the darkness of his apartment with the threadbare shades pulled wide so that he could see the wonderful lights cast upon the domes of St. Basil's Cathedral.

He had conceded, telling al-Ghazi that he would commit himself "to put the demons back into the box." He was no magician, not a conjurer, not even a man who could urinate without a burning sensation that caused him a pain far greater than his arthritis, which often plagued his bones in the cold Russian weather.

In truth al-Ghazi was right, he considered. As beautiful as it was outside his window, the way the lights lit the colored domes of the cathedral, *his* Mother Russia was forever gone.

During the latter part of the Cold War, Leonid Sakharov was a pioneering savant in the field of nanotechnology—leap years ahead of Russia's most brilliant scientists. In the mid-eighties when nanotechnology was in its genesis stage, the Russian and American tactical war departments realized that the use of nanobots, or nanoweapons, was the future of the arms race with far more devastating repercussions than nuclear devices. Billions of programmed molecules, unseen and indefensible, and with no need of special equipment to produce, could serve the military's needs in several ways.

Sakharov's duties were to conceive nanoweaponry such as nano-scouts, bots so small yet capable of transmitting data from foreign sources that went undetected and unseen. Other military applications were nanobots that acted as poisons or a force field. More measures taken into consideration by the Kremlin were the use of nanoweaponry such as mind erasers, whereas nanobots would settle in an insurgent's brain as micro fields, then fire off as small brain bursts that would wipe away sections of memory, and then reprogram it with new commands, new memories, and new ideologies that were suited for communist rule.

Additional applications such as nano-needles and water bullets were scrapped because of their non-lethal relevance that would ultimately achieve the Russian means to rule by military dominance, which was to kill from a distance with something one-billionth of the size of a man. But more importantly, to do so with something that was highly programmable.

It was just another matter of the race game between Russia, the United States, and the United Kingdom. But Russia had Leonid Sakharov, a brilliant physicist who realized that molecular nanoweapons were the next great superweapons. In order to get funding in a Russian economy that was slowly being whittled away by the war in Afghanistan, he explained in detail that the weapons were simple molecules converted by their atoms, and then those atoms would insert themselves into atomic systems which would transform molecules into tiny computers that raced through space like submicroscopic viruses capable of finding the enemy and then destroy them. After lobbying tirelessly for the sake, safety, and cause of Mother Russia, he got the funding.

However, his research did not come without tribulation.

Progress was slow at first—baby steps, really—a stagger here and a stagger there, the frustration worming its way into his core until he took to the bottle to take off the edge. And then gains became strides, strides became leaps, and Sakharov was elated at the advancement made toward the evolution of the atom.

He would spend nights on end with little or no sleep—his only true companions beside his underling associates were his colossal ego, and a bottle of the finest vodka rubles could buy.

But one night, in one of his celebratory moods after making a breakthrough, Old Man Sakharov took to lack of caution and, against the advice of associates, initiated a start-up program after he was warned about the consequences since no pre-tests were conducted to determine the hazardous effect of the nanobots under controlled conditions. But the old man gestured with a dismissive wave of his hand, his ego and the influence of liquor now the driving forces behind his decisions and started the program with the push of a button.

As he sat at a monitor behind a bomb-proof resistant glass wall, he watched his associates as they examined a monkey that was isolated in a separate room behind another glass wall. At first, there was nothing as the old man became flustered, angry, and not understanding what went wrong. And then a waspy hum sounded over the mike as the monkey became agitated. Within moments the hum grew in intensity, the nanobots replicating faster than anticipated. And then the monkey began to scream at a pitch that none of the scientists had ever heard from any animal.

Quickly, the rhesus's fur began to slough off by the handfuls, the monkey waving and swinging its hands wildly at something unseen. And then its flesh began to disappear as if eaten away by patches, revealing the muscle and gristle underneath, then bone. The rhesus raised its head in agony, its eyes dissolving within their orbital sockets, and then it shuddered one last time before falling. Within moments, like a time-lapse reel of a movie running in fast forward, the monkey dissolved down to skeletal matter. But it didn't end there. The bone quickly became polished, and then cracked, revealing the marrow that soon disappeared. And then there was nothing, not even the outline of dust. Everything that was carbon matter was gone.

And Sakharov smiled. "There you have it, gentlemen," he said over the intercom. "The future is finally here."

But the celebration was short-lived.

The hum of the nanobots sounded like a hive gone mad, growing louder, the speakers sounding off as if the volume was being turned up.

*No! No! No! They're replicating too quickly*!

Sakharov's mind began to go into panic mode, his two associates looking at him through the glass from the lab, wondering what was wrong.

And then the noise ceased, the waspy hum cut off as if on cue.

Not a collective breath could be heard as the two scientists stood as still as Grecian statues.

And then the glass that separated the two scientists from the rhesus lab began to crack. At first, it was just one spot, a pinpoint with spider-web cracks that blossomed into full designs. And then a second and third pinpoint, the cracks trailing across the pane until they met other cracks, the window becoming compromised, and then it blew outward with an explosive force, the hum now sounding like a freight train speeding through a tunnel.

Sakharov's associates began to slap at their coats, at their faces, as if swatting away annoying gnats or insects. And then the material of their coats began to disappear, and then strips and slabs of flesh. Their faces simply disappearing: the skin, the muscle, ultimately revealing the curvature of bone underneath and the empty sockets where their eyes once were. Their tongues no longer lolled, the meat stripped away, vanished. And in a last act of self-preservation, they clawed at the window that separated them from their mentor with the bony tines of their fingers, the digits of bones were seen as they ticked against the glass in macabre measure.

*What have I done?*

Sakharov watched with paralytic terror as the men slid down the glass leaving bloody trails against the pane.

And then a silence that was complete and absolute followed.

Sakharov looked at the speakers.

Not a sound.

And then it came as a single tick against the glass that separated him from his associates' lab. The glass divider between his room and his associates took on a single pinprick hole that was beginning to web out with a series of meandering cracks.

Acting quickly, Sakharov lifted the plastic emergency shield that covered a red button and slammed his palm down. A titanium wall came down and covered the glass. And then he pressed the button again. This time initiating a failsafe program that ignited the lab, burning everything within the room at more than three thousand degrees. Everything, including the nanobots, was incinerated.

Nevertheless, Sakharov was hailed by the Kremlin as a hero, whereas his associates were looked upon as collateral damage. But he knew differently. He had become drunk to the delight of his ego, casting aside all precautions and believing that nothing could have gone wrong when, in fact, everything had gone horribly wrong. And it wasn't too long afterward that he realized that such nanoweaponry was far too dangerous. According to an article by Eric Drexler, whom he considered to be his "near" equal, replication was much too fast if not contained. And within a week the bots could exponentially grow to such numbers that the entire surface of the Earth would be consumed by matter Drexler termed as "grey goo," which is to say everything alive on the planet would be devoured and anything to come within its gravitational pull would be consumed as well.

But the Kremlin didn't want to hear this side of the scenario. What they wanted were results, so funding was extended with expectations that Sakharov would be able to program the molecules to keep from replicating themselves and to better devise a way to control them from a computer monitor.

When Sakharov told them that such science was decades away, they simply told him that the "first" second of the first decade just ticked away; therefore, he wasn't to waste another moment.

For years he worked on methods and theories, having diagrams of buckyballs with scribbled notes wallpapering the walls. He worked tirelessly, honestly believing that he could be the next Nikola Tesla, the Serbian genius.

As months and years drew on, as the wall crumbled in 1991, and with it, communism, the new leadership refused Sakharov any true freedoms and placed him under the auspice of the new Directorate S, an updated version of Kremlin bureaucracy.

With pressure mounting and with Sakharov struggling with the bottle, his work went well beyond stress, so the gains were minimal. With more pressure being asserted by the powers that be, Sakharov finally snapped and erased almost ten years of data from all computers and their banks, leaving nothing to be retrieved.

This earned Sakharov nine years in the prison system where he watched inmates die around him in the most horrific conditions.

But he did not blame Mother Russia. He blamed himself, knowing that his ego was paramount and that his downfall and failures were of his doing.

He still loved his country, even though it was a marginal facsimile of what she used to be.

But he survived Vladimir Central. And by the time he was released, Russia had a new political face. And it turned up its nose at him by telling him that he was aged and forgotten.

*But my mind is as sharp as it always was.*

He smiled because this was true.

In Vladimir Central, he would draw diagrams and formulas in the mud, then commit them to memory before erasing them at the approach of the guards. Now that his mind wasn't addled with drink, he could think, configure, and institute new measures of control if allowed to do so. He would be diligent and careful. And though he quickly found a reason to press his lips around the mouth of a bottle the moment he was released from Vladimir Central, he would gladly give it up to prove to himself that he was not the failure Mother Russia believed him to be since she discarded him like yesterday's news.

He then raised the glass of vodka to his lips and drank, the alcohol going down much cooler than the urine that often left his body. *You're coming apart, old man.* But he smiled at the thought.

Regardless, he had lived a good life, developing weaponry he believed would serve as a deterrent against the United States, for which they would fear retaliatory strikes derived from Sakharov's wares. The old man genuinely believed that he was once the front line of his nation's defense, when, in fact, he was just a cog in the scheme of Russia's massive operation that was well beyond his comprehension.

He sighed. He stared. He thought. And he drank; knowing once he left this apartment, once he left for Iran, and despite the promises of reliving his glory years, Leonid Sakharov knew his time was limited.

Again, he smiled. And then he lifted a full glass of vodka and extended his hand toward the lights of St. Basil's Cathedral and proposed a toast. "To my beloved Mother Russia," he whispered. "I have missed you so. And I promise to make you proud." And then he drank until the glass ran empty.

# CHAPTER EIGHT

*Tehran, Iran, Three Days Later*

Deep in the center of Iran's capital, by far the largest urban city with a population of over eight million people, al-Ghazi found it easy to hide within the bustle of the major metropolis. After meeting with Leonid Sakharov, he took an immediate flight back to his central base.

The weather was hot and dry, the sky a deep blue, a cloud not to be seen. The stink of a big city was evident with the smell of fumes and exhaust permeating the air as if a sandstorm had swept through the streets, the atmosphere cloyingly thick with haze the color of desert sand. People milled about the bazaars where animal meats hung from hooks. And al-Ghazi took it all in as he sat at a table outside an eatery enjoying a Sharbat, a sweet drink prepared from fruits and flower petals. As always, he was impeccably dressed in a shirt so white that it cast a glowing radiance, whereas everyone around him wore the traditional *Shalvars* or *Sarbands*.

Patiently, while at leisure with his drink, al-Ghazi waited. His contact would be prompt, as always. So, at noon when his phone rang, he knew exactly who it was.

He recognized al-Zawahiri's voice right away.

"There is no doubt the Americans will eventually come after me since they murdered Osama," said al-Zawahiri. "After today I will stay in contact through couriers since I must now go into exile."

"I understand."

"Do you have the physicist?"

"Not yet. But arrangements have been made for him to arrive in Tehran shortly. My men will be there to pick him up."

"There will be problems getting him through customs, yes?"

"Not at all," he answered. "I have been given assurances by custom

49

agents at the Imam Khomeini International Airport that Dr. Sakharov will pass uncontested. If he does not, then it is understood that consequences will befall those who stay his passage."

"Is he capable of doing the job? My sources tell me that the physicist has grown infirm."

Al-Ghazi took a sip from his Sharbat, the outside of the glass sweating. "It appears that drink has taken his body, al-Zawahiri, but not his mind. So, what has become Russia's loss is now Allah's gain."

"Then you've done well, al-Ghazi. Allah truly shines upon you with favors."

"I am blessed, yes."

"Quickly, tell me of your agenda and then speak no more of it to anyone hereafter."

"The good doctor will arrive tonight and be taken to a safe house at the northern edge of the city where he will rest. On the following morning, he will then be taken to our base camp in the Alborz."

The Alborz is a mountain range in the northern part of Iran stretching from the borders of Azerbaijan and Armenia in the northwest, to the Caspian Sea in the south. The range also borders Afghanistan to the east and seats the tallest mountain in the Middle East, Mount Damavand, which is well over 18,000 feet tall.

The range is porous with caves, like Afghanistan. But unlike Afghanistan, the region is highly protected by President Ahmadinejad's forces since the area falls under Iranian sovereignty. To breach the area would be difficult. To find the exact location of the lab site would be almost impossible. And as far as al-Ghazi was concerned, he was untouchable.

"And you're ready, I presume?"

"Quite. This facility is located deep within the base of Mount Damavand. President Ahmadinejad was kind enough to create a state-of-the-art laboratory that will be activated by power cells."

"It appears that Ahmadinejad's nuclear program has more applications than just an energy resource as he claims. I'm sure he did not do this from the goodness of his heart."

"Of course not, but his stake is a simple one," he said. "In exchange for his use of the lab and his continued protection, he has respectfully requested that his team of scientists be given access to data regarding Sakharov's nanotechnology."

There was silence on the other end.

And then: "We have no other choice?"

"The facility is well protected, al-Zawahiri. And the equipment is something the good doctor may understand. Even with my schooling, I have no concept as to what they do. They are truly state-of-the-art, which gives us the promise of achievement that would bring us victory over the infidels in a final assault that would give Allah his true station above all."

"I may believe in you, al-Ghazi. And I may believe in Dr. Sakharov. But I do not trust Ahmadinejad. I'm afraid once this is all set and done, then he will take it all for himself."

"There will be a fail-safe against that," al-Ghazi returned evenly.

"And what would that be?"

"If President Ahmadinejad should fall back on his agreement, then I will make sure that the data will be compromised, rendering the entire operation useless."

"I see."

"There is a solution for everything," he said. "I will maintain all data so that a lab in Pakistan has the chance to emulate the progress of what we are doing inside Mount Damavand. If Ahmadinejad falls back on his word, then at least you'll have the necessary information to replicate the technology."

"You've considered your options well," said al-Zawahiri. "Impressive."

"I'm a soldier of Allah's army. I plan for every contingency."

"And what about the Ark of the Covenant?"

"It's safe inside the facility in Damavand," he answered. "Once the nano project is complete, then the Ark will come into play."

Although al-Ghazi could not see al-Zawahiri, he knew the old soldier held a pleased look about him.

"*Allahu Akbar*," the old soldier finally said.

Al-Ghazi nodded, smiled. "*Allahu Akbar.*"

The line was severed.

Al-Ghazi then removed the SIM card from the phone, destroyed it, and quietly watched the people of Tehran mill about as he sat back and enjoyed his Sharbat.

# CHAPTER NINE

*Vatican City, Domus Sanctæ Marthæ*

On the edge of Vatican City but adjacent to St. Peter's Basilica lies the *Domus Sanctæ Marthæ,* the residential quarters of the Cardinal Electors who are housed there prior to entering the conclave to elect a newly appointed official upon the passing of the pope.

Three days after his arrival, Cardinal Bonasero Vessucci took up residence in a dormitory room overlooking the Basilica.

To be back at Vatican City held something special for him, the air of the plaza bearing a uniqueness unlike anywhere else in the world. Or so he believed.

In the days that followed his arrival, politicking began, the camps congregating with discussions as to who would provide the best possible leadership and guidance, and whether or not the names bandied about were more conservative or liberal in ideology. Like last time, Cardinal Vessucci's name entered discussions as a leading candidate alongside Cardinal Giuseppe Angullo, whose camp banded with the late Pope Gregory's in the last election and caused Vessucci to lose by a marginal count and ultimately his exile by Gregory. In exchange for Angullo's collusion entitling him the papacy, Pope Gregory would grant Angullo Vessucci's old post as the Vatican's secretary of state, the second-highest position in the Church.

Now with less than a year under his belt and the leading title as the Church's secretary of state, Cardinal Angullo was positioned to take it all despite talks amongst the Electors that members within his camp had defected. No reasons were given other than that his position had been severely weakened with his major components of support now gone.

Nevertheless, Angullo's camp remained strong with Vessucci

trying to corral as many of the cardinal's defectors with powerful and persuasive politicking.

Vessucci was gathering momentum.

By the end of the third day, as the sun was beginning to set, Bonasero Vessucci made his way to the papal chamber. The doors were guarded by two members of the Swiss Guards, who were holding traditional halberds. When the cardinal stood before the doors the guards, out of obligatory courtesy, opened them and allowed the cardinal passage into the chamber.

The doors closed softly behind him, the snicker of the bolt locking into place barely perceptible to the cardinal's ears.

The room was vast, and the scalloped drapery hung motionless as Vessucci crossed the floor in a room that appeared more sepulchral than hallowed.

He stood at the threshold of the balcony that overlooked the city in its glory with the Egyptian obelisk and the colonnades within clear view. People milled by the thousands, vacationers mostly, with their digital cameras and touristy attire. And the sky was a perfect blend of reds and yellows with the onset of a darkening sky.

He quickly made his way to the stone guardrail, lifting the hem of his garment as he did so, and then laid a hand on the railing. The drop to the street below appeared farther simply by illusion alone. The height was no more than thirty feet. But for some reason, it looked twice that.

He looked over the edge and noted that the blood was gone, the bricks no longer holding any tell-tale sign that the pontiff's life had leeched out onto the surface below.

"A shame, isn't it? That the pontiff should lose his life so early during his tenure."

Vessucci started. He did not hear Cardinal Angullo enter the chamber, nor the closing of the doors after the guards let him in. The face that measured Vessucci was oddly hatchet-thin with a snout-like nose and grim lips fashioned above a weak chin. His eyes were so dark they seemed without pupil. And when he spoke, he did so in a discordant twang similar to the strings of an instrument being plucked.

Vessucci returned the same arduous glare. "Quite," he simply said.

"Are you here to reminisce of a time that once was? When you and Pope Pius once stood here talking about the Church . . . And of the dark secrets during his reign."

Vessucci immediately understood the cardinal's insinuation. He was talking about the Vatican Knights. The Church's clandestine op-group of elite commandos who were summarily disbanded under Gregory's rule, the pope declaring them an abomination to the Catholic faith despite the good they proffered to those who were weak and innocent. "The only darkness is the truth of what happened to Pope Gregory," he returned.

"Oh?"

Vessucci turned his gaze upon the plaza of Vatican City, then patted the railing with his hand. "I have stood here many times overlooking this city with Pope Pius," he said. "As I'm sure you have with Pope Gregory."

"I have, yes."

Vessucci looked at the railing, and at the carvings of angels and cherubs. "Then you know as well as I do that it is quite difficult for a man to fall over this railing since it is raised to a level to bar a man from leaning too far forward."

"It is quite obvious to me, Bonasero, that the railing is not high enough."

The cardinal drew closer. The railing reached the point of his abdomen.

But Angullo intuited his action. "Pope Gregory was taller than you," he said.

"True. But not tall enough for the brunt of his weight to carry him over the side." He turned to Angullo. "Unless he was pushed, perhaps?"

The cardinal cocked his head to one side the same way a dog would when trying to grasp the meaning of an uncertain moment. "If I didn't know better, Bonasero, I would say that you were insinuating that the good pontiff was murdered. And that you, at least by the tone of your voice, believe that it was by my hand."

Vessucci stood back from the railing. "Every shiny surface has a little tarnish underneath, Giuseppe. All I'm saying is that the case was closed much too quickly without the benefit of a full objective examination, simply for the belief that nothing truly reprehensible can happen at the Vatican."

"Come on, Bonasero. Do you really believe that Pope Gregory met his death by the hand of another rather than by the hand of Fate? He fell. Accidents happen."

"To fall over this railing is highly improbable since the railing was constructed exactly for that reason—as a safeguard to keep one from falling over its edge." He shook his head. "No, Giuseppe. Either he took his life . . ." He let his words trail. But a heartbeat later, said: "Or someone aided him in his fall."

The cardinal was taken aback. "What you say, Bonasero, is nothing but absolute nonsense—this talk of murder and suicide. Gregory was sound of mind the night of his death. He would never put the Church in such a position by taking his life."

"Exactly. And that leaves us with the other option, doesn't it?"

Cardinal Angullo's nostrils flared the same moment his brow dipped sharply over the bridge of his nose in anger. "The days of heresy have been abandoned by rational thought over the years, Bonasero. But if anything provides a strong case for such profanation, it's what you just stated."

"Is your memory so short, Giuseppe? Have you forgotten the attempt on the life of John Paul the Second?"

The cardinal bit his lower lip.

"What I say holds a measure of probability. Therefore, I will not turn a blind eye to the reality of what might have been."

Cardinal Angullo turned away from Bonasero, his eyes alighting on the landscape of Vatican City. "So, what will you do?" he asked. "Open an investigation when there are less than ten days left before we enter the conclave to vote on the successor?"

"Hardly. I'm simply voicing my opinion."

"But you believe the pontiff was murdered?"

Bonasero remained quiet.

"You do realize once the newly elected takes the Papal Throne, then you will return to Boston along with your foolish notion."

"Unless, Giuseppe," he faced the cardinal directly, "I'm elected to the pontifical post."

There, a laryngeal microexpression, a quick bob of his Adam's apple, was a sign of concern from Angullo.

"And if you are," Angullo returned dispassionately, "then what? You'll spearhead a quest to find something that does not exist? You'll just end up like a dog chasing after its tail, Bonasero. There's nothing out there for you to find. And if you are elected, don't you think you'd be better suited to apply yourself to the needs of the Church rather than the needs of yourself since you are newly appointed?"

"To seek the truth, Giuseppe, is always the need of the Church."

Whether Cardinal Angullo shook his head in disagreement or disgust, Vessucci could not determine.

The cardinal then looked over the railing, then back to Vessucci. "Do what you must," he told him. "Chase your foolish notions while I seek to better my position with the Electors. If I take the throne, Bonasero, let it be known right now that you will return to Boston and seek the truth from there. And believe me when I say that such notions will fall on deaf ears."

Vessucci smiled. "God is never deaf or blind to the truth, Giuseppe. And the truth will always find its way, whether I'm at the Vatican or across the ocean."

Angullo began to circle the cardinal, and Vessucci took a conscious step back away from the railing.

"Perhaps you think me the killer, is that it? Is that how you plan to win the Electors votes, by politicking with foolish and unfounded theories—that the good Cardinal Giuseppe Angullo murdered the pope? Is that your strategy, Bonasero?" The cardinal was now standing directly behind Vessucci, who could not see the man through either corner of his eyes.

Vessucci turned enough to offer a sidelong glance. "I politick with the strengths I offer as a newly elected and nothing more," he said.

"I see." Angullo maneuvered back toward the railing. And then: "I understand that your camp remains strong, even after Pope Gregory sent you to America."

"And yours a little less powerful."

Angullo smiled, nodded. "It will be interesting when the Electors take to the conclave. But tell me, Bonasero, should you be selected to the papal throne, will you bring these Vatican Knights, these abominations, back to the Church?"

"Whatever I do, Giuseppe, you will have no knowledge of my stance in any position within the Church, believe me."

"As the Vatican's secretary of state, I'm afraid you'd have no choice."

"Oh, but I do," he returned adamantly. "In the same manner that Pope Gregory has seen me fit to leave my post that you now hold, I would yield the same power of authority to see the same. Perhaps, Giuseppe, Boston would suit you well."

The cardinal nodded. "You forget one thing, Bonasero. You seem overly confident when everyone within the Church knows you were summarily sent to the Boston as something punitive. Your camp will dissolve on that tainted issue and your bid to seek the papal throne will end before it even begins."

"Is that how you plan to politick?"

The right corner of the cardinal's lip lifted into the beginnings of a sardonic grin. "Would I be lying if they learned the reason why you were dismissed to Boston, to begin with? That you were summarily dismissed from your post because of these Vatican Knights and the Society of Seven. These clandestine organizations within the Church nobody knew about?"

He had just played his trump card and the cardinal immediately picked up on it.

"I see," said Vessucci. "But you forget one thing."

"And that would be?"

"These Knights were highly beloved by every pope going back to World War Two. And no one loved them or pressed them more into duty than Pope Pius and John Paul the Second." He now stood before Angullo so that he faced him directly, almost toe to toe with his back to the railing. "Should you use this as a tactic, then you'd be besmirching the good name of John Paul, a man who is being sent up to sainthood."

Angullo's smile widened. "Bonasero-Bonasero-Bonasero, are you listening to yourself? When you speak, then you do so as a hypocrite."

Vessucci appeared quizzical.

"Did you not just say that 'the truth will always find its way'?"

"I did."

"Yet it's all right to keep the truth of the Vatican Knights from the members of the entire College of the Cardinals for fear that they may think of them in the same light as Pope Gregory, as mercenary abominations."

*Touché.*

Angullo turned away and headed for the chamber door. "There's no place in the Church for a hypocrite," he said over his shoulder. "I suggest you think your position over clearly and bow out before your image is so badly tainted that you'll end up in a parish somewhere in East Africa."

"Is that a threat?"

Cardinal Angullo hesitated at the chamber door, his hand on the knob, and studied Vessucci through obsidian eyes. "My stance with the Church is clear. What I want is clear. If you stand in my way, then I will destroy you."

"The same way you destroyed Pope Gregory?" As much as he didn't want to, he said it.

Cardinal Angullo let his hand fall and took two steps back inside the chamber. He shook his head. "Think what you will," he told him. "But the man died by accident and nothing more. Worse, you're beginning to sound like a man of desperation, which is sad since at one time you were highly esteemed."

"I still am, otherwise, you wouldn't have come here to share your game plan and intimidate me to fall out."

"I came here to talk about politicking, which we did. But you also accused me of possible murder. And that, Bonasero, is stepping over the line. Politicking is one thing; wild accusations are another."

In Bonasero's mind, he conceded. As strong a politic as he was, Angullo bested him at every corner, at every turn, his tongue sharp and his reasoning even sharper. He had turned Vessucci's considerations of Pope Gregory's death into the possible realm of one man's desperation, should it be spoken in certain circles. Secondly, in his statement of seeking the truth, didn't Angullo purposely use the Vatican Knights as the optimum example of why Vessucci's 'truth' was hypocritical since the Knights remained a well-hidden secret from the College? Wasn't keeping them a secret for fear of internal dissatisfaction within the religious hierarchy that was, in essence, a 'lie'?

Vessucci was beaten down on a political level, and badly.

Angullo reached blindly for the knob, his eyes remaining focused on Vessucci as his hatchet-thin face held the winning glow of achievement. "Think about it, Bonasero. Your weakness has become my strength."

"I have as much right to the position as you do," he finally said, but not as self-assured as before.

"As does anyone else," he said. And with that he left the papal chamber, closing the door behind him.

Vessucci exhaled as if he had accumulated his frustrations and vented them with a long sigh in catharsis. Nevertheless, he remained solid in his convictions to believe that Pope Gregory did not fall by his miscalculation.

He went back to the rail and peered over the edge to the bricks below. Despite Angullo's countermeasures, there was no doubt in his mind that he was not a desperate man, but a man of conscience and reason.

He would politick and try to sway the Electors that he is just as strong a candidate as he was during the last election within the conclave six months earlier. He would once again provide them with his strengths, his weaknesses, and lay everything out as to the direction the Church should head. And then hope that his bidding would secure him the throne.

People continued to mill about the Square. And once again Cardinal Vessucci sighed. Cardinal Angullo was a strong adversary whose name was thrown into the arena at the last election. And as secretary of state, he held the notoriety of being the pontiff's closest ally.

This was going to be an uphill battle all the way, he thought.

And with that thought on his mind, he dolefully returned to the *Domus Sanctæ Marthæ.*

# CHAPTER TEN

*Las Vegas, Nevada*

Kimball Hayden was working the trash canisters along the casino floor when Louie tapped him on the shoulder.

"You haven't given me an answer. And we have only five days left."

"I thought my lack of an answer was answer enough," said Kimball, tossing a trash bag into the cart. Around him, slot machines and video games chimed their wins and losses with the winning screens lighting up in cartoonish displays of coins dropping into the winner's trough.

"There's a treasure chest lying at our feet," said Louie, stabbing a finger in the air as if to harshly punctuate his point. "And all you have to do is get into the ring. But you're kinda giving me the feeling that you're gutless. Is that what you are, J.J.? Gutless."

Kimball smiled at Louie's adolescent attempt at peer pressure. "Look, Louie, I'm not interested in cage fighting. I never was and I never will be. Okay?"

"So, this is what you want to do for the rest of your life? To pick up trash?"

"It's an honest living. I told you that."

"You also told me that you'd think about the ring."

"I did . . . for about a second."

Louie shook his head. "You have all the tools, J.J. You even have the look. What an awful waste."

"So, I have the look, huh?"

Another nod. "You look like a warrior, J.J. It's in your eyes. It's in the way you move, the way you walk. It's all about you and here you are diving into trash cans."

"As I said, it's just a temporary gig. And then I'll move on."

Louie grabbed Kimball by the elbow. "Can I show you something?"

"If it moves you—yeah, sure."

Louie ushered him to the end of the aisle that led to the Sports Book. Once there he released him and pointed to an aging African-American who looked jaded, his face hanging as if perpetually distraught. Like Kimball, he was shagging trash bags from receptacles and discarding them into carts. "See that man right there?"

Kimball shrugged. "It's Tyrone. So what?"

"Tyrone said the same thing thirteen years ago," he said. "That exact same thing: 'It's temporary.' But look at him. He's become someone without hope or ambition." He turned to Kimball. "And that's going to be you, J.J.—a man without hope or ambition."

"So, fighting in a caged arena like an animal is supposed to give me a sense of hope or ambition? Is that what you're telling me?"

"All I'm saying, J.J., is to give yourself a chance to be what you were meant to be and to stop wasting your life." He looked at Tyrone, then back to Kimball. "We both know you were never meant to do this. You were meant to be someone special." Then in an imploring manner, "Don't become like Tyrone. Don't waste your life when there's opportunity knocking at your door."

Kimball looked at Tyrone and noted that the man looked older than his fifty years. His face hung with aged looseness. And his back began to take on the fatigued shape of bowing into a question mark.

"I can't, Louie. I'm not like that anymore."

"J.J., I can tell that you were a fighter at one time, a warrior even. The scars are all over you. But don't ever forget that you can never truly walk away from what you really are. A fighter will always be a fighter. A loser will always be a loser. And a dreamer will always be a dreamer. If you think for one minute this is only temporary, then you're sadly mistaken." He pointed at Tyrone. "Take a look at your future, J.J. I hope it ain't so, but take a good, long look."

Kimball did, seeing more than just the tired assemblage of a man who once dreamed that his life held so much promise, but eventually lost that potential over time, his dreams fading. When Kimball turned to say something to Louie, the man was gone.

He had finally given up on Kimball.

The fight was off.

And Tyrone was aging by leaps and bounds.

**While in Vegas**, Kimball had become a creature of habit. The moment he clocked out of work he bought his $1.99 parfait glass of shrimp, watched the overhead show of the Freemont Experience, and then went home. There were no back-alley surprises, no meth whores looking for a quick buck or gangbangers sizing him up as he passed them by. Unlike most nights, tonight was uneventful.

He sat in his apartment with the lights and TV off, nothing but dark shadows.

Nor did he shower—the stink of garbage all over him.

Louie had provided him with an opportunity. He also told Kimball the truth about himself, even though he tried to turn a blind eye to what he truly was: a warrior, a fighter, a killer. Not a man who was elbow deep in trash.

But Kimball was a man convicted to make a change.

But it was hard, if not impossibly difficult since the blood of a soldier still coursed through his veins.

The moment the Vatican Knights were disbanded by Pope Gregory XVII, Kimball wondered what lies in his future. Honest jobs with meager wages? Little hope of anything else other than to believe that one lousy job was just a setback? And that every job would be something 'temporary' until something better came along. What he learned was that life beyond the auspices of the Vatican was far more difficult than he had imagined.

Kimball stood up and parted the drapes, allowing a ray of gray light to filter in. In the distance, he could see the flashing lights along Boulder Highway. And to the west the dazzling lights that the Las Vegas Strip was known for.

Change was not easy, he told himself. And Louie's words were beginning to strike him hard.

He was growing older, like Tyrone. And whether or not he wanted to admit it, he was becoming just as jaded. 'Temporary' was becoming 'permanent.'

He then went to the refrigerator, pulled out a bottle of Jack Daniels, and rather than grab a glass to drink from, he returned to the window and drank directly from the bottle.

And then reality struck him like a hammer blow: *I kill people. It's what I do. It's what I'm good at.*

This had always been his mantra.

It was also a fact that those who contested him had also breathed their last breath.

"I kill people" he whispered. "It's what I do. It's what I'm good at."

Kimball closed his eyes, letting the effects of a buzz overwhelm him. And in his mind's eye, he could visualize the disappointment in Louie's face, could hear the admonishment in his voice: "*A fighter will always be a fighter. A loser will always be a loser. And a dreamer will always be a dreamer. If you think for one minute this is only temporary, then you're sadly mistaken.*"

Kimball brought the bottle to his lips and took a long swig.

And then in a whisper only he could hear, he said: "I . . . am . . . a warrior."

He took another long pull from the bottle and closed the drapes, immersing him in a gloom that was equal to his mood.

Within the hour the self-proclaimed warrior passed out from too much drink, his bladder loosening as he lay in mock crucifixion across his bed, only to awake six hours later totally humiliated by what he had become.

# CHAPTER ELEVEN

Leonid Sakharov had always been afraid of flying, which was actually an excuse to imbibe a few shots before boarding his flight to take away the edge. He also knew it would be the last time he'd be allowed to partake.

By mid-afternoon, he boarded an Aeroflot Russian Airliner. And though he found the economy class cramped with the hanging odors of unwashed passengers sitting around him, he at least found marginal comfort knowing it was a straight route to Tehran.

With his meal tray down, Sakharov had his notes out, little pieces of paper with drawing representations of molecular buckyballs and corresponding formulas. From his memory he had mined the information he created mentally while serving in Vladimir Central, the sketches derived strictly from recall as he doodled spherical molecular formations of the Buckminsterfullerene, the Carbon 60 molecule necessary for the structure of the nanobot.

Buckminsterfullerene is the smallest fullerene molecule in which no two pentagons share an edge. The structure of $C_{60}$ is a truncated icosahedron that resembles a soccer ball that is made up of twenty hexagons and twelve pentagons, with a carbon atom at the vertices of each polygon and a bond along each of its edge. This special molecule was discovered in 1985 at Rice University and was deemed very adaptable, smart, and able to contemplate its existence. A year later, Leonid Sakharov embarked on his scientific journey thousands of miles away by programming a chain of commands into the structure, the molecule then carrying the codes over to replicated molecules until the commands became a collective whole. And though the commands worked in the previous testing, the matter to slow the process to duplicate itself exponentially had fatal consequences. And this was the problem—to somehow give it a smaller lifespan half the length of the original, and then a half-life for every subsequent molecule thereafter until it fades itself out completely.

He examined his notes carefully, then made additional sketches and drew formulas with numerical designs that looked more like Greek lettering.

And he did this all the way to Tehran.

Once the plane touched down, Sakharov disembarked with the aid of airline personnel, who wheeled him across the terminal in a wheelchair and released him to al-Ghazi, who was waiting by the terminal doors.

Al-Ghazi, as always, was impeccably dressed from top to bottom. "And how was your trip, Doctor? I assume it was a pleasant journey."

"Pleasant? It smelled like ass all the way over," he said.

*As crotchety as ever*, al-Ghazi thought.

Once the doors opened, a plume of heat blasted into the doorway.

"It's hot as hell out there," said Sakharov.

"But it's a dry heat."

"I'll make sure to tell that to the ambulance driver as he's loading me into the back of the van. I'll just say to him: 'No rush. It's just a *dry heat*, so don't worry about the oncoming heat stroke.'"

Al-Ghazi rolled his eyes. Working with Sakharov was going to be difficult; he could tell.

Moments later they were in the back of a limousine cruising away from the airport. Sakharov had his full attention set to the passing landscape, marveling at the architecture.

Al-Ghazi smiled, intuiting the old man's thoughts. "It's not the mud huts and stone structures you thought it would be, is it?"

The old man looked out the window, noting the complexity and wide arrangements of design and culture taken into consideration of their planning. The buildings were stunning, elegant. But such praise of amazement was beyond Sakharov's makeup.

He waved his hand dismissively and sat back. "I've seen better," he finally answered. And then: "So now what?"

"Now, you will go to a safe house and rest. Tomorrow you will be taken to a facility in the Alborz Mountain Range, courtesy of President Ahmadinejad."

"Ahmadinejad? What the hell does he have to do with this?"

"He's providing a safe haven that neither Iraq nor Afghanistan can provide at the moment," he told him. "You will always be safe,

Doctor. And you'll be able to work knowing that you will not be disturbed."

"That's good," he said. "Those are conditions I can work with."

"But, Doctor, you will not be alone, either."

"What's that supposed to mean?"

"It means that you will have three aides of my choosing to help you with your research."

"Aides! I don't need any aides! There was never any discussion of assistants."

"The choice is not yours to make."

Sakharov nodded, "I see. Now that you have me where you want me, I'm now at your mercy. Is that it?"

"Doctor, I'm providing you with the best equipment, the best of everything, so that you can simply provide me with the best results. You will be pampered beyond your wildest dreams. And believe me, this lab will be something you've never seen before and something Russia could never duplicate. It'll be your playground. And these aides are there only to be at the mercy of your beck and whim, nothing more."

"Nothing more, huh? Well, I don't want any rookies, you hear me? I want somebody who knows their way around the lab and to do things without me watching over their shoulder every waking minute."

"Your three assistants, Doctor, are tops in their field of nanotechnology. Two were educated at the most prestigious schools in the United States, the other in the United Kingdom."

"Americans and a Brit?"

"Hardly," he answered with a hint of venom. "They are like me. They are Arab."

"You mean they're al-Qaeda?"

"Not particularly. No," he returned. "Let's say that they had no choice in the matter since their family members are at the mercy of my organization."

"I see," said the old man. "Recruitment by intimidation, is that it?"

"Ultimately, and in the end, the decision will be theirs to make."

"And if their answer is 'no,' then a good ol' fashion beheading is in order for their family members. Am I right?"

Al-Ghazi held his hands out in surrender. "What can I say," he said. "Business is business."

The old man looked out the window noting that the landscape was getting visibly downgraded as if war-torn, the buildings old and in disrepair. "Obviously, you're not taking me to a five-star hotel."

"Where I'm taking you, Doctor, is still better than that rat-infested apartment I took you out of."

"There were no rats in that apartment," he insisted harshly. Then in a more subdued tone, "They were just big-ass mice."

The vehicle turned onto a dust-laden driveway between buildings that were cramped with just enough space for single-lane driving until they came to a lot in front of a two-story rise with barred windows.

"This is it, Doctor."

Sakharov remained silent, but just for a brief moment. "Are you kidding me?" he finally said. "A bunch of fleas wouldn't live here. I think I'm entitled to a little luxury for what I'm about to do for you, don't you think? I want to stay in one of those fancy hotels we passed a while back with caviar and an all-you-can-drink bar. That's what I want."

"What you want is of no concern to me, Doctor. This is just a place to lay your hat for a moment while I'm in Islamabad finishing up business. And then off to greater comforts come the day after tomorrow."

Sakharov could do nothing but relinquish his bull-headed stance.


**"Why does everything** in this country smell like ass?" said the old man.

Al-Ghazi clenched his jaw, fighting for calm. The old man continued to test his patience.

The moment the old man opened the door he clearly noted that the room was small with horrible ventilation, the air so hot and stale that it hung like a pall. On the floor was a thin mattress with a blanket that had seen better days, its edges tattered like the ends of a flag that had waved itself ragged with the course of an unyielding wind. And the walls were cracked enough to reveal the mud bricks underneath. Even the roof bowed downward in a threatening manner.

"You do take me to the nicest places," Sakharov commented, shaking his head disapprovingly.

Al-Ghazi dropped Sakharov's bag to the floor with a loud bang. Apparently, he'd had enough of the old man's ravings of discontent.

"Regardless, Doctor," his tone held an edge to it, "here you will stay, and here you will rest. Come tomorrow and every day thereafter, there will be no time for leisure. This is it."

The old man chortled. "I had better accommodations in Vladimir Central."

Al-Ghazi closed his eyes and clenched his jaw once again, with the muscles in the back working. And then calm overtook him, his facial semblance taking on the features of gentle repose.

"I see it'll take patience to deal with you," he told him.

"Whatever." The old man shuffled his way across the floor and to the window, looking through the bars at a dirt lot. Children played with sticks and a ball, kicking up dust in their wake. And the old man now had regrets. *What have I done?*

"Doctor Sakharov?"

The voice sounded thin and tinny as if spoken from a great distance.

"Doctor?"

"What."

"Perhaps you could go over your notes to better acquaint yourself with the technology you have been away from for so long."

"The science is up here," he said, tapping the tip of his forefinger against his temple. "It never went away. It never goes away."

"Then you can replicate your findings of what you did in Russia in the Alborz?"

Sakharov turned on al-Ghazi. "I can do this with my eyes shut," he answered. "From the first day I started my sentence in Vladimir to the day you showed up at my apartment, I have thought nothing other than nanotechnology or how I could make it better." He took an awkward gait closer to the Arab. "All those years you reached me in Vladimir Central with letters and messages kept my hopes alive that someday I would be granted the opportunity to ply my trade once again. And for that I thank you. But don't you ever question or interpret the validity of my skills as a nanotechnologist again. Duplicate it I will, as promised for my early release."

Al-Ghazi nodded, somewhat taken aback by the old man's power to intimidate. "You do realize that we will be time-restricted."

"If you say you have the equipment as you claim, then time won't be an issue. I simply need to achieve the methods to program the fullerene molecules to nullify their lifespan by half upon every replication until they fade completely out of existence."

Al-Ghazi didn't have a clue as to what Sakharov was talking about.

68

"Yeah, well—I can tell by the stupid look on your face that you don't know what I'm talking about," said the old man.

If Sakharov had a skill, thought al-Ghazi, it was getting under a man's skin.

"Rest," he finally told him. "Food will come momentarily."

"Food? We ain't talking baboon eyes or anything like that, are we? No monkey nuts or something that'll make my stomach crawl."

Al-Ghazi, for the moment, had to wonder if it was worth keeping this man alive. As much as he wanted to say "no" and pass a sharp blade across Sakharov's throat, he had no alternative but to keep the old man upright. If nothing else, he considered, keeping him alive was imperative.

# CHAPTER TWELVE

*Vatican City*

The sole distinction of being the smallest country in the world belongs to Vatican City, which is roughly the size of a golf course. It also serves as a sovereign state catering to billions across the globe as the religious hub for Catholicism with its focal point the Basilica, which bears the designed floor plan of a Latin cross. Beneath it lays necropolis, the ancient city of the dead that was pioneered during Rome's Imperial times, and ultimately discovered by serendipity in 2003 when the earth was lifted to create a parking lot. Thereafter excavation began, the groundwork opening a few years later to restricted parties who were allowed to venture into the tombs by invitation only.

Those without restriction, however, were few.

Deep within the necropolis was the base command center of the *Servizio Informazioni del Vaticano,* the SIV, or the Vatican Intelligence Service. Since the Church had diplomatic ties with more than ninety percent of the countries worldwide, it was recognized as one of the most esteemed agencies in the world, rivaling Mossad and the CIA.

In a chamber beneath the necropolis and south of the Egyptian Tomb that was restricted to all parties except for the SIV and certain religious VIPs, lay a high-tech room behind walls of reinforced glass. Against the entire opposite wall hung large, high-definition monitors situated before computer consoles on tiered floors. And the lighting was constantly subdued, enabling the LED vision of the screens to be more crystalline in effect.

Those who manned the screens and tendered the consoles were not civilians at all, but Jesuit priests who were given the sole tasks to monitor hotspots across the world, especially the insurgencies that were brewing in North Africa and the Middle East.

On the screen was an aerial image of Jerusalem, most notably the Temple Mount. People milled about, their daily routine nominal beneath the desert sun as the satellite zoomed in with such clarity and proximity that their identities could be discerned with facial recognition software.

"It's as if nothing ever happened," said Gino Auciello. The Jesuit was tall, thin, and wiry with shock-white hair that was conservatively cut. His face was smooth and unlined, his complexion the color of tanned leather. And though he was pious to the core, he was also a scholar from Harvard University who graduated from the School of Theology, with minors in the sciences of politics and world studies. And it was this combination that suited him well for the role as the assistant director of the SIV.

Beside him stood Father John Essex, a priest who got his foothold of learning in London and progressed into the SIV for his economical patience regarding his penchant to gather and analyze pertinent data in regard to Vatican interests. He was short, stocky, and well-conditioned, the Jesuit often serving as a boxing coach for wayward children at the Boys' Center in Rome. With obsidian hair, ruler-straight teeth, a Roman nose, and sapphire blue eyes, John always drew the appreciable eye of the female constituency within the administration. "Nothing seems to ever happen," he finally answered, "because to them, nothing did. It's unlikely the government is going to inform them that the most jeweled treasure of our time was stolen from them beneath their very noses."

Father Auciello took a step forward with his hands clasped behind the small of his back. "Any intercepts?" he asked, his eyes remaining fixed on the monitor.

Essex nodded. "From the imprecise data collected from Mossad, it appears that an Arab faction may have taken the Ark and left behind the staff of Aaron and the golden pot of manna as proof of the true Ark. Apparently this faction contacted Mossad, saying the Ark would open its ills against all the infidels in the world. No further explanation was given."

"Do we know anything about the faction group?"

"No. From what we can surmise from the intercepts, the Lohamah Psichlogit believes the illegal excavation was conducted by al-Qaeda.

But they're basing this on an encrypted message they received and translated from an unknown source. Keep in mind, however, that this is nothing but inference since the partial communication has not been confirmed as viable. But as of three hours ago it's the only thing they have. And because it's the only thing they have, it's the only thing *we* have."

Auciello nodded. "Keep monitoring the channels."

"Will do."

For a brief moment, both men eyed the monitors in silence, both wondering if the holiest of treasures was truly in the hands of al-Qaeda. And both wondered the same thing: What will they do with it?

As that thought hinged on their minds the access door behind them whooshed open and a man wearing vestments stood silhouetted against the backdrop. "Gentlemen," he said, "how good it is to see you both once again."

Fathers Auciello and Essex stood rapt as the shape came forward.

**Cardinal Bonasero Vessucci** lifted the hem of his robe and carefully took the steps to the Tomb of the Egyptians. The air was dry and cool, the smell musty and moldy as all underground chambers were. The cardinal had ventured these steps many times in the past as the Vatican's secretary of state. Now he ventured them as a man stripped of his hierarchy, but a man respected by the ranks of the SIV, nonetheless.

With the alacrity of an aged man, he took the steps slowly as he descended, the way lit by electric lanterns. When he set foot on the bottom, he noted the old stone walls and the pathways, once erected by pagans, leading to the old burial chambers. He also took note of the trail that led to the SIV command center, a bullet-shaped archway that gave entrance to a vaulted doorway that had a mirror polish to it. Beside it was a keypad.

After punching in the buttons, the door opened, giving entrance to a pristine white booth where he was being scrutinized by a security camera, which was a small globe that hung at the top of the booth's corner marking the landmarks on the cardinal's face for facial recognition as he stood there. Once done, the second set of doors opened, and the cardinal was given access to a small, rounded chamber that was so ethereal in its whiteness that it seemed to give off a glow.

"Welcome, Cardinal Vessucci," said the security officer monitoring the facial recognition scanner on his console. It was a 3-D picture of the cardinal along with a brief dossier of the man's profile. "It's good to see you again."

The cardinal smiled. In the room's center was a single white desk. And the officer sitting behind it wore the traditional garments of the security staff, a pair of black pants and a scarlet jacket with the symbol of the Vatican on the coat pocket, the crisscrossing keys of St. Peter—one gold, the other silver—set beneath the papal tiara. The colors of the man's uniform were in dark contrast against the entire whiteness of the room.

"Ah, Emilio," he said, holding out his hand. "If only the circumstances were different."

The officer took the cardinal's hand and shook it. "I see you're part of the conclave once again."

"Twice in six months," he responded. "And in my book, that's twice too many." He looked past the officer to a smoked glass doorway. "Would the good Fathers Auciello and Essex be in by any chance?"

"They are."

"Would you be kind enough to give me access to the SIV Chamber? There are matters I must discuss with them."

"Of course, Cardinal." The officer pressed a button, and the smoked doorway gave access to a feebly lit stairway. "Be careful," he told him. "The rails will guide you."

The cardinal smiled. "I'm no stranger to the chambers, my dear friend."

The cardinal descended the stairway with a tight hand on the railing. Once he reached the bottom he noted the reinforced glass, the myriad of blinking lights and monitors, the casts of light coming from the faces of the PC monitors sitting on top of the consoles. Against the opposite wall stood a massive screen that offered a view similar to looking out a glass window. The clarity was that exceptional.

After punching in a code to access the chamber, the door whooshed open, and a blast of cool air met the cardinal as he stepped onto the threshold. Fathers Auciello and Essex turned, and the old man could see the surprise on their faces.

"Gentlemen," he said, "how good it is to see you both once again." And the good Cardinal Bonasero Vessucci stepped inside, the door closing behind him.


**Arms were extended** and hands were shaken. Fathers Essex and Auciello had missed their old friend, which was evident by the genuine smiles and congenial pats on the shoulders. After the greetings ended, the cardinal then took on a more sober look as he ushered the priests away from the monitors so that he could pull them into close counsel, so as not to be heard by the Jesuits.

In a tone barely above a hushed whisper, the cardinal said, "It's a shame about Pope Gregory."

Both men nodded.

"So, tell me, what do you know about his passing?"

Auciello took the advance and spoke for Father Essex as well. "That it was an accident, the pontiff leaning too far beyond the railing."

But Bonasero's instincts had always been quick and sharp, his assumptions not always correct but at least close to the truth. In his regard, he had viewed Gregory as a deeply careful and prudent man who considered every facet of life with the utmost caution, which was an embedded trait of his polished conservatism. *So, what was he doing at such an early hour on the balcony? Was there something on the cobblestones below calling him from the shadows of the blue night like a siren? Or was it truly an accident as everyone believed: that the man simply fell to his death?*

The questions nagged at him and wouldn't let go; a marked trait as staunch in him as conservatism was in Pope Gregory.

"Is everything all right, Bonasero?" asked Essex.

Bonasero feigned a smile and placed a caring hand on the Londoner's forearm. "Everything's fine," he told him. "But tell me, when I left, did the good pope inquire about the nature of the Vatican Knights?"

Auciello nodded. "He did. But only through the good Cardinal Angullo, who wanted to know everything including the activities of the SIV."

"Such as?"

"Angullo wanted to be apprised about everything regarding the Knights," he said. "As well as all SIV matters pertaining to the Knights, and how deep the SIV looks into on-site matters and situations across the globe. To me, it seemed as if the cardinal was acting more on his interests rather than that of Pope Gregory's since the pope already knew about the magnitude of our responsibilities—global or otherwise. It appeared to me that the good cardinal was gleaning knowledge for his sake rather than the sake of the pope."

Bonasero nodded and listened, consuming everything with avid interest.

"But he is the secretary of the state," he added. "So, we could not deny him what he requested to know."

There was no doubt in Bonasero's mind that Cardinal Angullo was grooming himself to be omniscient in worldly affairs. He also knew Angullo to be overly ambitious to fulfill his needs to achieve greater heights within the church's hierarchy. The man was politically skillful in negotiations, quick with his wit, and articulated well with a sharp tongue. In a power grab, he also maneuvered himself to usurp Bonasero's position as secretary of state; better positioning him to the papal post should it become vacant, which it had six months after the last Electoral vote.

And in that short tenure while Gregory reigned, Cardinal Angullo learned the secrets of the Church and placed himself in a position to know everything, should he happen to take the papal throne.

Cardinal Bonasero found the whole scenario disturbing, however. The power of the Church was squarely within Angullo's grasp and his power would have no boundaries, should he be chosen.

Bonasero took a step closer to the screens, the view of the Middle East and Northern Africa as clear as peering out an unblemished window, as his mind continued to roil with the thoughts of Angullo possibly garnering the papal post. What he couldn't let go of was the fact that there was something deeply hidden, if not forever buried, that Cardinal Angullo ambitions to succeed the throne outweighed his moral compass, and even considered that the cardinal's ambitions had become so paramount that the life of Pope Gregory was snuffed out by the cardinal's committing hand.

Letting a sigh escape, Bonasera closed his eyes with the realization that corruption within the Church was not just a medieval constitution, but a conviction of a black soul who was convinced that their actions were for the overall good.

And Bonasero prayed that this was not the case, hoping above hope that Pope Gregory's death was truly a mishap rather than the dark machinations of a lost soul.

He washed the thought away and turned toward the screen, reminiscing of a time when he used to view and direct the Vatican Knights to the hot spots around the world to save countless lives. And then he wondered how many souls were lost due to the refusal of the Church to send forth a unit to protect the citizenry of the Church within the past six months.

Under further consideration, it was amazing to the cardinal how one man had the power to change the lives of so many with a single command or wish, each thought directed by the convictions of what Pope Gregory believed to be right or wrong, good or evil.

And then his consideration went one step further: *How many people died over the past six months under the pope's tenancy when they could have been saved?*

As he stepped closer to the visual on the mounted wall screen, Cardinal Bonasero Vessucci could only wonder.


**"Tell me—" said** the cardinal, pointing to the live feed "—why you are observing the Temple Mount."

Fathers Essex and Auciello joined the cardinal by his side, the men focusing on the actions playing out before them.

Father Auciello answered in his usual stately manner. "You have been gone for too long, my friend," he said. "If you were still secretary of state, then you would have a live team in place."

"Are lives in jeopardy?"

"No," said Auciello. "But we are getting invalidated reports through encrypted codes from Mossad that the true Ark of the Covenant may be in the possession of an al-Qaeda faction."

Bonasero appeared astonished. "The Ark of the Covenant? At the Temple Mount? Has it always been there?"

"We're still trying to determine that. But all indications are that the Covenant was located in an uncharted chamber approximately a half kilometer to the east."

"And how did it come into the hands of al-Qaeda?"

"Again: we don't know for sure. Everything is just speculation at this point. But Mossad seems to be highly active at the location we're now watching."

Bonasero Vessucci remained riveted in his stance, his eyes cast forward, watching. If Pope Gregory did not disband the Vatican Knights, then there was no doubt that they, along with established members of the SIV, would be onsite gleaning information rather than speculating from satellite feeds and encrypted notes. "Al-Qaeda will use it for nefarious purposes only—we know that. It's an interest of the Church to be shared by all, not just the Church itself." He then turned to Fathers Essex and Auciello. "Is the Camerlengo acting on this?"

Auciello nodded. "No," he said. "He's more focused on the pope's burial and the upcoming election."

"As well he should be."

"And we haven't enough data to support the need to act. And even if we did," he added dolefully, "we longer have the resources to intervene."

The cardinal turned back to the movements on the screen, the people milling about on an obvious hot and dry day. Auciello was right, he considered. The Vatican Knights were the only true resource to act on behalf of the Church in affairs of war and battle, in which the lines drawn were not specifically done so at the Vatican door. Most interests were in foreign lands with diplomatic ties which were well beyond the reach of the Church, some halfway around the world. Now that the value of the Knights had been cast to the wind, there was little or no salvation beyond Vatican City for those with the most need.

Furthermore, al-Qaeda was a faction of opportunity. If they truly were in possession of the Ark, then they would capitalize in such a way that would subsidize terrorist campaigns for years to come. How they would benefit was the question that lingered in the cardinal's mind. But they were talking about al-Qaeda.

And al-Qaeda would find a way.

"Bonasero?" Father Essex sounded almost contrite. "If I may be candid."

"Of course."

"Since the times of Pope Gregory and Cardinal Angullo, we have been somewhat revoked to act accordingly."

Bonasero Vessucci understood. Without the Vatican Knights to act upon pertinent information that may prove detrimental to the assets and interests of the Church, or to its citizenry, then there was no point in having the SIV other than to convey rudimentary intelligence.

"I hear you," he said, and then he ushered them away from the

Jesuits once again. When they were in the pooling shadows with a minimal light cast from the screens, Cardinal Vessucci spoke to them with open objectiveness. "As you know, I am impotent to act in the manner deemed necessary by my station."

"Then perhaps you'll elevate to the next level so that you can."

"It's not a secret that I'm seeking the papal throne. But Cardinal Angullo is a formidable candidate who seeks the throne as strongly as I do."

"Should Angullo succeed the throne, others will suffer due to the Church's inability to protect them. So, tell me, Bonasero, if you take the papal throne, do you plan to bring back the Vatican Knights?"

There was a moment of hesitation, and then he nodded, a single bob of the head. "It would be my wish to do so," he answered. "But the good Cardinal Angullo would stand in the way since he refuses to see their necessity in the scheme of things. If al-Qaeda is truly in the possession of the Ark, then we need to react before such a treasure is lost forever—or before it's used in ways not meant to be."

"I hear his camp has weakened," said Essex.

"But still formidable. Remember, gentlemen, he has strength by being the secretary of state and as Pope Gregory's close friend. Those two facts alone make my journey a difficult one to achieve."

There was a momentary lapse of silence.

And then, with forced spirit, the cardinal smiled. "We must be patient by waiting to see how His will plays out," he said. "If the good Cardinal Angullo excels to the throne, then so be it."

"You know as well as I do that if he does, then the Church suffers greatly. It's not only His will, Bonasero, but there's a human element involved as well."

"From where I stand, I can do very little. But if my peers see me as a suitable replacement for Pope Gregory, then the SIV will be brought into play . . . as will the Vatican Knights."

Essex and Auciello did not smile, nor did they betray their thoughts or emotions. But deep inside they wanted the cardinal to take over the papal throne and the privilege to protect the interests of the Church, its sovereignty, and the welfare of its citizenry, which could only be done with the Vatican Knights under his rule and the rule of the Society of Seven.

They hoped.

They prayed.

They needed.

And the only person who stood in Bonasero's way was the all-powerful Cardinal Angullo.

# CHAPTER THIRTEEN

*The outskirts of Tehran, Iran*

Night had come to Tehran. And the old man lay on the ultra-thin mattress recalling the moments when such a luxury would have been a blessing in Vladimir Central Prison.

*Just a simple item,* he regarded, as he lightly brushed his fingertips over the coarse fabric. The little comforts that better a man's life, he told himself, can be by the most minimum of degrees.

On that first day when the doors of the Vladimir Central Prison closed behind him, Leonid Sakharov couldn't even begin to comprehend the meaning of hardship or fear or degradation until the bodies of his comrades began to pile quickly at his feet.

After having his head shaved, the cuts and scrapes testament of a dull blade, he was then placed in a cramped cell with three other men. Two nights later, with the situation serving as a psychological breakdown as much as physical, they were ordered out of their cell to the showers, told to spread their legs and feet as they placed their hands against the wall, and beaten with a baton or rubber truncheon until they had little reserve left to drag each other back to their cell.

Those who later complained to the authorities of the brutality were singled out for worse punishment, which is why Sakharov remained submissively quiet by giving in to the totalitarian rule that governed the system.

During the nights in his quarters when he froze and his bones seemed to be as fragile as glass when not-so-alien screams sounded pained and distant, he kept his mind active and his eyes closed, drawing mental pictures of buckyballs and formulas in his mind before committing them to memory.

Often in the mud-laden yards, whenever possible, he would draw diagrams and formulas with the tip of his finger, finding it easier to actually *see* what his mind was conceiving, and then filing it away in his memory if the concept were scientifically feasible.

The buckyballs, the formulations, everything was an escape in a world that was brutally harsh and unyielding. Cellmates came and went, always a different and interchangeable face on a seeming rotation to fill the gaps left behind by those who died by raging disease, torture, or suicide. But Sakharov hung on while his body slowly caved to alternative sicknesses stemming anywhere from lung ailments to fever. And whereas his body began to regress, his mind continued to remain sharp.

On the climatic cusp of weather change, when the conditions were about to become abysmally cold due to the onset of fall and winter months when the tines of his nerve endings began to ache in concert, redemption came to him in the form of a man he had never met before.

It began on a damp morning, the old man huddled beneath a threadbare blanket on his bunk, his knees drawn up in acute angles in a feeble attempt to keep himself warm. In the early morning light, he could see the cold, wintry vapor of his breath, causing him to pull the blanket tightly around him as though it were a second skin.

And when he heard the footfalls of the coming guards he closed his eyes, feigning sleep.

The door of his cell slid back, the un-oiled squeal of metal against metal as brutal as life inside Vladimir Central, and then the hard nudges against the old man's side with the tip of one the guard's baton.

"Get up and come with us," he said in typical clipped Russian.

The old man learned long ago never to question a guard or to look him in the eyes. Laboring to his feet, shedding the blanket to one side, Sakharov stood and simply waited for the next command with his head submissively lowered so that his eyes were cast to the floor.

One of the guards pressed the baton across his backside and used it to usher the Old Man out of his cell. "Out and to the right," he ordered.

Sakharov closed his eyes. 'Out and to the right' normally meant one of two things: either he was about to be beaten unmercifully with a truncheon, or he would be forced to act on behalf of the guards and beat another prisoner as they watched. He hoped it was the latter.

As they reached the far end of the right quadrant, the guard shoved the old man with the stick to drive him in another direction, towards the yard where inmates were allowed one hour of 'outside' time.

Once there, the old man was shoved into the yard and the door closed behind him. He was not alone. In a frozen muddied lot surrounded by twenty-foot concrete walls and a chain-link fence serving as a ceiling of sorts to prevent escape attempts, he stared at a man who was tall, dark, and well dressed. His beard was perfectly trimmed, framing a thin face marked with the color and features of a man from the Middle East.

The man held his ground, appraising Sakharov with his hands deep inside the pockets of his jacket. His vapored breath came in equal measures. "Doctor Leonid Sakharov?" he asked in perfect Russian.

Sakharov looked immediately away; the man having been institutionalized long enough to be submissive at every encounter.

"Come, come, Doctor," he said, taking a step toward the old man, "I'm a friend. There's no need here to look away since we are equals, yes?"

Sakharov looked into the man's eyes. "Why am I here?"

The well-dressed man circled Sakharov as if sizing him up, his hands remaining inside his jacket pockets. "You don't look so well, Doctor. You look—what? Twenty, maybe thirty years older than when you first came here a few years ago?"

"What do you want?"

"I think the question should be, Doctor, is what we want from each other."

The old man appeared small, the upper half of his body folding like the curve of a question mark, as he remained silent.

"You want what only I can give you," the man added. "And in recompense, you give me what only you can give me."

"And that would be?"

"Your skills, Doctor. What I want are your wonderful skills."

"As you can see, I'm a broken old man. I have no skills."

"I'm not talking about your body or soul. I'm talking about your mind."

Now it was Sakharov's turn to appraise the man, to size him up. "Who are you? What's your name?"

The man smiled handsomely. "My name is Adham al-Ghazi."

"And why would a man from the Middle East want with my mind, as you so pleasantly put it?"

"It is said that you possess the theories of a certain technology we are most interested in."

"We?"

"The group I work for," he answered.

"And what group would that be?"

The man's smile diminished, but slightly. "A group that is willing to fund your way out of Vladimir Central Prison."

Sakharov straightened up at this the same way the ears of a dog would perk up at something interesting.

"From the looks of things, Doctor, it appears that you won't live another four months and we both know it. Now I can give you back the freedom and comforts of life, or I can leave you here to rot in this facility."

"You want to know about nanotechnology."

"I want to know certain applications of it, yes."

Sakharov squinted to study the man and moved closer. "You know why I'm here, don't you? You know that I was impatient and foolish, which cost the lives of two good people my government dismissed as collateral damage."

"I won't deny that."

"Then you also know that I foolishly destroyed the subsequent tests because of the nature of the program—that it's too powerful to manage."

"You became a drunk who fought with and lost a battle with his personal demons, Doctor. Don't kid yourself. There's nothing altruistic about your nature. You do what you do because you know that you can do what no other man on this planet can. This technology is too valuable to waste. If your government refuses to see that, then there are those who will value you for who and what you are . . . I can give you peace of mind, Doctor. Or as I said, leave you here to rot. It's your choice. But if I walk away from this prison, then I walk away for good."

Sakharov slowly bent back into position, his mind mulling over the proposition. He was a man dying by the inches, a man who often watched his cellmates come and go in a crafted box of cheap wood.

For years he formulated theories in his mind and stowed them away, only to get the chance to one day utilize them once again. For years he romanced and fantasized the idea of once again being in the lab to correct the errors of his past and to learn due diligence. It was the only thing that kept him alive over the past few years. Without it, he would have given up long ago like so many others who died without hope.

"Who are your people?"

"Is it important?"

"If I do this, then I need to know who I'm working with."

"First of all, Doctor, you won't be working with anyone. You'll be working *for* me and the constituency I represent."

Sakharov cocked his head studiously. "You're from the Middle East?"

"I am."

"Then why would I work for you? A man from the Middle East?"

"If you want your freedom, Doctor, then ask me no more questions and leave it at that."

"Are you al-Qaeda? Do you want to use my technology for weaponry? Is that it? At least give me the courtesy of knowing the people I may work for."

"Al-Qaeda is a strong word, so we'll leave it at that, Doctor. And you're running out of time. So, give me your answer."

The old man pulled in a breath of cold air, and his lungs rattled with awful wetness. "What must I do?" he asked flatly.

"Simple: stay alive while my people negotiate a sum for your release. It may take a while. It all depends upon the greed of these people. It could take a month, a year, who knows."

"And if you can't settle upon a sum?"

"Then you will die. But their greed is paramount, so I wouldn't worry. The moment we attempt to back off, then they'll give in. In the meantime, the guards will be paid to see that your accommodations are better, the meals more plentiful, and that you stay alive, if possible."

"And if I'm released?"

"There are other hurdles my constituency is trying to solve at this moment to acquire the necessary accouterments and location to serve your needs. Once done, then I will locate you and request that you fulfill your half of the agreement."

*And once I'm free and disagree to fulfill my obligation to them?* The answer was clear to Sakharov: *Then they will kill you in a manner far worse than Vladimir Central ever could.*

"Your answer, Doctor."

"If you could expedite the matter, then that would be greatly appreciated. It isn't exactly the Ritz in here."

Al-Ghazi gave a quick perusal of the area. "That's quite apparent," he said.

The man from the Middle East began to walk to the door and without looking back, he said, "In time I will find you, Doctor. Do not forget our agreement should the sum of your release be agreed upon."

And that was the last time the old man saw al-Ghazi until the moment when the Arab showed up in his apartment to cash in his chips.

From that point after the meeting, he was then ushered to a different cell that was larger, yet still cramped with the bodies of other prisoners, who were told that Sakharov was a man walking with a hands-off policy. If anyone so much as lay a menacing touch on the old man, then not only would they fall victim to a guard's truncheon, but most likely end up as pulp inside a pauper's coffin. The gruel was plentiful by Vladimir Central's standards, and a heater was provided as promised. The greatest luxury, however, was not the warmth or the additional gruel, but the wafer-thin mattress. Instead of lying on a cold wooden surface, he slept in marginal comfort.

So here he was, in Tehran, on a mattress reminiscent of his time in a Russian prison, a mere luxury.

And until the moment the old man fell asleep, Sakharov was caressing his fingers over the mattress.

# CHAPTER FOURTEEN

*Vatican City*

Standing before an open window in the *Domus Sanctæ Marthæ*, Cardinal Angullo stood looking out at the Basilica, musing over the fact that the conclave was just under two weeks away and that he, along with three others including Cardinal Bonasero Vessucci, were part of the *Preferiti*, those who were the most preferred to succeed the papal throne by the College of the Cardinals.

Politicking was a way to promote and nothing more. But it was the individual's choice as to who would succeed that was kept close to the vest. Those who divulged their candidate while entering the conclave stood the chance of ex-communication. Therefore, to build camps and alliances, and to share with them the strengths and ideologies of a *Preferiti* brought to the table beforehand, was paramount.

But Angullo's camp had weakened over the past six months, his ideologies not coinciding with the pontiffs, and therefore enacted unwarranted challenges toward the pope with subsequent discussions that often became heated between them. By exhibiting more power than was granted, with his management sometimes uncontrollable by the way he acted before the pope, caused his members to disassociate from his camp, the one-time respect for the cardinal now lost.

And this did not go unnoticed before his eyes.

By the inches, he was losing his foothold to be the next in line for the papal throne, yet his camp remained strong. But as time moved forward his power diminished. And so was the opportunity to sit upon the papal throne and rule a constituency of more than a billion people.

So, he acted accordingly and provided his opportunity.

On the eve of the pontiff's death, he spiced Gregory's meal with a poison that made him sick and feverish and somewhat disoriented. As the hours passed, as the blue shadows traipsed slowly across Vatican grounds with the trajectory of the moon, he waited in the shadows of the pontiff's chamber with saintly patience.

When the pope exited from the bed with the poison coursing through his veins like magma, and then making his way to the balcony, Angullo could not believe his luck and chalked it up to God's will. His original intent was to place a pillow over the pontiff's face and snuff the life out of him. And with the aged man dying in his sleep, a way of life in which the world would view as God's will, no questions would be asked. But when the large man stood at the rail of the balcony overlooking Vatican City, it was as if God was allowing him a lasting panoramic view of St. Peter's Square, a final goodbye with the Basilica, the obelisk, and the Colonnades clearly defined within his mind.

But Gregory's mind was clearer than he thought, the pontiff calling out in the darkness of his suite, somehow knowing that he was not alone, which caught the cardinal off guard.

Like a wraith that appeared to glide inches above the floor rather than walk across it, he quietly made his way to the balcony with a hand raised, and with a mighty shove sent the pontiff airborne, the big man clearing the railing and falling to the cobblestones below.

From his vantage point, he watched the life bleed quickly out of the man and across the stones, the old man raising a clawed hand skyward, towards him, accusing him one last time before it fell the moment, he took his last breath.

Angullo closed his eyes at the memory of what he had done so clear in his mind's eye. But the images of what he did that night never haunted him, his conscience remaining clear and undisturbed. And at that very moment, he had come to terms believing that what he had done was truly justifiable—and that upon his succession to the throne he would rule the Church the way Gregory should have.

And then he opened his eyes and raised his hand before him—the murdering hand, he considered, the one willed by God to shove Pope Gregory to his death for the good of the Church.

And since it was against Vatican law to perform an autopsy on the pope, the poison would never be discovered. And the cardinal was convinced that this was all due to the Lord's wishes. Lowering his hand, his eyes once again returning to the Basilica, Cardinal Angullo realized that another within the *Preferiti* stood in his way. And should

Cardinal Vessucci garner enough steam before the conclave, then God may see fit that Cardinal Vessucci follow the same fate as the late pontiff.

After all, he told himself, it was God's will.

# CHAPTER FIFTEEN

*Islamabad, Pakistan, The Following Day*

In the eyes of the Islamic Revolutionary Front, Umar al-Sarmad, although not a leader, possessed the qualities to become one. He was twenty-eight, brash, and full of bravado, the young warrior always romancing the idea that fighting in the name of Allah was a prestigious one.

For the past four years, he held the front lines along the Afghan mountain range, always the first into battle, the last to leave. Often, he would pray alongside his fellow combatants in the complex cave system as bombs hurtled over their heads, with the tremors beneath his knees or the cascades of dust falling from the cave tops affecting him little.

But in reality, Umar al-Sarmad had constantly prayed to a god that was not his and fought alongside the revolutionists with bravado that was nothing more than veneer.

For Umar al-Sarmad was not as he seemed.

His true name was Aryeh Levine, a Hebrew growing up outside the city of Jerusalem.

And he was Mossad.

At the age of twenty-four and having served three years in the Israeli Army and then an additional three years as a commando, Aryeh Levine caught the eye of one of the most recognized, if not the most legendary, intelligence agency in the world.

He was smart with the ability to make snap judgments hinging on instinct rather than the timely process of deductive reasoning. His judgments were usually correct in the most difficult situations—his leadership was recognized and never questioned. So, he was recruited for the welfare of the state of Israel.

From day one, he was "processed" as though he were a prisoner and had gone through rigorous interrogation techniques to withstand any punishments meted out, should his role as an infiltrator be compromised. He learned the enemy's language and dialect, their culture, and prayers. And the transformation from Aryeh Levine to Umar al-Sarmad was a successful one that culminated in a final makeover as an Islamic terrorist.

His commencement began in Yemen, at the Zaydi Great Mosque, where his anti-sentiment rants against the United States and Israel caught the attention of radical fundamentalists. Within months his seemingly sound reasoning earned him prestige within the Circle, which subsequently became a call of duty to serve Allah on the battlefield alongside his al-Qaeda brothers. Within three months, which was from the time he entered the mosque to the moment he first set foot on the battlefield, Aryeh Levine had successfully infiltrated the Islamic Revolutionary Front.

It wasn't, however, too long thereafter when he caught the eye of his leader, Adham al-Ghazi. On a frigid day deep in the mountain terrain, al-Ghazi's team happened upon a counterforce of a dozen troops who were killed in an ambush, their bodies scattered, bloodied, and unmoving. In the event, however, two survived the skirmish, both wounded, one holding his bullet-ridden arm, the other weak with a badly rented shoulder.

When they were forced to their knees before al-Ghazi, their eyes resigned to the fact that their lives were about to come to a horrible and violent end, the same way that a cat plays with its prize before the kill.

And al-Ghazi was that cat, his quiet demeanor as powerful as a feline's paw swiping at them, his dark eyes serving as the talons that drove deep beneath their skins by peeling back the layers to reveal their inward secrets until he knew who and what they were without even questioning them. Without a second thought or consideration, he simply knew they were Mossad.

They had stumbled upon a recon mission.

In his manner of questioning them, they gave little, most likely false data in the form of red herrings, as they were trained to do under such circumstances. To make his point, however, al-Ghazi shot the man with the gravely wounded shoulder dead, with the black-edged bullet hole emitting a ribbon of smoke from the man's forehead as he knelt a brief moment before falling dead beside his aide.

"*The truth,*" al-Ghazi said, his voice cold and flat and naturally uncaring to the surviving Mossad. "*I want . . . the truth.*"

But the truth never came. Instead, al-Ghazi was met with silence.

"*Very well, then.*" And at that point, he handed his pistol to Umar al-Sarmad, to Aryeh Levine, and without looking at him said, "*You know what to do.*"

The moment he hefted the pistol and regarded its weight in his hand, he turned to the agent. At the same time, the agent turned his oily and soiled face to the mouth of the weapon, then to the eyes of Levine. In an instant his eyes started, recognizing Levine, even with the growth of his beard. It was a fatal mistake. Within a measure of a heartbeat, Levine pulled the trigger. The bullet diced the man's brain and killed him instantly.

In al-Ghazi's eyes, Levine knew he had made an impression. But deep down he agonized over the trigger pull, having been forced to kill one of his own to maintain his cover.

In the aftermath he notified Mossad, telling them it was an unfortunate necessity. And in the end, the Mossad chalked it up to collateral damage that could not be avoided.

It was also the move that put Aryeh Levine under al-Ghazi's wing as his trusted trigger man who killed anyone at al-Ghazi's say without impunity. And by doing so, Al-Ghazi had elevated himself as a man with ultimate power by having others kill for him. *Anyone can take the life of a man,* he always said. *But to get others to do it for you is* absolute *power.* And it was this idea alone that he relished.

And Aryeh Levine was all too happy to oblige him, as long as he maintained his cover. Soon, he thought, he would kill al-Ghazi as a courtesy of Israel and its allies with the gun he had been handed.

Over time he had become stellar in his duties, promoting himself as a trusted officer within the ranks, but more so in the eyes of al-Ghazi, which prompted a call from the high-ranking official to serve as his aide in an impromptu mission.

In al-Ghazi's office in Islamabad, Umar al-Sarmad—and whenever he heard that name he inwardly cringed—sat before al-Ghazi's ornate desk with the black marble top. Despite the notion of al-Qaeda living in abject poverty within caves and landscapes that were harsh and brutal, they were not without their luxuries, either. His office was spacious with top-of-the-line furniture surrounded by Arabic wares, vases, and tapestries that proved costly. And scarlet drapery with scalloped hems that adorned the windows overlooked the stunningly beautiful city.

Like always al-Ghazi was impeccably dressed as he sat in a chair made of Corinthian leather, one leg crossed over the other in leisure. With his elbows on the armrests and his fingers tented with the tips resting beneath his chin, the Arab smiled at Umar, at Levine, showing off the fine rows of bleached-white teeth. "How are you, my friend?" he asked.

"I'm fine, Adham. Yourself?"

"As well as could be," he said, leaning forward. The Arab then reached into a draw and removed a manila envelope. Inside was a photo that he removed and placed on the marble top of his desk. "I need your services," he told him.

Levine sat and waiting.

"I need you to serve as an aide for this man" He slid the photo across the desktop, a black-and-white glossy of Leonid Sakharov. "He is a scientist working on behalf of our organization," he said. "But I need someone who will watch him since I have other projects in the making and cannot be there as I would like."

"You want me to serve as his bodyguard?"

"Not so much as I want you to serve as my eyes and ears when I'm not there," he said.

"There?"

"Tomorrow, you and I will be escorting the good doctor to Mount Damavand in Northern Iran."

Levine's mind reeled. *Iran?* The country was not exactly open to al-Qaeda operatives, he thought. But since he was programmed not to question al-Ghazi's judgment, who thought he was acting on behalf of Allah—and that the sin of not "possessing faith" in everything Allah warranted was usually meted out with a good old-fashioned beheading if questioned—thought it best to remain silent.

"Where we will take part in creating a glorious history," he added dreamily.

Levine realized he had to get a message out to his sources immediately. With al-Qaeda making a pact with the Iranian leadership, their alliance would galvanize Israeli and western agencies to take the required action in the form of sanctions or military strikes. His first inclination was that it had something to do with the development of

92

Iran's nuclear program and that Sakharov the key to putting it all together.

But Levine was wrong. His inclination was way off base because it was something far worse than the advancement of nuclear weaponry.

"I would be honored," he finally told him.

"Good. Then we leave for Mount Damavand first thing in the morning with the good professor along. But I must warn you now, Umar, the man is exceedingly difficult to get along with."

"I'll cope."

"Get a good night's sleep, then. Tomorrow we begin to make history and shine in Allah's eyes once again."

*Whatever.* "Then I must assume, Adham, that this will be a lengthy mission?"

"That will depend on Sakharov."

"Then may I leave the compound for a moment of leisure."

Al-Ghazi stared at him long enough for Levine to think that he may have triggered suspicion.

But then: "Not tonight, Umar. I cannot allow anything to happen to you. This opportunity is so dire that I must insist on your lockdown."

Levine conceded by nodding. He would have to figure a way to contact his sources once at Mount Damavand—a terrible risk to be sure, but a necessity, nonetheless.

Levine got his feet and bowed his head in respect of al-Ghazi's leadership. "*Allahu Akbar,*" he said softly. *Allah is the greatest.*

Al-Ghazi smiled in return. "*Allahu Akbar,* my friend. *Allahu Akbar.*"

# CHAPTER SIXTEEN

*Tehran, Iran*

For the past two days, Old Man Sakharov sat by the window watching children play in the dust of inhospitable land. The air held a wonderful dryness to it, and the sun blazed whitely overhead. As the children played on in the heat of a mid-afternoon sun without a care or worry of the atrocities brewing around them, he wondered if these kids would fall victim to the fundamentalist guiles of people like al-Ghazi, who were far more determined to put a gun in their hands in the name of Allah, rather than to teach them the ways of proffering an olive branch to their enemies.

But were they any different than his government who routinely embedded the seeded hatred against the United States during the Cold War? *No*, he answered loudly. *There was no difference, whatsoever.*

For two days the old man waited patiently, often daydreaming by creating buckyballs within his mind, often taking on a detached look by staring at nothing in particular and smiling dreamily at the thought of a second chance.

But when al-Ghazi walked into the room Sakharov didn't dare tip his hand that he wielded all the excitement of a child gearing up for the holiday season, as if gifts were mounting under the tree or placed next to the Menorah.

He was ready.

"About time," he said curtly. And then he noticed that al-Ghazi was not alone. "And whose little boy is this?"

Al-Ghazi was dressed in fatigues and wore the traditional black turban of war. Beside him stood Levine, just a measure shorter than al-Ghazi, but beefier and broader along the shoulders. He too was wearing fatigues and a turban similar to al-Ghazi's.

"His name is Umar al-Sarmad," he told him.

"Is Sarmad going to be my babysitter? I'm not a child, you know. I thought we had this discussion."

"We discussed the matter of your *scientific* aides bearing the knowledge and skills to assist you in the lab. Umar will be standing in as my proxy since I will not be there as much as I would like to be. Since I have cabals to direct, he will act as my eyes and ears when I'm gone."

"In other words: the man is going to be my babysitter?"

"No, Doctor. He's like I said—my eyes and ears." He stepped deeper into the room with his hands clasped behind the small of his back. "For you to work uninterrupted, we were only able to secure this lab in collusion with Ahmadinejad's blessing, as long as your work is shared with his regime."

Levine's ears prickled at this.

"However," he continued, "Ahmadinejad is not entirely a man of integrity. But a man who often says something to those who wish to hear something positive but does something else entirely different to promote his self-interest. Umar al-Sarmad will make sure that *my* interests will be protected when I'm not there."

"Is that how you look at me, as an interest?"

"I look at you, Doctor, as an asset to me, to my people, and Allah. And I made that quite clear to you on the day I visited you in the courtyard at Vladimir Central Prison, did I not?"

Sakharov remained silent.

"Umar will make sure that your progress will be recorded, and then forwarded to our sources for our safekeeping, should Ahmadinejad fall back on his promises to unite our findings."

Sakharov raised a hand. "Wait a minute," he said. "If Ahmadinejad falls back on his promise, then what will happen to me?"

"Do you want me to lie, Doctor, and tell you that nothing will happen once the testing is completed? That there is no risk involved? Or do you want the truth as I believe it to be?"

"What do you think?"

"Ahmadinejad has given me his promise that no harm will come to you or to anybody as long as we share a mutual interest in your work. But I cannot ultimately control the man's actions should he fall back on his word."

"I'm not so sure I want to take that risk," he returned.

Al-Ghazi feigned a half-smile and leaned forward so that his lips were inches away from Sakharov's ear. "If you do not do this, Doctor, then be assured when I tell you that if you do not go forward with my wish from this point on, then I will have you diced into cubes of human flesh by my people starting from the feet up. And be doubly assured when I tell you that I will make sure that you live long enough to see the pieces of your body placed beside you before they are fed to the dogs. Now, do you have any further questions for me?"

Sakharov tried to square his feeble shoulders in defiance. But it didn't work, the old man looking comical in his attempt, which turned al-Ghazi's false smile into a real one.

"Good," said al-Ghazi, stepping back. "Then we are in full agreement." Al-Ghazi turned his back on Sakharov and started for the door. "Gather your things," he told him over his shoulder. "We'll be flying off to the Alborz very shortly."

"How shortly?"

"Fifteen minutes." And then he was gone, leaving Levine in the room with Sakharov.

The old man squared off with the al-Qaeda operative, looking intently into the man's steely eyes and seeing nothing but resolve.

"Just to let you know that I'm a grown man who's not about to stand by and let someone like you intimidate me," he told him. "I've been around the block a few times and dealt with people much tougher than you."

Levine stood idle, saying nothing.

"I've been to Vladimir Central, you know. There isn't a tougher place in the world than Vladimir Central. And I survived that."

The operative took a step forward. "Now you have fourteen minutes."

Sakharov began to pack.

*Tehran, Iran, Imam Khomeini International Airport*

The chopper lifted off accordingly with al-Ghazi, Old Man Sakharov, and Levine, who sat in the helicopter's bay, watching Tehran pass quickly beneath them as they headed north toward the Alborz mountain range.

The trip for the most part was a silent one except for the rotor blades thrumming overhead. And it was during this downtime of the flight that each man held to his thoughts. Al-Ghazi considered the future and the opportune consequences that Sakharov's ingenuity would bring to the major cities of the United States and its allies, most notably Israel. Sakharov on the other hand, resurrected illustrations of buckyballs within his mind's eye, seeing with microscopic clarity the Frankenstein's monster he was unknowingly creating, due to his lack of visualizing anything beyond his colossal arrogance. And Aryeh Levine, or Umar al-Sarmad, sat trying to decipher ways to contact his sources without drawing undue attention or to risk an unwanted sacrifice should he be discovered.

So, the Israeli's mind toiled, always thinking. But until he saw the Comm Center of the facility in the Alborz, or until he understood what exactly Dr. Sakharov was working on, only then would he act.

Levine leaned forward and yelled over the noise of the rotating blades. "So, Doctor, what is it that's so important that you're working on?"

Sakharov turned to him. "What's your name again? Omar, right?"

Levine nodded in a way to correct the old man. "It's Umar," he said.

"Omar?"

Levine tried to shout above the sound of the rotors. "U . . . Mar," he pronounced.

Sakharov shot him a thumbs-up. "Gotcha, Omar!"

Levine wanted to roll his eyes and considered that Al-Ghazi was right when he said that Old Man Sakharov had a way of crawling beneath your skin and staying there.

"So, what do you do?" he asked again.

"Buckyballs," he answered.

"What?"

"Nanotechnology."

Levine fell slowly back into his seat. He knew nothing of nanotechnology, having only to be a quick study in regard to nuclear or biological warfare. But nanotechnology, although not exactly new, was alien to him since its applications were relatively in the genesis stages since the 1980s.

"What about it?" he pressed.

And then al-Ghazi intervened by raising a hand, a gesture for the discussion to cease and desist immediately. "What the good doctor does, Umar, is not open for discussion until we reach the facility. Once you become his aide, only then will you become an implicit part of the program. As long as we are in the company of others not privy to the project," he pointed to the two Iranian pilots sitting in the cockpit with headgear capable of washing out noise and listening in, "then there are to be no further discussions. Trust no one at this point."

How spot-on he was, thought Levine. Trust no one, especially the man who was sitting beside him wearing the guise of al-Qaeda when he was actually Mossad.

Playing his part as the duty-bound soldier, Levine fell all the way back into his seat, closed his eyes, and for the remainder of the flight let his mind wander, often dreaming of a safer Israel, while Sakharov dreamt of buckyballs.

*Mount Damavand, Iran, The Alborz Mountain Range*

The chopper floated effortlessly over the helipad near the top of Mount Damavand. The mount itself was one of the tallest within the range at over 18,000 feet in elevation, but the facility was located just above the base at roughly 3,000 feet above sea level. Nevertheless, the air was cold. The mountain was capped with pristine layers of snow. And the anticipation had boiled to a point where Old Man Sakharov's heart began to beat with the pace of the swinging blades of the chopper. As if to placate his condition, the Russian placed a soothing hand over his chest.

The helicopter hovered above the pad, giving a view of the facility's grounds. Above the cave entrance that led to a vault-like door, was a machine-gun nest manned by two soldiers. Below that entryway, where the gravel road began to wind its way toward the cave's mouth, stood a second MG nest, also manned by two soldiers.

And Levine took it all in, making mental calculations by noting the landscape, entry-points, and manned positions.

When the chopper landed and the blades stilled, the helicopter's door was swept open, and a soldier stood in silence as if appraising each man individually.

Levine immediately recognized the man's uniform. The soldier was wearing the identifiable attire of a Quds' operative, the uniform a tan camouflage with matching tan beret and Quds' insignia. His beard was marginal, a stunted growth of hair, and he wore sunglasses to protect his eyes against the harsh sunlight. With a wave of his hand, he motioned for the people within the helicopter to disembark and yelled something out in Farsi, which was taken to be an order to hasten their activity since patience did not seem to be a virtue with this man.

Once the three disembarked, they were ushered to a nearby Jeep and gestured to get in by the soldier who carried an assault weapon.

Levine leaned to within earshot of al-Ghazi. "They're Quds," he whispered.

"I expected no less from Ahmadinejad."

The Quds Force is an elite unit of Iran's Revolutionary Guard who once reported directly to the supreme leader Ayatollah Ali Khamenei. However, the uprising in the last presidential election in 2009 and its post-election suppression, indicated that the political power of Ahmadinejad was surpassing the power of the Shiite clerical system, leaving Ahmadinejad as the supreme ruler. With the Quds Force now under his rule, they remained subject to strict, military discipline presumed to be under the control of the highest levels of Iranian administration.

In hindsight, Levine just realized that his game had become more difficult by countless times. These guys were not to be trifled with.

As the Jeep took the road to the cave's entrance, Levine noticed the concern on al-Ghazi's face. Apparently, al-Ghazi's sudden illumination of the matter was surprising, given the fact that he formerly mentioned that Ahmadinejad was not to be trusted. Obviously, the presence of Quds Forces posed a threat to his program, or at least that's what Levine discerned from al-Ghazi's expressions.

In gesture, al-Ghazi rubbed a nervous hand over his face and chin.

When the Jeep came to a stop at the cave's entrance, both al-Ghazi and Levine took note of the machine-gun nest situated in the rocks above the cave's maw. Levine also took quick note of the .50 caliber machine gun pointing in their general direction. Sakharov, either in blissful ignorance or he simply didn't care, maintained a preamble of a smile.

*Now what?*

The Quds driver said something in Farsi, which al-Ghazi understood, and gave the driver a faux-pas salute the moment the driver sped away.

It was at that juncture that the vault's door, which held a mirror polish to its metal and about twenty feet within the mountain's recess, began to open outward. When the aperture was wide enough, a dozen

Quds' troops sprinted toward the three men with assault weapons well within their grasps but not pointed at them, but more to the ground at their feet.

Taking up the rear but walking as a man of leisure, a forged smile on his face, was a small and delicate man, hardly a soldier, but someone al-Ghazi and Levine immediately recognized.

His name is Hakim al-Sherrod. And in the circles of intelligence, it was believed that he was the most trusted of Ahmadinejad's aides. In fact, some believe that al-Sherrod was the true voice of Ahmadinejad, persuading the president on most decisions, earning him the nickname "The Devil's Companion."

With his arms held out in greeting, al-Sherrod pulled al-Ghazi into an embrace. And Levine saw al-Ghazi tense for a moment as al-Sherrod corralled him in.

"Ah, Allah has blessed you, I see." The man's smile widened, showing small, yellow teeth resembling kernels of corn.

"And why is there a Quds Force here?" al-Ghazi asked in a measured tone.

"For protection. Why else? You must remember, my good friend, that this facility is unchartered. Should the Israeli's learn of its position, then they may see fit to hand down retribution should they prove the true meaning of what we are about to achieve here, yes?" He then released al-Ghazi to square off with Sakharov, the man still smiling as his hatchet-thin face moved up and down the old man in appraisal. "And this is the esteemed wizard, yes? The man who will change everything?"

When Levine turned to see the man appraising him, he could feel his scrotum crawl the moment he wondered if this man had the uncanny insight to see him for who he truly was, the Mossad.

"And you would be?" he asked.

"Umar al-Sarmad," he answered evenly.

"He is my most trusted aide," al-Ghazi intervened. "And he will act as my proxy when I am not available. During my absence, he will act as the good doctor's aide."

"Aide?" Al-Sherrod faced al-Ghazi with his hands clasped behind the small of his back and looked at him questioningly. "It was my understanding that we have already provided Doctor Sakharov with the required aides."

"It was also the understanding that the good doctor would have an aide of my choosing, should my presence be needed elsewhere."

The man stared at him for a long moment, and then he beamed a smile. "Of course," he said jovially. "Of course!" And then he gestured to the open vault. "Please, come and settle in," he added. "We've much work to do, yes?"

Al-Ghazi, Sakharov, and Levine entered the facility in front of the suspicious eyes of the Quds' troops, the door closing behind them, and then the massive bolts sliding into their circular sockets, locking them in.

# CHAPTER SEVENTEEN

*The Alborz Mountain Range, Inside The Facility*

Levine's first assumption was that the facility was an unchartered station within the Alborz initially created to engage in nuclear or biological weaponry manufacturing. But as they walked by the glass-encased laboratory he barely recognized some of the hardware involved. In fact, he recognized none of it.

In a two-tiered lab that was massive and well lit, the bright lighting gave it somewhat of an antiseptic white-wash glow to the point where the area seemed to hold an ethereal glow. Technicians were completely in white, the color of their skin the only contrast to anything around them, as they tendered to electromechanical components and hardware. To the left was a tube-like structure Levine would come to learn as the molecular assembler. There were infrasonic equipment and probe microscopes, vacuum environments to avoid the scattering of bots, and the most advanced Electron Optical System available. And by Sakharov's expression, he could tell that the old man was salivating internally.

Whatever they were planning to do was definitely on a molecular level. Whether it was nanotechnology as the good doctor professed or nuclear research for warfare as intel believed, he knew he had no other choice but to contact his sources for a probable strike, even at the risk of his life.

And time was critical.

Acting as a guide, al-Sherrod led al-Ghazi's team to their quarters, which was through a tunnel drilled by a cylindrical bore since the walls were perfectly round and smooth. Overhead tracks of lighting gave off a pearlescent glow. And the smell of baked meats wafted from the mess hall not too far from their quarters, making them yearn for a fine meal.

At the next turn, al-Sherrod stopped with his hands clasped before him. His features betrayed no sense of emotion, no sense of what he was thinking. Behind him was a channel that went as far back as thirty meters before hitting a wall, the living quarters. And from Levine's viewpoint, he could tell they were prefab capsules built into the walls.

"Here you will rest," said al-Sherrod. "Mess call will be at eighteen-hundred hours. If you are late, then you will not eat. Everything here is regimented. So, I need you to keep that in mind."

Nobody said a word; the tense silence an awkward passing between them before al-Ghazi finally stepped forward and bowed his head as a show of marginal respect. "We accept your hospitality," he told him, "and much gratitude."

Al-Sherrod nodded. "What I do, I do for Ahmadinejad, as you know. But what we do together, we do so for the sake of Allah, yes?"

Al-Ghazi concurred with a nod and a smile. "*Allahu Akbar*," he added. Allah is the greatest.

"*Allahu Akbar*." Al-Sherrod then side-stepped al-Ghazi and moved with disciplined economy to the end of the corridor where it came to the T-juncture of the branch before stopping to face off with al-Ghazi and company one again. "One more thing," he began. "There is a hallway leading from the lab to a special compartment," he said evenly. "Inside is a great treasure which lays the purpose as to why you are here. Should your curiosity pique, you may enter in the presence of its glory but only under the watchful eye of the Quds." He hesitated while surveying Old Man Sakharov, internally commenting how this feeble-looking troll held the key to success. And then: "Remember, 1800 hours and not a moment later. *Allahu Akbar*."

"*Allahu Akbar*."

The moment al-Sherrod and his Quds unit left al-Ghazi and his team; al-Ghazi let his tension drip away by letting his shoulders fall slowly into the crookedness of an Indian's bow, the shape of a man slipping into relief. "I don't trust him," he said lowly. "The Devil's Companion is never without his wiles, no matter how accommodating he may seem."

"Perhaps he trusts us as much as we trust them. Which isn't much at all," said Levine.

"I can see Quds here as a factor to protect the facility since it bears a uniqueness, and would no doubt fall under foreign inquiry should its true purpose be discovered. But al-Sherrod's presence disturbs me greatly," he added. "He sees everything, which I'm sure is why Ahmadinejad placed him here, to begin with. So be careful, Umar. Don't let his smiles draw you into a false sense of security."

Sakharov was taking this all in but said nothing. After seeing the equipment, nothing else seemed to matter. In fact, he appeared to have a passive, almost dreamy appearance about him.

"When he told us of the hidden treasure," he told Umar, "he was also telling us that Quds will be everywhere."

Levine picked up the same notion—that al-Sherrod was surreptitiously telling them that as much as he was the eyes of Ahmadinejad; the Quds force would be the eyes of al-Sherrod.

They would be everywhere.

Levine then closed his eyes and clenched his jaw, causing the muscles to work. Doing recon throughout the facility is going to be difficult to achieve, especially under a constant and watchful eye. To get a message out to his sources, to proffer them the correct coordinates, was going to be an accomplishment.

He opened his eyes. Tomorrow, he thought, he would survey his surroundings and mine it for information before breaching the Comm Center and setting forth a series of communications that would likely cost him his life.

There were just too many eyes, he considered, too many obstacles to overcome. But since the safety of Israel was paramount, then his life was purely insignificant. This was something every agent was fully imbibed to believe: *That the life of Israel as a whole is worth more than the cost of the individual. Should the individual give up his life for the whole, then he shall become heralded to greatness.*

Still, Aryeh Levine found little consolation in this.

Suddenly al-Ghazi clapped him on the back, stirring him from thought. "Rest, Umar. Tomorrow we begin to seek the glory of our task, yes?"

The question was rhetorical, so Levine didn't answer.

Instead, his mind wandered and tried to find a viable solution that would enable him to contact his sources and enlighten them of the horrible truth within.

**As fatigued as** Umar al-Sarmad was, he could not sleep. The room was in actuality a prefabricated capsule fitted into a recess that was bored into the stone wall. Although it gave enough head clearance, it was still cramped and quite spartan. The bunk bed was riveted to the left side and a small desk to the right. Embedded into the walls were rows of fluorescent lighting. At least in Levine's mindset, it was nothing more than a glorified holding cell.

As he lay there with one arm crooked behind his head, he had to figure a way to get at the control panel and send a message.

But like any idealist, he knew there was no practical approach to the situation since there would be guards and personnel manning or protecting the consoles, the situation of making outside contact impossible to achieve. But the word "impossible," at least for Levine, didn't mean that something could not be done. It simply measured the degree of difficulty, which in this case, was at a remarkably high degree.

Still, he believed there was a solution for everything. And over the next few days, he would seek the measure to accomplish the means after he digested everything he needed to know about the facility. He would watch, he would learn, and he would inform the proper authorities to engage in a series of military sorties.

With his mind constantly working to focus on his game plan, he reached out and turned off the light, the room completely swallowed in darkness.

Lying with sleep hours away if it was to come at all, Aryeh Levine, now Umar al-Sarmad of the Islamic Revolutionary Front, a covert operator for Mossad, prayed not to Allah but to Yahweh, for a resolution where casualties could be kept to a minimum.

Idealistically thinking, he prayed that His answer would be "yes." Realistically, however, he knew His answer would most likely be "no," since realism always seemed to triumph over idealism.

Nevertheless, Aryeh Levine continued to pray.


**On the following** morning after Levine awoke from minimal sleep, he learned of al-Ghazi's departure during the night.

When commandeering cells independently, work was never done.

Levine gathered himself and dressed accordingly, which also meant donning the black turban of war, and headed for the mess where he sat alone at a table under the watchful eyes of Quds soldiers who often tossed derisive—yet out of earshot—remarks in Levine's direction, the comments drawing laughter from other Quds officers.

But Levine ignored them, thinking how funny it would be if he coordinated a military strike against the bunker ultimately swiping away those cynical smirks right off their proud faces.

A preamble of a smile came to his lips as he toyed with his food briefly on his plate with his fork, before bringing a morsel to his mouth.

When he completed his meal, he placed the plate and utensils at the counter and left the hall. Voices in Farsi called after him, more derisive remarks that went completely ignored.

Walking the facility, he made mental notes and filed them away. In his observations he saw Sakharov wasting no time as he busied himself in the lab, the old man moving with more of a bounce to his gait. With him were two lab techs dressed in lab coats—one manning the helm of a keyboard that managed a high-definition wall screen, the other jotting notes on a Plexiglas clipboard as he tarried around Sakharov making notes on everything the Russian did.

Machines came to life, emitting energies Levine could never begin to understand. And then he wondered if even the reinforced windows separating him from the lab were enough to contain any measurable damages, should the so-called failsafe neglect to perform as required. After all, Sakharov was manipulating atoms.

Wherever he went Levine was not alone. Keeping several paces behind him were two Quds soldiers with their sidearms holstered. So, Levine meandered, absorbing everything, the two soldiers always behind, not too close but not too far, either. When it came time to contact his sources, he would have to take them out to achieve the means. He would do it quickly, quietly, and efficiently. This he was sure of.

On the second-tier level overlooking the lab, also fully encased in bomb-proof glass, he observed a room in subdued darkness; the surrounding walls lit up with pinprick beads of light and display monitors.

*The Comm Center.*

He saw technicians speaking into their lip mikes as the accompanying software translated words in Farsi onto the screen. Other monitors depicted areas outside the bunker such as the machine gun nests, the helipad, and the mountainous lanes and winding paths.

Making an approach to the facility would be all but impossible without being seen.

He then turned. The soldiers were still there, making it quite clear that there was nothing covert about their actions and that Levine would be under their constant scrutiny.

"Taking in the sights, I see." Al-Sherrod exited from the Comm Center with his yellow teeth as visible as a Cheshire grin in the quasi-darkness. "I thought you'd be with the good professor in the lab. After all, are you not his personal technician?"

"When Dr. Sakharov makes a request for me, then I shall answer."

"I see."

The diminutive man stood there for a long moment surveying Levine's eyes. And Levine wondered if the man had the insight to see the true intentions that lie beneath his façade.

And then: "Yes." As he said this, he did so with a honing eye squinting in a manner of suspicion. "Your presence here is quite specific," he told him. "You are Dr. Sakharov's aide and nothing more. Therefore, your movement in this facility is quite minimal."

Levine bowed his head. "My apologies. I was not told."

"You are here only because it was agreed upon by al-Ghazi and President Ahmadinejad that, at least for now, we work together for a common goal when, in fact, the truth is that this agreement is between two men who do not trust each other. You watch me. I watch you—except I have more eyes." He pointed to the soldiers behind him. "Be that as it may, the agreement is that you are allowed to forward all of Sakharov's findings to al-Ghazi as a failsafe that your faction has all the detailed information to duplicate the doctor's finding outside the lab. But only under the strictest measures of the protocol."

"Which means?"

"That you will only forward Sakharov's findings under very watchful eyes—most notably mine. You're here only to verify that the information sent to al-Ghazi is true. And don't think for a minute, Umar, that I don't know that your al-Ghazi's watchdog in the same manner that I'm Ahmadinejad's. Therefore, you will be restricted to the common areas on the main tier. Everywhere else is off-limits. Is that clear?"

"Very."

The Devil's Companion smiled in a way that was genuine, which often ingratiated himself to be trusted just before he struck them dead, and then clapped a hand on Levine's shoulder, turning him away from the Comm Center. "Be as it may," he began, "Doctor Sakharov's findings will be glorious. And it will be your people who will destroy the Great Satan and the infidels of Israel. And it will be done with the blessing of Allah."

"I know not of a specific plan regarding my people."

"Al-Ghazi did not tell you?" he asked.

"No."

"Then I will tell you this," he said. "It all begins with the relic below."

Levine cocked his head questioningly. "Are you talking of the holy relic?"

Al-Sherrod's smile flourished, showing his irregular rows of teeth, and nodded. "I've something to show you," he told him. And then his face beamed with the pride of a champion.

# CHAPTER EIGHTEEN

*Tel Aviv, Israel, Mossad Headquarters*

Two days after the Lohamah Psichlogit lost communication with their operative working on the terrorist front, Yitzhak Paled sent a covert contingency force to the Afghan region to team up with CIA operatives to reevaluate the situation and retrace Levine's last position since he was a high asset to both sides.

It was later discovered that Levine did not make his routine connection with his courier as scheduled; therefore, red flags surfaced.

Satellites were immediately set to target Afghan hotspots, but the mountain range was too massive, the satellites failing to pick up anything of significance other than insurgent squads walking mountainous trails. So, after three days of searching, after three days of the operative missing his contacts, it became clear to the principles of the Lohamah Psichlogit that Aryeh Levine was missing.

*But to where? Was his position compromised? Or was he dead?* These questions worried Paled tirelessly since Levine was an A-1 asset that took years to implement as a plant. Due to his solid and consistent intelligence networking over the years, the thwarting of insurgent missions on Israeli and American fronts proved successful on several occasions with numerous lives saved. But with Levine missing and no intel serving as the conduit to *"keeping your enemies close,"* both the United States and Israel were gnawing on their proverbial lower lips in anticipation of what was to come now that the window of collecting data had been abruptly closed with Levine's absence becoming critical in the wake of his disappearance.

Yitzhak stood still examining the wall-sized screen in the Lohamah Psichlogit monitoring lab. He stood there rubbing his chin thoughtfully as he studied the many angles of the Afghan and Iranian Fronts, the satellite images zipping from one picture to another while homing in on the coordinates of Levine's last points of contact.

But this exercise of making detection of any kind, he knew, was nothing more than a futile attempt at serendipity.

The voice beside him didn't startle him like it would most people when someone comes up from behind without sound or announcement. Paled simply stood unmoving as the man spoke. "Anything?" he asked.

Yitzhak Paled shook his head—a single nod. "He missed his contact in Tehran," answered.

"Aryeh is exceptional at what he does. If he's out there, then he'll contact us." Benyamin Kastenbaum was a large man who had served on every level of the Mossad except for the Director's position, which he declined on more than one occasion simply for the fact that he enjoyed his position as an intelligence officer so much that there was little else, he wanted outside of what he already was. When he spoke, he did so with a booming voice that rattled the air around him, his bass so deep it seemed to stimulate the atmosphere. But he was becoming old, his hair had gone gray a decade ago, his body had grown soft from muscles that used to be rock solid. But his mind remained clear, his memory forgetting little over the years.

Yitzhak nodded. "If his position has been compromised, Iran will not hesitate to execute him. I fear he may already be gone, Benyamin. And if that's the case, then we are surely crippled on the Iranian Front."

"There are others."

"But Aryeh was our deepest asset."

"Then we must take into consideration that Aryeh may be dead or captured and move on. Let our sources maneuver into position to gather whatever information is available regarding al-Ghazi and the Revolutionary Front. In the meantime, continue to watch the Fronts if it soothes you. But remember this: It's all right to empathize, but never sympathize. Once you sympathize, then you will lose your ability to lead. Personal emotions must be set aside, Yitzhak. There will always be others who can take his place." And then: "This is war. It always has been."

Yitzhak sighed. Kastenbaum was correct and his assessment was even more so. This was a war that was unbridled and vicious, and most likely a war without end. But all wars had their components when it came to winning or losing. Assets were a premium. And Levine was one such asset.

"Maneuver others carefully into red zones," he said. "And maintain a vigil on both fronts."

The old man placed a soft hand on Yitzhak's shoulder. "I know you're friends," he told him. "And I pray for Aryeh. But if you don't recognize that what we do benefits the whole and not the one, then you will fail us all."

"Although I respect you, Benyamin, and love you like a brother, don't you ever lecture me again about my position here. I lead the Lohamah Psichlogit because I'm capable of doing so. The loss of one man, even if it happens to be a friend, will not deter me from performing my duties." He turned to the old man whose face had become crestfallen in surprise. "Is that clear?"

Benyamin nodded. "I'm sorry, Yitzhak. You're right. I was out of place."

And then Yitzhak spoke gently as if the matter was already forgotten. "Is there anything else?"

"Just one matter," he said. "We received the data regarding the carbon dating of Aaron's staff."

"And?"

"It's the real thing, Yitzhak. It's been confirmed to be thirty-seven hundred years old."

Yitzhak focused his attention back on the screen, his eyes glossing over. Then in a whisper to no one in particular, he said, "Then it truly is the Ark of the Covenant."

# CHAPTER NINETEEN

*Inside Mount Damavand, Iran, The Alborz Mountain Range*

Umar, or Levine, entered a chamber with al-Sherrod and the two Quds officers in tow. The room was perfectly square, not too large, but big enough to hold its prize. In the room's center situated on a foot-high platform was the Ark of the Covenant, which gave off a gold nimbus of light beneath the conical beam of a lamp shining down from above.

Slowly, the operative's jaw dropped in typical awe. He knew that the Ark in Axum, Ethiopia was a facsimile. But there was something about this particular Ark, a discharging of energy that was tangible and intangible at the same time, something wonderfully magnetic.

"Do you sense it, as well?"

Levine ignored al-Sherrod and stepped closer with his hands held outward with every intention of placing his palms against its surface. The history behind this box, he thought, the power of its simple presence, was overwhelming.

Slowly, he pressed his palms against the gold that shined like the surface of a mirror—could see the color reflect off him as he stood next to the precious icon. His clothes, his flesh, everything about him became the color of gold within its glowing presence.

He did not feel the fatal electric charge that was alleged should the Ark be touched by open hands. Instead, it was cool and smooth to the touch, its texture like the even surface of glass. And then he grazed his fingers gingerly over the golden seat, then over the cherubs facing away from each other with the tips of their wings touching, then over the golden loops for the carrying poles. Everything he laid a hand on rang of legitimacy. And in his heart, he knew this was the true Ark of the Covenant.

"Where did you find it?" he asked, tracing the tips of his fingers over the shell.

"Does it matter?"

"What does this have to do with what's going on here in this facility?"

Al-Sherrod moved closer, the glow of the Ark now catching him within its aura. "Al-Ghazi truly did not tell you, did he?"

"Al-Ghazi informs cells as to their directives. In order for them to succeed, he must keep secrets in case one cell is compromised so that others can remain ignorant to keep them from forwarding information to the enemy. Even cells need direction from someone. And al-Ghazi is that someone. He tells me only what he must."

"But for him not to trust in you, Umar?"

"It's not a matter of trust, but a tool of defense."

Al-Sherrod circled the Ark and ran a slender hand around its frame. "Do you know of the Ark's tale? Of what the Christians believe will happen should the cover be lifted?"

Levine stood silent.

"Al-Ghazi lifted the cover. And do you know what happened?"

More silence.

"Nothing," al-Sherrod said. "Inside were two tablets of stone, a golden bowl of manna, and an ancient cane."

Levine knew the story of the dark angels within should they be released from the Covenant, the demons hunting down those close by who were filled with black wills instead of the Light of His glory, devouring them.

"It is nothing more than a box laden in gold and superstition," he added. "But the good Doctor Sakharov is going to change all that."

Levine turned to him, the features of his face already asking the question: *How?*

Al-Sherrod smiled. "If al-Ghazi did not tell, nor will I," he answered. And then he grazed his palm lovingly over the structure, a gentle caress.

"Will you destroy the Ark, then?"

Al-Sherrod nodded. "The Ark was given to the prophet Solomon as a sign of His devotion to him. No, Umar, the Ark is only a vessel that is finally coming into its own as something it was meant to be all along—a tool by Allah to finally diminish the infidels given the prophecies. Once the lid is open, then the demons will rush forward to destroy those not within Allah's grace."

Levine suddenly felt his chest tighten. *A vessel of destruction*, four words that caromed off his mind over and over again, the words resounding in hollow cadence: *A vessel of destruction.*

"Your role will be a prominent one once the good doctor has completed his tasks to al-Ghazi and to Ahmadinejad. So, you deserve to see it this one time. But after today, Umar, you will not come near this chamber again. Is that clear?"

Levine grazed his fingers over the cherub's golden wings. "Clear."

"Keep to your tasks by serving Doctor Sakharov and keep yourself to the areas classified as non-restricted."

"Understood."

Al-Sherrod smiled at him with those yellow teeth. And then: "*Allahu Akbar.*"

With a lack of commitment in his tone, Levine uttered, "*Allahu Akbar.*" And was escorted from the chamber sensing that a bulls-eye was just drawn on his back by the man they called the Devil's Companion.

# CHAPTER TWENTY

*Las Vegas, Nevada*

"I'll do it." The three words were spoken with little conviction as Kimball stood before Louie's desk in a quaint little office whose walls were covered with corkboards, pushpins, and memos that overlapped each other. The blunt of a cigar burned in an ashtray that read WHAT HAPPENS IN VEGAS STAYS IN VEGAS, sending a corkscrew ribbon of blue smoke ceilingward.

"You'll fight?"

"I need the money."

"We all need money," he said, smiling. Louie immediately went to the phone and tapped in numbers on the keypad and fell back into his seat. There was a look about him, thought Kimball, of victory due to the way his mouth tilted with smugness, how the arch of one eye was raised higher than the other.

"Yo, Mario, set me up for the undercard on Friday's fight. I got my boy wonder here to go a few with whomever you have available." There was a long pause as Louie nodded his head, imbibing every word Mario had to say. And then: "Is he any good?" There was another pause. "Six fights and six wins, five of them by knock out. Well, it seems that my boy here has his work cut out for him then . . . What? . . . Yeah, Friday night . . . All right then." He placed the phone gingerly onto its cradle, grabbed the stub of his cigar, and set it at the corner of his mouth while surveying Kimball with a steady gaze. "Why the change of heart?" he asked.

"As I said, I need the money."

Louie shook his head. "I ain't buying it."

"I'm not trying to sell you anything. So, either you believe me, or you don't. I don't care. If you want a fighter, then here I am."

"Oh, yeah," he said, his smile growing into a wide arc. "I got me a fighter, don't I?"

"So, I take it that I'm on the undercard on Friday night?"

Louie nodded. "You'll be fighting a guy named Tank Russo—a big mother from back east. New York, New Jersey—they're all the same. But he's good, J.J. Five knockouts in six fights. And I mean flat-out, star-seeing knockouts that sent three to the hospital. This guy is up and coming," he added. "Another ten fights, he should be seeing rock-solid numbers from the purse."

"And how much will I get?"

"With my fifty percent—"

"Twenty-five," he corrected.

"Thirty-three?"

"Twenty."

"Twenty? You're going the wrong way, J.J. When you negotiate, you're supposed to come to a happy medium. How about twenty-five percent?"

"Twenty. You're not the one going into that ring against a wrecking machine."

The smile washed away from Louie's face, which had become as sullen as stone. "All right twenty. But you better win, J.J. The purse for this fight is one thousand for the winner and five hundred for the loser. If you lose, I only get a C-note."

"That's not bad for a phone call."

Louie fell back into his chair. "No, I guess not. But if you lose, J.J., you won't climb, especially coming out of the gate with a losing record."

"I won't lose."

"You seem pretty sure of yourself."

"Sure enough," he answered. And then: "How many fights will it take to get to the top?"

"I'd say about fifteen, maybe twenty if you have a loss. It all depends upon how exciting of a fighter you are. If you're good, you move. If not, then you'll be trolling for trash as long as you work for this casino."

"And the purses?"

"They grow as you do. Once you hit the mainstream, once the TV's focus on you as a supreme fighter, then you're easily looking at five to six figures."

Kimball couldn't afford the television networks to reveal his true identity. Should a government constituent recognize him, then his life would be in jeopardy, and he'd become the target of indigenous forces sent to silence him for the black ops he once performed for them and the dirty little secrets he held, including the sanctioned assassination of a United States senator.

No, he told himself. He would only bankroll enough money and leave Las Vegas before he made any type of impression with the network brass. Perhaps to Montana and buy a small spread to get started, and then grow from there. He would live a quiet life, alone, under a new name, a new identity, and pay taxes. He would wake up to the colorful streamers of light at dawn, then sit on the porch at dusk in a rocker watching the day's light fade to obsidian darkness where the night sky sparkled with countless pinprick lights as stars glowered against a most gorgeous canopy. A soft wind would blow through the trees, the leaves singing in concert. It was all quite simple, he thought. Ten fights, maybe twelve. Just enough to get him started.

And then he would once again try to escape from his true nature.

"I knew you'd come around," said Louie. "You can't run away from who you are. I always told you that, didn't I? I always said that you were a fighter, J.J. I could see it in your baby blues."

Kimball nodded. *You're right, Louie. I can't escape from who I really am, can I? A fighter . . . A warrior . . . And don't forget killer.*

"Take the rest of the day off," said Louie, standing, the cigar hanging precariously at the corner of his mouth. "Tomorrow, too. I'll tell the bosses you went home because you were sick. But I need you rested. This fight ain't gonna be a cakewalk."

Kimball left without a spoken word and kept to his ritual as much as he could. He went and bought his parfait glass of shrimp and walked beneath the overhang of the Freemont Experience. But it was still light, and the overhead was not activated. So, he walked to his apartment passing the homeless, the addicted, the forlorn, and the wasted. He walked without a hitch in his step and his head held low.

The homeless begged him for money, their bony hands greased and caked with dirt held out for meager wages—a penny, a nickel, or perhaps the jackpot of a dollar bill. But Kimball ignored them the same way he ignored the lifeless-looking nymphs who were ready to pleasure him for enough money to buy a bindle of meth.

Montana was looking better with every stride.

When he got home, he went to the bathroom and gazed upon his features. He looked deep into his cerulean blue eyes, wondering what it was that Louie saw. Did they have a certain look about them? Something that gave insight to what he truly was? Were they the telltale signs of a killer in dormancy?

He raised the tips of his fingers and brushed them against the reflected images of his eyes—the blue eyes, so beautiful in their color, so deadly in their meaning.

Kimball then went to the refrigerator and pulled out a bottle of vodka from the freezer, sat on the edge of the bed, popped the cap, and took a long swallow.

This is how he geared up for the fight, by first taking on his demons.

# CHAPTER TWENTY-ONE

*Vatican City*

Upon the passing of the pope, politicking was paramount to succeed to the throne. The two leads within the *Preferiti* were Cardinals Vessucci and Angullo. Cardinals Bass and Botelli were considered third and fourth respectively in the rankings, but still within striking range, even though both cardinals gravitated more toward the principles of a more liberal state.

To politick outside the walls of the Sistine Chapel prior to the conclave was acceptable. To politick for the papal station once the conclave was in session invited ex-communication. By the time the door to the chapel was sealed minds should be made up, a successor chosen on the merits of what he could bring to the Church.

After a day of true debate among his constituency, Cardinal Bonasero Vessucci had been diligently patient while listening to others. What had come to the fore is that Angullo's camp had weakened considerably after the secretary of state often disputed the pontiff's decisions and openly criticized the man for his judgment, which drew the ire of the pope and a growing distance between them.

In some eyes Angullo was seen as intolerable and uncompromising, causing many to withdraw from his camp, which in turn weakened his support. Others, however, stood firmly by him because they wanted to remain in the good graces of the man holding the second-highest position within the Vatican.

And this was good news for Bonasero Vessucci, who was highly respected within the College of the Cardinals as someone who debated with skill and tolerance and had the pedigree of serving behind one of the most revered popes ever to reign by serving as secretary of state prior to his removal by Pope Gregory and further viewed as a man of altruistic conviction.

While his following ran deep, Cardinal Angullo's was running far and dry and fast, the unspoken polls rising in Vessucci's favor.

As he stood before an open window of his dormitory at the *Domus Sanctæ Marthæ* overlooking the Basilica, he reflected over the possible changes to come. Without hesitation, he would reinstate the Vatican Knights to protect the sovereignty of the Church, its interests, and its citizenry beyond the reach of the Swiss Guard. For those who could not protect themselves, the Vatican Knights surely would.

Standing idle watching the sun slowly set, the sky turning from a deep blue to reddish-orange, Cardinal Bonasero Vessucci sighed. Even with the polls serving in his favor, he knew he had an obstacle to overcome as long as Cardinal Angullo remained steadfast. If nothing else, he thought, the man was ambitious to a fault.

And sometimes, ambition could warp a man's sense of conscience.

With a preamble of a smile, the cardinal continued to admire the sunset, the sun's tendrils finally fading toward the darkness of night.

**As Cardinal Vessucci** stood at the window of his dormitory, so did Cardinal Giuseppe Angullo.

He stood there as a dry wind caressed his skin—the same dry wind that was blowing on the fatal night of the pope's death.

As the sun settled, so unsettled was his nerves.

Although silver of tongue, his past association with Pope Gregory had proved to be a slow undoing of his grip over his camp. Those whom he considered his closest allies had quietly defected, his numbers growing weaker at a time that was becoming more opportune. In whispered circles he heard that some had defected and became a part of Vessucci's growing numbers, propelling him to the top of the *Preferiti*, whereas others gravitated to other aspirants. Either way, Angullo was slipping.

Closing his eyes, he could feel his ambition torture him like something hot and writhing in his gut. The seat was but a conclave away, a position he glorified since he was ordained as a priest in Florence. And here he stood after becoming second in command of the Vatican through Machiavellian means.

If he ousted Cardinal Vessucci once, then he could do it again. But time, he knew, was crucially limited with the conclave only days away.

He exhaled, knowing the task to be a difficult one. How could he dethrone Vessucci before the throne even fell to him? Tell the cardinals of Vessucci's past when he sanctioned the Vatican Knights, a group of mercenaries? But that would also malign Pope Pius, who also sanctioned the group. And to malign Pope Pius in the eyes of the College of the Cardinals would certainly end his political push for the throne.

The man grits his teeth, feeling cornered.

And then he raised his right hand and held it up against the backdrop of the full moon, examining it. It had been the hand that pushed Gregory from the balcony, ending his life. It was also the hand that put him in the position to succeed Gregory by placing him at the helm of the papal throne.

It was all in the right hand.

Lowering his arm, Cardinal Angullo's mind began to work.

He clearly recalled the moment inside the papal chamber as Gregory lay on the deathbed in gentle repose after the body was appropriated from the bloodied cobblestones beneath his balcony. In keeping with medieval ritual, the Camerlengo took a silver hammer and tapped the pope's forehead three times, calling out his Christian name. When there was no response, the Camerlengo then announced to those present that the pope was dead and proceeded to remove the Fisherman's Ring from his finger, an act of dethroning. Once done, then the proper authorities took over, namely the coroner.

But keeping with papal law he knew the pope could not be autopsied, the poison in his system crippling him that night would never be detected, the crime going unnoticed. It had been papal law since the inception of the Church, a loophole for murder no doubt used many times over—at least in Angullo's estimation.

But such a law did not apply to cardinals or bishops or clergy. Not everyone was immune.

In the darkness of night, Angullo sighed with pent-up frustration.

Should he apply the same fate upon Vessucci as he did with Pope Gregory, there was no doubt in his mind an autopsy would follow, and an investigation conducted by Roman authorities would ensue. The death of a *Preferiti* so close to the death of the pontiff would certainly draw suspicion, especially if the poison that weakened Gregory was discovered in his system.

But Vessucci had been slowed by age. His steps were becoming shorter, his gait becoming more labored. Surely these were signs of an aging man falling into ill health.

Once again, he held his hand aloft against the round frame of the full moon and flexed his fingers before drawing his hand into a tight fist. As he did on the night of Gregory's death, he would enter Vessucci's dormitory room and apply a pillow over the man's face, smothering him. He would then set the body in gentle repose, the man dying in his sleep of natural causes.

However, a telltale sign of dying by this method always left the victim's eyes bloodshot.

This much he knew.

But with the Conclave days away it was a risk he was willing to take since God, after all, would be watching over him.

This he was sure of.

So, with his clenched fist held high, with the backdrop of the full moon framing his tightly balled hand, Cardinal Giuseppe Angullo was feeling more than triumphant.

*Soon, Bonasero, the papal throne will be mine.*

*Soon.*

# CHAPTER TWENTY-TWO

*Las Vegas, Nevada*

Friday night in Las Vegas is a night of anarchy in most cities, a place with no discipline and no sense of order. Although Sin City is a city cast in liberal shadows, it is also a city of tough laws. Prostitution is illegal in Las Vegas, although most casinos have their own stables hidden away and usually for high rollers; alcohol is never allowed while driving, although open containers are acceptable while walking the Strip; and the perception of lawlessness or unrestrained actions would likely guarantee a criminal charge and several days in the Clark County Detention Center, most likely ruining a vacation by spending it in a facility that always smelled like dirty laundry.

But certain venues held the Thunderdome likeness of Ultimate Fighting. The cages were surrounded by fanatical fans bent on brutality rather than boxing. Their screams and cries erupting as the contestants entered the cage knowing that only one would leave, and the other would lie as a broken tangle.

In the undercard bout at Caesar's Palace, Kimball and Tank Russo, a huge man with broad shoulders and pile-driving arms, entered the ring. Tank regarded Kimball with a warrior's glare, that straight-on look of a champion who was not afraid with his chin raised in defiance; and a prognathous brow scarred from past combats with every crooked line a badge of honor. And then he rolled his shoulders and neck to loosen up, the large bands of muscles writhing.

Kimball stood idle, staring at the 4-ounce gloves on his hands and flexing his fingers, these types of gloves alien to him.

"He's a big dude, J.J." Louie called out from the first row. "Be careful!"

Kimball turned to him and saw the concern on Louie's face—could read the scripted lines of his features openly, the man having little faith in Kimball after seeing the size of Tank Russo.

And then he looked into the stands, at the scores of people who wanted to witness unbridled violence. Their faces masks of hungry rage.

*Welcome to my world.*

Tank moved closer to the ring's center, throwing jabs into the open air. Kimball, with all the ease of a man taking a leisurely stroll, moved forward when the ref beckoned him to the center.

Whereas Kimball appeared uncaring, his opponent appeared bull-like; a man who wanted nothing more than to beat him down to paste simply because he could.

After the ref gave the final directions both men parted, Tank Russo taking a defensive stance, hands up, knees bent, eyes focused, whereas Kimball stood straight with his arms by his side and a smile on his face as if saying "what's this all about?"

When the ref gave the signal, Tank closed in. And Kimball could see in Tank's eyes that he thought this was going to be an easy victory, the opponent in Kimball too green.

In a sweeping motion so quick, so fluid, Kimball swung his leg out and then up until his leg was straight up in the air, and came straight down with an ax kick, the heel of his foot coming down on Tank's head, the force behind the blow snapping Tank's head viciously to the side, his eyes then rolling into slivers of white before he buckled as a boneless heap to the floor, the man rendered unconscious inside of seven seconds.

Kimball stood there looking down at his opponent, and then he turned to Louie who was standing in paralytic awe, his cigar threatening to fall from the corner of his mouth as Kimball shot him a thumbs-up. "Is that it? Am I done?"

Louie stood in stunned silence along with the rest of the crowd. Whereas they saw the makings of a true champion, he saw dollar signs. And then to no one in particular he whispered, "He's gonna make me a millionaire." And then in a celebratory manner by pumping his fist high, he yelled, "A millionaire!" It was the rallying cry that got the crowd going, the quasi-silence now turning into a cacophonous riot of absolute noise and cheer.

Louie ran to the cage and curled his fingers through the rubber-coated links. "I knew you were a fighter!" he told him. "Damn if I didn't know you were a fighter, J.J."

"Is that it? Are we done?"

But Louie just ranted. "That was an ax kick," he said. "A perfectly performed ax kick."

"Louie, are we done?"

Louie's smile broadened. "Until next week," he told him. "Next Friday night."

"Bigger purse?"

"After this? I'd say so."

"I need the money."

"Don't we all," said Louie, a ribbon of smoke curling lazily from the cigar's end. "Don't we all."

**In the locker** room with distant cheers of the next fight coming through the cinderblock walls, Kimball sat on the bench undoing the tape that was wrapped around his wrists when Tank Russo was helped to a nearby medical table with his trainers aiding him into a supine position.

Kimball glanced up long enough to see Tank wave off his team before going back to the unwrapping.

Tank turned to him. "That was just a lucky kick, dude."

Kimball ignored him.

Then: "Dude?"

Kimball faced him, his features appearing taxed. "What."

"That was a lucky kick."

"If you say so." He went back to undo the tape.

A short lapse of silence followed before Kimball spoke, his eyes focusing on the tape as he unwound the strips rather than looking at the man on the table. "Are you OK?"

Tank nodded, his eyes looking ceilingward. "A little dizzy," he answered. "And I can feel a headache coming on."

"You need to get yourself looked at—make sure you don't have a concussion."

Tank turned to him. "J.J. Doetsch," he said. "How come I never heard of you before? It's obvious this isn't your first time to the rodeo."

Kimball smiled. "I thought you said it was just a lucky kick."

Tank proffered his smile, an icebreaker between burgeoning

125

friendships. "That was just my ego talking. You know how it goes in this business."

Kimball finished with unrolling the tape from his wrists, tossed them in a trash can, and walked up to Tank who lay there with partially glazed eyes. But intuitive eyes as well.

Tank saw the scars, lines, and bullet pocks along Kimball's ripped body, the obvious wounds of battle. "You ain't new to this, are you?"

"Cage fighting? You were my first."

"Seriously?"

"Seriously," he said. "You're my first cherry pop."

Tank faced the ceiling. "Lucky me," he said.

Kimball placed a kind hand on Tank's shoulder and smiled. "Yeah. Lucky you."

When Kimball returned to the bench Louie was standing there with eight crisp Benjamins fanning out from his grasp. "Your take," he said, "as we agreed upon."

Kimball took the money and stared at it for a long moment. It's not that he had never seen that amount before or held them for simple homage. It was the way he earned it—by ritualistic brutality that catered to the whims of the masses.

It was blood money.

He took the bills, folded them, and slipped them into his shirt pocket that hung on a hanger in his locker. "Thanks, Louie."

"I'll see you tomorrow at work, then. We'll talk about next Friday night." After pumping a victorious fist in excitement, Louie was no doubt heading for the Blackjack tables with his roll.

"You're going to be a champion someday," said Tank. "You know that, don't you? You're going to be right up there because you give the people what they want: a vicious wrecking machine that takes his opponents out without conscience or care."

Kimball sighed, and then said evenly, "Without conscience or care, huh?"

Tank nodded. "That's right, buddy. And that's why you're going to be a bankable star in this business. When I first saw you, I thought you were just a stupid greener just standing there. Just cool and calm is what you were. Grace under pressure like I've never seen before. You showed me nothing as though you were completely empty."

Kimball stared briefly into open space before turning to the lump of bills bulging from his shirt pocket within the locker. It was so easy, he

126

thought. The money. An obvious pull since he was good at it. But what panged him to no end was that Tank Russo instantly saw in him what others have been saying about him since the beginning: that Kimball Hayden was a man without a conscience.

And a man without conscience can never see the salvation within God's eyes.

Kimball was suddenly full of regrets.

# CHAPTER TWENTY-THREE

*Northern Iran, Mount Damavand, The Facility*

Although Leonid Sakharov worked more than ten hours straight, he did not allow his fragility to slow his pace. In fact, Sakharov appeared to have more of a bite to his stamina, more of a hitch to his gait as he roamed from one unit to another, from one monitor to the next.

While Levine stood sentinel by the bay doors, one of the few spots in the lab afforded to him by Sakharov, he watched the old man operate the nanoscopic machines with an eagerness that had been missing in the old man since leaving Vladimir Central, and subsisting on the memories of someday returning to his one true love: nanotechnology.

And here he was, inside a lab with the most advanced technology the profits of oil could buy despite the UN sanctions that crippled the country.

In the fore of the lab, Sakharov was seated before the most powerful microprocessor in the world that had millions of transistors just a few dozen nanometers wide, a nanometer being a billionth of the size of a meter. The technology was a marvel in the eyes of Levine, the machinery incomprehensible since something manufactured that was a billionth of size truly existed. But the Holy Grail was the Assembler, Sakharov's pride and joy. The machinery was state-of-the-art technology that built nanobots molecule by molecule until molecular chains were created, the chain itself becoming the fusion of the nanobot.

With quick efficiency drawn from memories, Sakharov expertly crafted molecular chains that would take on a programmed life of its own and replicate. To program a lifespan and to give it a platform to perform to the will of their Creator was a different matter, a different process. So for years, he had sketched theories in his mind. And now that he was handed the opportunity to accomplish the means during the twilight of his life, Sakharov was creating with much success. Within hours he created the chains. Within days he designed a program to imbue in the molecules. Within a month he would become a God.

The makeup within the nanobots was a predesigned half-life with every subsequent bot living approximately half the lifespan of its predecessor. This was a safety feature to keep the nanobots from replicating exponentially, based on Drexler's theory that unrestrained growth would cause the bots to consume all organic material on Earth within weeks.

With half a lifespan with every replication, their time would always be minimized to the point where every bot would exist down to a trillionth of a second, which was hardly time for them to exist long enough to do any damage. And it was also Sakharov's goal: Maximum damage in the beginning, but zero to none thereafter.

At the end of the day and at a specific time, Sakharov would create a disk of the day's acquired data and proffer it to Levine who was summarily escorted by two Quds soldiers to the Comm Center. This was the only time he was allowed into the communications station per the agreement between al-Sherrod, al-Ghazi, and President Ahmadinejad. Since the data was crucial and a tenebrous alliance was born between factions with a common goal, and since trust remained at a bare minimum, Levine was able to, via imaging satellite, speak to al-Ghazi, whose image appeared slightly grainy on the live feed on the monitor screen.

After placing the disc into the required slot of the computer, Levine spoke into the lip mike. "Download today's data," he said evenly.

On another screen designs of molecular chains, nanobots, and buckyballs, along with scientific equations, formulas, and rows of text, all downloaded with the screen becoming a cyber script of symbols and rune-like designs. Once the material was downloaded, he said, "Send specifications to given address: Tehran. Al-Ghazi."

The data moved through cyberspace within the blink of an eye, the information relocating to al-Ghazi's location and downloaded onto a disc on his end.

And then: "And how are you, Umar?"

"I'm fine," he answered.

It was here that al-Ghazi would look for particular facial tics on

Levine's face, with certain tics meaning certain things. If the data proved false or doctored, then he would give a subtle wink with his left eye; if under duress, then a wink with his right, two separate gestures with plenty of meaning behind them. Should Levine give off the impression of either, then al-Ghazi would counter with a gesture of his by blinking his eyes twice, a signal to Levine to use his very particular set of skills to kill Sakharov, ending the concord between the alliances. But his features remained stolid, meaning that Ahmadinejad was, at least for now, complying with the conditions of the agreement. To get this message across that everything was pretty much copasetic, he would then tent his hands in mock prayer and bounce his fingertips off the base of his chin.

Whenever he did this, he could see relief fall over al-Ghazi's face. At least for now, Ahmadinejad was keeping to the agreement that the data should be shared between alliances, even with marginal distrust between them.

"Good," al-Ghazi said from the other end. "It appears he's making incredible strides."

"Sakharov knows exactly what he's doing. He's done it before."

"And you, Umar?"

"I know little of his project," he told him. "But the techs he's working with seem to be grasping his theories quite well."

"How much longer do you think it will take?'

Levine shrugged. "If I was to hazard a guess, I'd say maybe two weeks, three at the most."

"Excellent. Is that what he told you?"

"In so many words, yes."

"Al-Sherrod must be pleased."

"He is. So is President Ahmadinejad."

"With UN sanctions crippling his nation, he will now have some leverage against Israel should they commit to a military strike against their facilities. But it's not the nuclear programs they should be worried about, but the program of Doctor Sakharov."

Levine fell back in his chair. The room was dark all around him with the occasional glow from the monitor screens and blinking lights from the surrounding computer modules. He had to get word to his contacts, that a bunker not within the eyes of his country's satellite system is developing a weapon of mass destruction far more devastating than a nuclear device.

"Umar?"

He snapped aware. "Yes, al-Ghazi."

"I will speak with you again tomorrow, same time."

"Yes, al-Ghazi."

"And watch over the good doctor, yes?"

"I will."

From his end, al-Ghazi gave him a cursory salute. "*Allahu Akbar.*"

"*Allahu Akbar.*"

The monitor winked off.

In a dash of a moment before he stood, he took quick note of the other monitor screens, taking in that they were surveillance monitors of areas within the facility and outside with NVG cameras watching the areas surrounding the MG nests, paths leading to the facility, the helipad, and the banks of fuel cells lining the ridge, the power source for the facility. Fuel cells, he knew, were extremely volatile. Explosions by themselves might not destroy the facility. But coupled with a military strike from Israeli fighter planes, the missiles would certainly cause the bunker to collapse.

Since he was constantly being watched he knew he would have to act sometime before Sakharov finished his project. But if he killed the doctor, then he would have no way to contact his sources since he would no doubt be executed. Worse, the doctor had finished enough of the process for the Iranian scientists to pick up where he left off. Now he had no choice but to compromise his position and order a strike to destroy the bunker and the data, quashing the project and the minds contained within.

And then there was al-Ghazi. He knew where he was and the threat he had become now that he possessed much of the unfinished data.

It was time to make a move. But first, he would need to fathom a plan rather than act hastily.

A rough hand touched down on his shoulder, the hand of a Quds soldier. In Farsi, he barked an order. It was time to leave the Comm Center.

Standing, Aryeh Levine knew that his time was limited on this planet. But he also understood that the romance of being an operative was over. He had done his job and done it well. Now it was time to cash out and he would do so in a large way, in a blaze of fiery glory.

After all, he was saving Israel. And more likely other parts of the world, as well.

Therefore, Sakharov must not finish.

The bunker cannot stand.

And al-Ghazi cannot survive the week.

Being directed toward the exit by the rough hand of a Quds soldier, Aryeh Levine's mind was already working.

# CHAPTER TWENTY-FOUR

*Vatican City, The Start of the Conclave*

Before the election, the cardinals hear two sermons: one before entering the conclave, the other once they are inside the Sistine Chapel. The sermons are intended to spell out the current state of the Church and to further suggest the qualities necessary for a pope to possess at that particular time.

Over the past few days leading up to the conclave, Cardinal Angullo had worked his silver tongue and once again garnered the favors of those who had once gravitated away from his camp back into his pull, placing himself as a favorite within the *Preferiti* alongside Cardinal Vessucci.

As the first sermon was coming to an end, Cardinal Angullo viewed Cardinal Vessucci with a long and calculating look. The cardinal was kneeling with his hands tented in prayer with an onyx-beaded rosary and silver crucifix dangling from his fingers, the crucifix reflecting a diamond spangle of light whenever it spun pendulously from side to side.

Closing his eyes and tenting his fingers in his sense of prayer, Cardinal Angullo went back to his entreaty to God, his lips moving wordlessly until the final moment of the Eucharist.

At noontime, on a day with a uniform blue sky and white-hot sun, the cardinals gathered in the Pauline Chapel of the Palace of the Vatican, and then proceeded to the Sistine Chapel singing "Veni Creator Spiritus."

Cardinal Vessucci was at the head of the procession, singing in chorus. Behind him, Cardinal Angullo also sang and did so in accord, the overall melody between the cardinals sounding more like a harmonious Gregorian chant.

Once inside the Sistine Chapel, the cardinals took an oath to observe the measures set down by the apostolic constitutions that upon election, should he be elected, understand that his optimum duty was to protect the liberty of the Holy See; disregard the instructions of secular authorities on voting; and above all else, maintain secrecy.

In keeping with age-old practices, the Cardinal Dean, the president of the College of Cardinals, then read the oath out loud in order of precedence, while the other cardinal electors stated—while touching the Gospels—that they promise, pledge, and swear to uphold the policies of the Church.

Cardinal Angullo was most vociferous.

After the cardinals had taken the oath, the Master of the Papal Liturgical Celebrations then ordered everyone other than the cardinals and conclave participants to leave the Chapel, a very slow progression as if in mourning, leaving behind the cardinals, the Master of the Papal Liturgical Celebrations, and an ecclesiastic designated by the Congregations prior to the commencement of the election to make a speech concerning the problems facing the Church, and once more on the qualities the new pope needed to possess.

The ecclesiastic was an aged old man with wizened crow's feet and a man who hunched inwardly at the shoulders. With his gray eyes, he held innumerable intelligence, and the tone of his remarkable voice remained honey-smooth as he spoke words learned verbatim from the script.

As he spoke Cardinal Angullo decided that he had all the qualities and tools required, had all the solutions to the problems plaguing the Church, ticking them off in his mind as the Vatican's new savior. Cardinal Vessucci, on the other hand, appeared studious and rapt, hinging on the ecclesiastic's every word, imbibing everything he said.

When the ecclesiastic finished, he moved with a shuffling gait beyond the Chapel doors, leaving behind the Master of the Papal Liturgical Celebrations to stand sentinel. Once the cardinals of the conclave were ready to proceed, the Master of the Papal Liturgical Celebrations closed the door before them and wrapped a chain with a papal seal on its lock around the door handles from the opposite side, locking the cardinals within the Sistine Chapel.

The click of the lock resonated throughout the chapel in echoing cadence, like the gunshot sound of finality, the galvanizing shot marking the start of the procedure of electing a new pope.

**In voting, the** cardinals use simple note cards for ballots with the words "I elect as Supreme Pontiff ___" printed on them, the open space to be filled in with the name of the elector's choosing.

By afternoon, the first ballot was held. However, no one garnered enough votes to win the pontifical seat, including Angullo or Vessucci, neither one getting the required two-thirds of the assembly's vote to win the papal throne. How much was received by Angullo, Vessucci or the other two cardinals of the *Preferiti* remained unknown.

It was also the only ballot of the day.

On the following morning as a battleship-gray sky threatened to open with torrential rain, the conclave continued with two additional votes, both failing to come to a clear and decisive decision as to who should lead the Church.

As each day passed, Bonasero Vessucci was beginning to lose hope. Whereas Cardinal Angullo smiled with all the pompous glory of a victor with the edges of his lips curling with the smug and anticipatory grin of someone who believed that the throne was within his grasp. With every passing of the ballot, things were beginning to look very bleak, whereas things were starting to look golden for Cardinal Angullo.

During the day's recess between the second ballot and the beginning of the third ballot, Cardinal Bonasero Vessucci stood alone, the man musing as he appeared detached from the moment until Cardinal Angullo invaded his space.

"Bonasero," he said.

Vessucci's eyes settled on the cardinal who held a smile. "It's becoming quite obvious that the throne is under the strong union of those who wish to see the most qualified to receive the papal station."

"Isn't that always the way?"

Angullo leaned forward, his smile widening, but marginally—more of a vindictive smirk than a gentle grin of congeniality. "Yes," he finally said. "But it appears that your camp has weakened significantly over the past few days. Since you were the alleged leader in the *Preferiti*, then the casted votes should have marked you as the pontiff within the first three ballots. That means, my Dear Cardinal, that something else is in the wind, wouldn't you agree? People are perhaps considering other factors."

135

"Like you perhaps?"

Angullo closed his eyes and gave a small tilt of his chin in acknowledgment. "Perhaps," he said. "But I am the Vatican secretary of state, which would serve others well if they should cast their votes on my behalf."

"So, you offered favors to those to bolster your camp?"

"No. Never. People see that I am a man of position. And who does not want to be in the same circle as a man of position? No, Bonasero. People by nature are self-centered, even if it's to the smallest degree. They're ambitious and they have the need, and the right, to excel to the next level. People, Bonasero, like to be in a circle with those in power and position, those who can help promote." And then: "Whose circle are you in?"

Bonasero Vessucci simply stared at him. Not a glare, just a studious look in which he was seeing Angullo as a man of true Machiavellian conviction.

"I see," he finally answered. "But keep in mind, Giuseppe, that it takes two-thirds of the votes to secure the position. There are others in the *Preferiti* whose votes may be diluting the overall percentage. It doesn't necessarily mean that you, I, or anyone else in the *Preferiti* has an advantage over the other. It simply means that patience should be viewed as a virtue."

"An exhibited virtue," he repeated. His smile broadened. "Yes, Bonasero, exhibit your virtue should it give you comfort." He then stood back and smiled in a way that was truly Machiavellian in nature by the simple curvature of his lips.

"Don't cast your shadow upon the papal throne yet, Giuseppe. The votes may not be in your favor."

"Perhaps not," he said. He then backed off, turned, and began to walk away. "But then again," he added over his shoulder, "perhaps they are."

# CHAPTER TWENTY-FIVE

*Las Vegas, Nevada, The Following Day*

The night before Kimball Hayden fought at another venue, his third fight in ten days. His second bout was all about a quick execution of his skills with a flurry of blows and a roundhouse kick to the jaw, leaving his opponent on the mat as a complex heap in less than two minutes. After two fights the crowd loved him. By the third fight, they hailed him as the Second Coming.

But it was Louie who told him to slow down the pace and make the fights last longer, draw them in and "*Make them love you more than they already do. And then give them what they want. Give them the total annihilation of your opponent.*"

Kimball sat in the quasi-darkness of his apartment drinking straight from a bottle of Jack. Behind him, the drapes were closed with marginal light slipping in through the seams where they met, and the air was hot and humid and stale with the smell of dirty laundry hanging in the air.

*Make them love you more than they already do. And then give them what they want, which is the annihilation of your opponent.*

*Is that what people want, Louie? An annihilation of somebody else?*

*That's the bottom line, buddy. That and the money, of course. But when you think about it, it all comes down to human nature. It's what they want, J.J. And you're the machine that drives them.* Louie then turned toward the crazed and applauding crowd like an emcee and opened his arms, the downed opponent at his feet beginning to come to. *Look at what you brought, J.J. Take a good look around and see what you've done.*

A day later, the words continued to echo throughout his mind as if they were spoken from the end of a long and hollow tunnel.

*Look at what you brought, J.J. Take a good look around and see what you've done.*

Kimball took another swig, a long pull until a bubble surfaced inside the bottle, and then laid it on the armchair of the seat and stared straight ahead into the darkness.

Last night was his third fight with the promise of more to come. His opponent was short and stocky with a bull-like neck and blunt limbs with tree-trunk thickness. It was obvious to Kimball that he fought his battles up close and personal due to his strike range being limited. So, he thought that this was going to be a quick and clean kill like the other two. But his opponent was tough and mean and could take mind-numbing punches as if they were glancing blows. His lips were split and parted, a cut slashed over his eye, bleeding profusely. But he kept coming, defying Kimball's well-placed jabs, his punches, and his many scored kicks to the facial and chest regions.

The crowd was going crazy.

And his opponent kept coming, throwing quick jabs with undeniable power behind each blow, landing, scoring, and often driving Kimball off balance. And then a right-cross to Kimball's face, a bruising blow which raised a knot above his eye, the bright light of intense pain soon following.

This guy was good.

Either that or Kimball was losing his edge.

Trading blow after blow, strike after strike, the fight waged on until the third round when Kimball found a brief opening and took it, driving a straight-on power punch like a pile driver into his opponent's jaw, the bone shifting horribly to the left, breaking, with the snap audible over the din of the crowd.

And then his world seemed to move with the slowness of a bad dream.

The raucous cry of the crowd moved in a slow drift as if the cries were weighted down, the shouts deep, long, and drawn out, becoming a sigh of tragedy and awe.

For a brief moment, his opponent wavered and teetered as his eyes went to half-mast, his face horribly disfigured with the crook of his jaw threatening to punch through his skin. And then he fell, hard, the fighter landing in a grotesque shape, his knees bent in oddly acute angles.

And then Kimball's world hastened, catching back up to the light of reality. The crowd cheered wildly as people applauded and raised their thumbs high. The decibels of their ovation carried across the air in concussive waves, the atmosphere moving, shaking, the walls closing in from all points of the arena, the effect finally striking him as a maddening drumbeat of cheers.

*Look at what you brought, J.J. Take a good look around and see what you've done.*

He looked down at the man on the mat, who was now receiving critical aid. And then he looked at his fist, at the glove, and then slowly unclenched his hand. He never realized that Louie was standing beside him, didn't realize that the ref had raised his other hand in victory. Kimball Hayden had lost himself in the moment and blotted out the noise, the crowd, becoming detached.

Within thirty minutes he received his pay, a thirty-five-hundred-dollar bonanza for less than ten minutes of work.

But Kimball remained somewhat vacant; Louie's words nothing more than a distant drone whenever he spoke, the money doing little to bolster his emotions as the bills lay curled in his hand.

He took another swig.

On the counter were bills in hundred-dollar denominations. Between his three fights, he earned just over six grand. Not a bad take for less than two weeks. Maybe within a month, he thought, maybe two, he would have enough to start elsewhere, to be somebody with a remote future.

*Forget Montana. Too cold.*

*What about Myrtle Beach?* And in the darkness, the corners of his lips edged up into a dreamy smile.

*I always wanted to live by the beach—to have my own business. Start anew.*

He then lifted his hand and let his fingertips run over the knot above his left eye and a reminder from his fight the night before.

A few more fights, he told himself, to build the till. And then I'm gone. Like that.

After a sigh, and with the images of beachscapes and waves pounding the surf, the noise alive in his ears as he closed his eyes, Kimball dreamed.

And he drank.

Pulling from the bottle long enough for a drunken stupor to overtake him, with the images of the coastline remaining on his mind as he fell asleep, the bottle finally slipped from his hand and to the floor, the contents spilling onto the threadbare carpet.

*Vatican City*

Inside the Sistine Chapel, another ballot was taking place, the second partaking on the third day.

For the past two days, the people standing within Vatican City saw only black smoke spiraling from the chimney, the color meaning that an elected had not been chosen. However, the cardinals had congregated between ballots and refocused their thoughts as to who shall lead them. Names of the *Preferiti* were bandied about, each man providing the pros and cons of the four main candidates, the arguments between liberal and conservatism, a judicial gathering of thoughts finally reducing four to two.

On the day of the ballot the cardinals voted, the votes cast then presented to the first of the three Scrutineers. Raising the container high, he shook it, and then passed the ballots among the three of them to be counted with the last Scrutineer writing the name down, and then calling the name out loud.

. . . *Cardinal Giuseppe Angullo* . . .
. . . *Cardinal Giuseppe Angullo* . . .
. . . *Cardinal Bonasero Vessucci* . . .
. . . *Cardinal Giuseppe Angullo* . . .
. . . *Cardinal Bonasero Vessucci* . . .

Both men could feel their nerves tightening, their hearts racing, palpitating, the ballots casting a final decision.

. . . *Cardinal Giuseppe Angullo* . . .

Bonasero closed his eyes and waited for the next name.

. . . *Cardinal Giuseppe Angullo* . . .

And then he began to lose confidence, knowing that two-thirds of the vote was needed and Angullo's name kept rolling.

And then:
. . . *Cardinal Bonasero Vessucci* . . .
. . . *Cardinal Bonasero Vessucci* . . .
. . . *Cardinal Bonasero Vessucci* . . .
. . . *Cardinal Bonasero Vessucci* . . .

He opened his eyes.

. . . *Cardinal Bonasero Vessucci* . . .

*. . . Cardinal Giuseppe Angullo . . .*

This was getting too close, thought Vessucci.

When he turned to face Cardinal Angullo, he could see the man looking at him with the intensity of a scalpel. His hatchet thin face was directed at him, eyes as black as onyx and a stare as cold as ice.

*. . . Cardinal Bonasero Vessucci. . .*

*. . . Cardinal Giuseppe Angullo . . .*

*. . . Cardinal Bonasero Vessucci . . .*

And it went on until a pope was finally chosen and white smoke billowed from the chimney.

Finally, the people in Vatican City cheered for the newly elected.


**After the election**, the Cardinal Dean summoned the Secretary of the College of Cardinals and the Master of Papal Liturgical Celebrations into the hallway where the Cardinal Dean asked the Pope-elect if he assented to the election by stating in Latin: "*Acceptasne electionem de te canonice factam in Summum Pontificem?*" Do you accept your canonical election as Supreme Pontiff?

Cardinal Bonasero Vessucci nodded in affirmation and accepted the post by citing the proper Latin phrases.

The Cardinal Dean stepped forward and asked him for his papal name. "*Quo nomine vis vocari?*" By what name shall you be called?

"I choose the name . . . Pope Pius the Fourteenth."

The Cardinal Dean nodded, and then led the way back to the conclave where the Master of Pontifical Liturgical Ceremonies created a document recording the acceptance and the new name of the Pope. Once the traditional motion was complete, Bonasero was then led into the "Room of Tears," a small area inside the Sistine Chapel where he dressed into the pontifical choir robe; the white cassock, rochet, and red mozzetta before donning the gold corded pectoral cross, a red embroidered stole, and zucchetto—all in preparation for the masses.

When Bonasero was ready, the Cardinal Protodeacon went to the main balcony of the basilica's façade with his hands held out to the people of the Square and proclaimed the new pope in a voice that was loud and projecting: "*Annuntio vobis gaudium magnum: Habemus Papam! Eminentissimum ac Reverendissimum Dominum, Dominum Bonasero, Sanctae Romanae Ecclesiae Cardinalem, qui sibi nomen imposuit* Pope Pius the Fourteenth." Translated: "I announce to you a great joy: We have a Pope! The Most Eminent and Most Reverend Lord, Lord Bonasero, Cardinal of the Holy Roman Church, who takes to himself the name Pope Pius the Fourteenth."

When Bonasero walked onto the balcony he saw the world differently. Throngs of people lined up so thickly he could barely see an inch of space between them, the cheers maddening. And somewhere, he knew, Cardinal Giuseppe Angullo was entirely livid with the outcome.

As he waved to the crowd, Bonasero knew he was now within Angullo's crosshairs.

**The day was** done, and the ceremonies were over.

As the moon traversed the sky, Cardinal Giuseppe Angullo stood before the open window of his dormitory room at the *Domus Sanctæ Marthæ* watching its slow trajectory. His mind, however, was detached from the reality of actually watching the moon as different images played within his mind's eye.

He had been so sure that his campaigning on the basis that he was a man 'bathed in the old tradition,' would garner the guaranteed ballots needed. But he was wrong. Cardinal Bonasero Vessucci won, taking the post he coveted to the point of pushing Pope Gregory over the rail because it was God's will to have him pave the way to the papal altar, for which he was to preside over. Now with Gregory gone and Pius the Fourteenth standing in the way, Angullo could feel something alien and familiar at the same time. It was the feeling of losing control, which was buffered with the need to do something about it in order to bring it back under his rule. Unknowingly, as he considered this, he clenched his right hand slowly into a tight fist as if grabbing something tight within his hold, the courses of blue veins tightening against translucent flesh as the knuckles of his bony fingers turned white.

Control was vacating him.

And he needed to curb this loss, this emptiness.

Stepping away from the window, the moon traversing overhead at a glacially slow pace, Cardinal Giuseppe Angullo began to outline a course of action against Bonasero Vessucci. He would have to be clever and sly. And he would succeed believing that there was a solution for everything.

Standing before the bathroom mirror, Angullo studied his

reflection.

For an odd moment words punctuated his thoughts, words he had never considered in the past or why he thought them. They simply came: *Mirror Friend, Mirror Foe.*

He examined his features further without emotion or movement. He stood as still as a Grecian statue, looking with impenetrable onyx eyes that never wavered in their sockets.

*Mirror Friend, Mirror Foe.*

Finally, he traced his fingertips over his image.

*Mirror Friend, Mirror Foe.*

*Yes, Bonasero*, he thought. *There's a solution for everything.*

Deep down he began to feel something familiar.

Control was beginning to seep back into his soul, something that was black and twisted, something very ugly.

In the mirror, his reflection took in a deep breath and exhaled in an equally long sigh. *Yes, Bonasero, there is a solution for everything.*

Behind him, the moon continued to move in its guided path, albeit with the slowness of a bad dream.

# CHAPTER TWENTY-SIX

*Mount Damavand. The Alborz Region, The Facility*

Leonid Sakharov did little to acknowledge the techs or Aryeh Levine. Instead, the old man focused more on the electromechanical components and hardware, showing more adulation toward the molecular assembler, the infrasonic equipment, probe microscopes, and the vacuum environments created to avoid the scattering of bots. He catered lovingly to the most advanced Electron Optical System available, rather than the living tissue that surrounded him. This was his entire world—the world of science. Everything else was immaterial.

While Sakharov seemed oblivious to those around him, he walked with more spring to his gait. And Levine couldn't help noticing that the old man was sweating profusely while his hands shook with the symptoms of neurological disease. The old man was drying out, he thought, the spirit of his mind overcoming his constant need for alcohol.

As the lab techs worked the consoles imputing data, Levine stood back, arms crossed, watching the monitors and finding with great fascination the simulations being cast on the high-definition wall-screen. Chains of molecular nanobots were replicating and self-sustaining themselves, the program giving them the intelligence to learn from experience as they evolved, essentially giving them life.

As Levine watched the chains move in serpentine fashion on the screen, the glass door opened, and al-Ghazi entered the lab with al-Sherrod behind him. Two Quds soldiers followed in their wake.

Al-Ghazi smiled when he saw Levine. He was wearing camouflaged attire and a black turban. "How are you, my friend?"

Levine greeted him, feigning a smile that looked uniquely genuine.

"It's good to see you. I had no idea that you were coming."

"I'm here on a last-minute invitation, Umar. I understand that the good doctor has performed all that was required of him and that we are ready to proceed with the testing on live subjects."

This was the first time Levine heard anything about this, al-Sherrod keeping him in the dark.

"Testing?"

Al-Ghazi sported his dazzling white teeth in the form of a broader smile. "It appears that the good Dr. Sakharov is ahead of schedule and is excited to show us his program regarding the nanobots."

Levine looked at the doctor, who was tapping instructions into the keyboard, noting that Sakharov chose to ignore those in the lab by remaining oblivious and cognizant of their presence at the same time.

"Doctor." Al-Ghazi stepped toward the scientists with his hands clasped behind the small of his back. "This must be an exciting moment for you, yes?"

The doctor gave a cursory nod, nothing else, not even a flicker of emotion.

"Then let's get started, shall we?"

One of the two techs went into one of the vacuum environments, a glassed-in room, with a canister the size of a liter bottle. It was cylindrical, the container metallic with a mirror polish. On top was a screencap, an opening. He placed it gingerly on the table and left the room as the second tech brought a goat into the chamber tethered to a leash, the animal bleating. While removing the tie from the goat's collar, the first tech returned with a cluster of indigent plants and placed them on the table beyond the goat's reach. Once done they exited the room, the door closing behind them with the subsequent whisper of the seal tightening that made the room inescapable for anything living—including a single cell, virus, bacteria, or nanobot.

"The canister, Doctor, will be larger for our purposes when the time comes, yes?"

"No," he answered crustily. "The nanobots have been programmed to reproduce exponentially. But every succeeding life will have a half-time, which means that they will eventually shrink themselves to a time limit where they cannot harm anything organic. For this experiment, the bots have been given a primary lifespan of one minute, its replicated life form will be half that, thirty seconds; the third chain, fifteen seconds; and so forth until their span shrinks down to a point where they don't exist long enough to do further damage. They will always exist since a trillionth of a nanosecond is still a measure of time, but too little to cause destruction. It's a safety measure to keep the nanobots from creating Drexler's theory of grey goo."

"Grey goo?"

Sakharov ignored him.

And then: "But is one canister enough for our needs?"

"More than enough," he answered. "In that one canister is a nano swarm that will act as a whole that can wipe out an entire city. So that you know, you can fit one hundred thousand nanobots on the head of a pin. It's more than enough."

Al-Ghazi gave off an expression denoting that he was impressed. "I see."

Levine took everything in. His curiosity piqued.

"And what about the plants, Doctor? What's their function?"

Sakharov set up the monitor for the final click of the button. "The bots have been programmed to attack organic matter, things that are alive or at one time were alive. Everything else—glass, metal, plastic—should remain unaffected."

"I see. But why isn't anything happening? I see that the container has a screen top. I assume it's open."

"It is."

"Then why is nothing happening?"

"Because," he let his finger hover over a button on the keyboard, "the nanobots are stimulated through sound waves. Once they are, then their programming kicks in and they take on a life of their own, doing what I programmed them to do: To evolve and to learn by experience."

"Life," he said.

Sakharov nodded. "I'm creating life."

After a moment of silence, as the doctor held a wavering finger above the keyboard, everyone waited with childlike anticipation.

And then the finger dropped, a single button pushed, the program initiating.

The goat bleated without care or caution, pacing the glass enclosure.

And then a waspy hum sounded over the speakers, growing in sound.

"It's activating," commented Sakharov.

Within thirty seconds the goat began to shake its head wildly as if buzzing flies were annoying it. Its bleating becoming more agitated, more terror-stricken. And then its coat began to ripple as if something alive was undulating beneath its skin, rolling. The creature then raised its head and wobbled upon weak legs as sores opened and pared back from its joints, exposing blood-laced bones. Its eyes bulged in terror, but only for a moment as they dissolved within their sockets, decaying. The meat of its tongue was now gone. Its flesh, disappearing. And within seconds its hide became a wild tangle of hair that appeared to move as the bots broke down the animal to nonexistence.

On the table the plants were decaying just as quickly, the organic material breaking down like a film in fast motion until nothing was left.

And then they waited, the glass holding, the buzzing sounding over the loudspeakers in a raucous din.

But within five minutes the drone of the bots was gone, their lifespan shrinking to the point where they could no longer be effective.

Al-Ghazi smiled and clapped a hand on Sakharov's shoulder, causing the old man to finally bring a smile to his lips. He had achieved his goal, he thought. He had done what Mother Russia refused to give him credit for—the ability to achieve where others had failed.

"My good Doctor, you truly have an amazing mind."

"I know."

Levine, however, was beside himself. Here was a technology far more devastating than any nuclear device, a weapon that could be programmed to kill without impunity or conscience—entire cities, towns, and populations gone without damage to the surrounding infrastructure. No doubt Israel was on that list.

"Ahmadinejad will be most pleased," stated al-Sherrod. "Since sanctions have made Iran the largest leper colony in the world, this will provide the means of leverage should Israel decide to bomb our nuclear facilities. Its allies will also fall under Allah's wrath—city by city, infidel by infidel."

Levine's fate was now clearly stated: He had no choice but to put himself in a position to contact his sources. Not trying to tip off his thoughts, he nevertheless gave a cursory glance to the Comm Center on the second level and noted the wall monitors through the smoke-stained glass. He would have to be swift and efficient. First, he would have to take out the two Quds soldiers that constantly shadowed him, no easy feat, then work his way to the center and send his coordinates for a military strike.

He then closed his eyes, a thought forming. He had lived a good life, an exciting life. But he saw no way to survive this mission but by the grace of God. He would, at least, try to escape through the mountains, finding avenues to the north. But the cold of the mountains was brutal, the attempt unrealistic, if not suicidal. But it was the only course of action available.

Al-Sherrod maintained his smile. "Then we are ready to move forward?" he asked al-Ghazi.

Al-Ghazi nodded, and then he turned to Levine. "Umar, I understand that you have seen the Ark."

"I have."

"Then your role has become much larger."

"How so?"

"The Ark will possess the good doctor's discoveries. I will need you to introduce the Ark as a faith of goodwill to the Zionists of Israel, the Catholics, and the Muslims. Iran cannot take an active role in this because they will be targeted should it be discovered that they had an active role in promoting the good doctor's creations. You will act as an emissary on behalf of our organization to promote a false image of good intentions. We would like a gathering of all heads of state, as well as the heads of religious denominations, to attend the opening of the Ark for the possessions within to be shared by all since all have an interest in what's within the Ark. Mossad already possesses the staff of Aaron and the golden pot of manna, as proof that the true Ark exists. However, we still possess the tablets containing the Ten Commandments. Such an opening of goodwill should be shared by all. But when they open the Ark, they will be greeted by the demons of Dr. Sakharov's making."

Sakharov clenched his jaw, causing the wiry muscles to work.

"But the Muslims?"

"Collateral damage," he said with indifference. "Since Solomon was selected to maintain the Ark, then it is believed that Allah favored him. Therefore, Muslims must be present so as not to draw suspicion as to the Ark's true intention."

"And my position?"

"You will negotiate the trade of the Ark for the good of all religions when, in fact, the opening of the Ark is to happen at a place of my choosing, my Ground Zero. A team of onsite operatives will coordinate the attack by initiating the program at the location. Laptops and experience will be necessary. Of course, their deaths being martyred."

"And what will your role be in all this?"

"My position will be minimal since it is my continuing duty to direct cells to perform certain missions throughout the regions. Therefore, I must remain covert. Iran, however, will deny culpability in this matter to keep sanctions from crippling them further. It is our intention to test this technology before we take it one step further."

"And that would be?"

Al-Ghazi nodded. "Should the doctor's finding prove as fruitful as to the events we have just seen, then we will place a canister in every major city in Israel, the United States, the United Kingdom, and to anyone who does not relinquish to our rule. Sanctions will and must be lifted from Iran. The infidels will give in to our demands. If not . . ." He let his words trail.

"And where will Ground Zero be for the initial run?"

Al-Ghazi's smile lifted into a sardonic grin. "In a most appropriate place," he told him. "We will open the Ark in the heart of Vatican City."

# CHAPTER TWENTY-SEVEN

*Vatican City, Three Days after the Conclave*

Inside the papal chamber, Jesuit priests Gino Auciello and John Essex from the *Servizio_Informazioni del Vaticano* sat before Bonasero Vessucci, the newly appointed Pope Pius XIV.

Both men sat with their knees crossed in leisure while the pontiff sat more stiffly, more agitated, his hands tented as he rested the points of his fingertips against the bottom of his chin, as if in thought.

"This is good," said Essex, his London accent quite apparent. "Your position here is deserving and long overdue."

"Thank you, John. I feel where I need to be," he said. "But I do have concerns."

"And they would be, Your Holiness?"

"I have reason to believe that Pope Gregory may have been murdered."

The Jesuits stared at him incredulously.

"The last time I visited you in the SIV chamber, the day you were watching the Temple Mount on the monitors, do you remember?"

"Of course," answered Father Auciello.

"I had my suspicions even then."

"But you said nothing."

Bonasero nodded. "At that time, it was just a notion," he said. "But now . . ."

Father Essex's face maintained the look of incredulity. "But why? And who?"

Bonasero Vessucci hesitated a brief moment as if choosing his words carefully. And then: "Cardinal Angullo," he finally said.

"Angullo." The simple word came from Auciello's lips as a whisper, almost too light for anyone to hear. He leaned forward in his chair. "Your Holiness, do you understand the magnitude of what you're saying?"

"Clearly," he stated. "The rule of the pope not coming under the guidelines of an autopsy is due to the very reality that popes have been murdered in the past, and that said proof would divulge the unbelievable corruption that exists within the shadows of the Basilica. Centuries ago, there were outward signs that poisons were used, but never spoken of."

"You think Cardinal Angullo poisoned Pope Gregory?"

"I think Cardinal Angullo is a very ambitious man with a very aggressive agenda," he said. "I believe the man's life has become a monstrous corruption whose soul has been lost, his sense of morality shattered. I believe that he has allowed his ambitions to take him away from the true nature of God."

"And you have proof of this?"

Another hesitation: "No."

"With all due respect, Your Holiness," said Essex, "may I ask what is prompting this suspicion?"

"Intuition. Observation. This man conspired to usurp my position as secretary of state to position himself for the papal throne upon the expiration of Pope Gregory. Six months later Gregory is gone, setting him up as lead *Preferiti*."

"Again, Your Holiness," said Auciello, "other than intuition, what is there?"

"Gregory was a strong man. When another man's ambition turns to impatience, then he makes his path to Glory."

"But surely Pope Gregory would have defended himself. He was a powerful man."

"Not if he was sick or knew his murderer, placing him in a position of vulnerability or complacency."

"I don't know," said Farther Essex. "Cardinal Angullo may be a man of moral questioning, but murder?"

"On the night of Pope Gregory's death, did you check the monitors of someone, anyone, moving through the hallways in the early morning hours around the time of the pope's death?"

Auciello nodded. "We did, Your Holiness, thoroughly. But there was nothing there except for Vatican Security, who were stationed at the entrance of the hallway. And they maintained their position throughout their shift."

Bonasero sighed, his eyes searching for thought as if it was imprinted in open space. "The old tunnels," he finally said. "Are there cameras situated in those passageways?"

"No."

"So, someone with the knowledge of Vatican schematics, someone who knows where the security cameras are positioned, could pass unseen?"

The Jesuits nodded. However, it was Essex who spoke.

"The passageways are all but known to a few—mostly by Vatican Security and the SIV."

"And to those within the Vatican hierarchy such as the secretary of state," he added. "Those tunnels are historic, and excavations are providing us with a history as discoveries are made. But they're there and Cardinal Angullo is a cunning man."

"Again, Your Holiness, and with all due respect, everything is speculation on your part."

Bonasero had to agree. No images on the cameras, nothing to alert the guards standing post that someone had unlawfully breached the corridors leading to the pope's chambers, nothing to indicate that Cardinal Angullo was even there. It was as Father Essex had said: pure speculation.

"Regardless," he said, "I may be in a place of position to fear for my life."

"If you wish, we can double the efforts of security."

"I have something better," he said. "I will give the cardinal the chance to prove me wrong. He will either act on his compulsion or surrender to it and do nothing. But most men who have lost their way often give to their temptations."

"And what is it you propose?"

"Before I left for Boston, I asked you to do me a favor. Do you remember what it was?"

Essex nodded. "You asked us to maintain the whereabouts of the Vatican Knights."

The pope nodded. "And where is Leviticus?"

"In Rome," said Auciello. "He's a civilian working with an Italian security agency specializing in measures dealing with identity theft for companies abroad."

"And Isaiah?"

"He's in Mexico working with the mission you adopted him from."

Bonasero nodded. Then: "What about Kimball?"

There was a hesitation on the parts of the Jesuits.

"Kimball?" he repeated.

"He's living in Las Vegas," said Essex. "He's working in a casino under the alias of J.J. Doetsch."

"As?"

"A janitor," said Auciello. "The man's a janitor."

Bonasero did not judge Kimball for what he was, which was a man seeking a simple life after living an incredible life of hardship. Perhaps it was the best thing for him, he considered.

"And there's something else," said Father Auciello.

"And that would be?"

"He's involved with cage fighting," he said.

"What?"

"There are fighting venues in Las Vegas where men fight against men for money. Kimball has been involved in three fights . . . He nearly killed the last man."

Bonasero closed his eyes, feeling the encroachment of a certain sadness creep over him. Some people cannot run from their fate, he considered. No matter how hard they try.

And then: "You are SIV and what we say here is confidential, yes?"

"Of course."

"I want you to contact Leviticus and Isaiah," he said. "I want them to find Kimball and bring him back."

"And if Kimball decides not to return?"

"Then he does so with the decision of his choosing? But I want to afford Kimball every opportunity to make his decision based on free will. Make sure he knows that my need for him is paramount. Tell him of my concerns."

"Of course, Your Holiness."

"But the ultimate decision is his."

After a congenial valediction, the Jesuits left the chamber. Bonasero then went to the balcony and traced a hand over the smooth railing where Gregory took his fall. There was no doubt that everything he considered was based on intuition. But it was intuition that guided him all these years, which, in turn, taught him how to handle each person differently based on his convictions regarding God and religion. It was his intuition to promote the Vatican Knights once again as a unit to save the lives of those who could not save themselves.

The air was sweet like honeydew, the breeze soft and caressing, the day clear and the sky blue, but as magnificent as everything appeared to be, he couldn't help the feeling that dark clouds were brewing and that a terrible storm was on the horizon.

It was his intuition that told him this—a voice he had come to trust and recognize, a voice that never failed him.

Under the canvas of an immaculately blue sky, he sighed.

# CHAPTER TWENTY-EIGHT

*Mount Damavand. The Alborz Region, The Facility*

Three days after Levine was informed of his future role in the scheme of Sakharov's discovery, he'd been deciding on the course of action to take, working the steps through his mind. The Quds that shadowed his every move had to go, quick and efficient kills. Then he would have to make his way to the Comm Center on the second tier, forward Sakharov's findings, the facility's coordinates for an illegal sortie into Iran, and take out the facility using the fuel cells as triggering mechanisms to implode the lab and turn it into a coffin.

Secondly, he was not about to be so cavalier to do this at the sacrifice of his life. The Comm Center was also the monitoring station and a means to open and close facility doors. He would open the vault door to the outside, during darkness when the shadows would become his ally, and hope that the machinegun nests wouldn't cut him down during his flight to freedom.

Feeling his heart palpitate with the reality of the moment, he took in deep breaths and released them as a reaction to settle his nerves. Getting into the proper mindset, he left his residential capsule and entered the hallway.

The trailing Quds soldiers were there wearing their prescribed tan uniforms of the elite force, their berets set to specs at the proper tilt, their eyes filled with disdain and suspicion, staring him down.

Levine gave a nod that went unacknowledged and walked past the soldiers. As expected, they followed, trailing ten meters behind, which posed a problem since he needed to get up close and personal and take them out with his particular set of skills.

As he passed the lab, he saw the Quds reflections mirrored against the glass, watching and carefully maintaining their distance.

He continued to walk as if in leisure, entering tubes and taking bends, listening to their footfalls as they followed, whereas he wore soft-sole footwear to mask his.

Rounding another bend, he finally took to a wall, his body rigid, waiting.

And when they rounded the corner, he acted.

Levine came across with the blade of his hand, chopping the first Quds soldier across the throat, the man's eyes widening in surprise as he fell to his knees clutching his neck. The second soldier went for his firearm, his hand falling on the stock as Levine forced the heel of his hand into the blade of his nose, forcing the bone into his brain and killing the man instantly.

The first soldier got to his feet, wobbled, and tried to recalibrate his stance. But Levine was on him within the second, grabbed the soldier by placing a hand at the point of his jaw, another hand at the base of his neck, and wrenched the man's head with such incredible force that his neck broke with an audible snap.

And then silence, Levine listening for backup of more Quds. But no one appeared.

Levine then dragged the bodies to a nearby capsule that stocked supplies and piled them into the given space. He then took their weapons, placing one firearm within the waistline of his pants while managing the other with a tight grip.

Now to the Comm Center.

Levine did not hesitate in his approach but moved quickly.

Running along the landing of the second tier he could see the monitors through the smoke-screened glass, could see the myriad of blinking lights—the nerve center of the facility.

The two techs never saw him enter but heard the whoosh of the door opening. When the first turned to see who entered, a well-placed bullet struck him in the forehead, throwing him against the console, blood and gore exploding from the back of his head and against the wall in a wide fan, the bullet exiting into the background monitor, shattering the glass and causing a cascade of sparks to fly, dance and die out.

The second tech put up his hand as if to ward off the blow of the coming shot, a feeble attempt at self-preservation as the weapon went off, the first bullet taking off two fingers, the second shot finding the tech's left eye, which caused the man's head to snap violently back, with his good eye detonating with surprise before he slid off his chair and to the floor.

In a fleeting move, he took to the chair, keyed up the board with typing commands to accept verbal instructions, put on the headgear, and spoke quickly and articulately. As he spoke, words appeared on the screen as code-red data requiring an immediate incursion into enemy territory with the intent to annihilate the facility with extreme force. Coordinates were given, the intentions of the use of nanotechnology forwarded, as well as the location of the Ark.

Time was limited, he knew, so the data proffered had to be minimal with the confidence that the information given could be deciphered by Mossad. He did not state what the Ark was going to be used for—no time to expound on that fact. He figured that the Ark could not be saved since the technology, the data, and the facility needed to be leveled.

As he spoke, it was always on the back of his mind that time was running short. There was no doubt that the reports of his gunfire galvanized others to react.

And then the sirens went off in a shrill that told him that time had run out.


**Al-Sherrod raised his** head from his pillow unsure if what he heard was the report of gunfire. There were three in total, or perhaps it was some obscure dream for which he could not remember.

With his head slightly raised, he continued to listen.

Silence.

And then the wild keen of internal sirens sounded off.

Al-Sherrod shot up from the bed bleary-eyed, his heart pounding, and quickly threw on a shirt and grabbed his firearm. Stepping into the hallway, bullet-shaped lights mounted above the doors blinked in calibrated flashes as sirens blared.

Quds soldiers stood in the hallway looking disheveled and lost, their shirts buttoned incorrectly as they rushed to get into uniform.

"Where's it coming from?" yelled al-Sherrod.

"We don't know," said a soldier.

"Then find out!"

The Quds grouped then branched out with the points of their weapons forward, the teams searching. Al-Sherrod took the rear with his head on a swivel, purposely hanging back, the man's true courage lacking since he was more of a politician than a warrior. The gun in his hand was a simple prop that made him feel secure and nothing more. It was also unlikely that he possessed the skills to hit a target of any kind, even one that was stationary. But the weapon was far better than an empty hand.

"Find the problem! Quickly!"

The Quds fanned out, searching, their weapons poised to kill.

#

Levine spoke quickly, giving as much information as he could, checked the screen before forwarding the information, deemed it proper, and then hit the SEND button.

With the speed of cyberspace, data was downloading at another point. His mission was done.

Now it was time for self-preservation.

Levine checked the console, the instructions written in Farsi.

No problem.

He noted the monitor giving a specific view to the cavern's vaulted entrance and tapped the quick instructions labeled on the keyboard beneath the screen. With another tap of the SEND button, the vault-like door leading to the outside began to open with a horrible slowness that was almost too much to comprehend at such a moment.

Grabbing his firearm from the console, Levine left the room and began to make his way out of the facility.

**The Quds quickly** converged, seeking the source of the warning.

From the second tier, Levine peered over the edge, a gun in his hand. Quds were moving with due diligence, searching.

And then they saw Levine with a firearm in his hand, a serious breach of his right to possess one inside the facility. As Levine fell back out of sight, bullets stitched across the wall where he just been standing, decimating it.

He ran down the hallway as the Quds took the steps to the second tier, nearing.

More gunfire, the report of the assault weapons outmatching his firepower at an unimaginable scale, the bullets missing as he took a bend, the floor and the walls of where he had just been taking on additional damage, the air chalked with dust.

Levine could sense that the air was noticeably cooler, the door of the vault opening enough to allow the cold mountain air inside, while leaving a sizeable aperture of escape.

He ran.

At the end of the corridor, he saw a glass partition that overlooked the first tier, a twenty-foot drop. Fifty meters beyond that was the Alborz region.

He lifted his pistol and shot the glass, the tempered chips falling like a cache of diamonds to the floor below. Standing along the edge of the upper tier, the floor below looked more like a hundred-foot drop rather than twenty, he gauged his landing.

More bullets passed around him in waspy zips, prompting him to leap.

Although he performed admirably by bending his knees and rolling with the motion of the flow upon landing, twenty feet was too much and the impact too great. Levine struck hard, rolled, the snap of his ankles sounding out like gunshots, the bones shattering to the degree that his feet hung at awkward angles.

Gritting his teeth in agonizing pain, Levine refused to cry out. His weapons skated across the floor beyond his reach.

*At least*, he thought, *I gave a valiant effort. Long live Israel*!

As he lay there, shadows poured over him. When he looked up, he noted multiple barrels of assault weapons directed at him.

Within moments al-Sherrod made his way until he stood over Levine.

For a long moment, he looked at Levine with a searching and calculating look. "Who are you?" he asked. "Who are you really?"

Levine remained silent.

"You are not al-Qaeda, are you?"

More silence.

"It appears that al-Ghazi has made a grave misjudgment in your character."

Levine lowered his head to the floor. His life was over, and he knew it.

A Quds officer burst through the line. "Al-Sherrod, the techs in the Comm Center are dead. And it appears that a message was sent."

"Find the point of contact," he ordered.

"Yes, al-Sherrod." The soldier was gone.

Al-Sherrod bent over Levine. "Umar is not your real name, is it?"

Levine wanted to spit in the man's face.

"Are you Mossad?"

No reply.

"Is that what you did?" he asked. "Did you contact Mossad?"

Levine finally groaned, his nerves becoming a tabernacle of pain. Al-Sherrod smiled and then set a foot upon one of the operative's broken ankles, causing Levine to bark out in exquisite pain. "I can do this all night," he told him. He ground his foot and the injury, causing Levine to clench his jaw and tears to run down the corners of his eyes. "What did you send to Mossad?"

Levine's breathing was becoming erratic, the man slipping into shock.

Al-Sherrod once again ground his foot against Levine's injury, driving another cry from Levine. "What did you send to Mossad? I will not ask again."

"Then don't . . . ask. You're just wasting . . . your time."

Al-Sherrod sighed, and then looked at the man with contempt. "Your pathetic life is over. You know that, don't you?" And then to his team: "Close the vault and secure the facility," he said. And then he looked at the man's broken ankles with a measure of admiration at the awkward way the feet were turned backward. "Prepare the vacuum chamber and carry this man inside," he ordered. "Let's see firsthand how the good doctor's discoveries work against the organic matter of a man's flesh."

Levine was lifted harshly off the floor, his seemingly boneless ankles flopping horribly against the tile as he was dragged away.

"Keep him alive for another day," he said. "I may need to mine him for information." The truth was, however, that he wanted Levine to suffer pain beyond endurance, beyond human comprehension, and then snuff out his life with a simple order.

Al-Sherrod, the Devil's Companion, did all he could to suppress a smile of satisfaction.

# CHAPTER TWENTY-NINE

*Tel Aviv, Israel, Mossad Headquarters*

Yitzhak Paled stood in the Comm Center watching the screen with his arms folded defensively across his chest. The large man, Benyamin Kastenbaum, stood beside him maintaining the same pose, his colossal frame dwarfing Paled's.

The room was dark, their forms silhouetted before the high-definition screen as encrypted notes downloaded from coordinates in the Alborz Mountain region, specifically from Mount Damavand, an odd point since there had never been verification of activity there.

"Aryeh's alive," Benyamin commented.

"From Mount Damavand in northern Iran . . . Of all places."

"What's he doing there?"

"I guess we're about to find out."

They watched the screen load up with rune-like characters, letters, numbers, and symbols, the techs playing the keyboards to decipher the codes. The data coming forward in five different segments:

2BEL4o69Zvwb45I1PyFVXr2nnebQliV53ZDboAv1Miat±Av%2F
y%2BFYQTxb9aonEsWDeRHwZBd73Jf%0AoCgOklgcitM90βM1iV
ifu%2Bftv≥€∞pJhQkVRRuLascUEzrgGz5F%2B34EibZQZUoUkfaVr
mvcPcHIXbq12D%0ATrq5d6Wlμ

GQDPfLFnAzafwKeNI0Aixcn12twrk7baXja7dDEJpBO9tbsl2QI3
b%0AtHbbABZgmRBBGk44an02VRlhcv%2FFWNg7jum1%π%2BO
N2sERIyla55%2FVp%2BvH2VX368%2F7M5nf%0AGYQ3LnJAxdj
LRp%2BEYSknuWFO£∑πα≠×ÅÄ¥ŭ

1pwyG%2Bj3D5uu69ee4QB0xAzdLQctkIf8X%0Aj4HZuiGuxrsn9

CbliKMSOecwUEiNs5Z4pV4sM0%2Bk%2Bg%2Bt%2FaY3T5qc8%
2FpaGPRitLV1QZFx4Bu5Ta4Z%0AjmYlUWQt2Sg8fGbMiB3Wu7a
GS3MSnsCETQ1u6TkMfoWK2RN


%2FXPgm%0Ax50TAUhWpn4v3epCVw4jCMJcAu8yHsuRoJqaa
Afl%2Bk2xGcQ72dpsLxvT2ForGKD6dJzT9QowA%0AhnumrRZUv
y%2BLV1DjnylkV0vf7KCdPKwVtq5jsDmg7hHuBWZYcx4clAT%2
B%2FNCpEJnWgNsAz6GL10qW%


2FpaGPRitLV1QZFx4Bu5Ta4Z%0AjmYlUWQt2Sg8fGbMiB3Wu
7aGS3MSnsCETQ1u6TkMfoWK2RNybls232BXrLsmkKy%2BON2s
ERIyla55f48rgI%0APlwfdZTHQiWnWji1beBt18RiJYYJFdIRYg5%2
FyETojJr33t%2FqkDMQbdUFZiJvE

The encryptions became clear, the markings and symbols conforming to Yiddish text. There was no doubt. Aryeh Levine was alive in a complex hidden deep within Iran's Alborz region inside a covert facility near the base of Mount Damavand. The exact coordinates were given for a preemptive strike.

The second verse touched upon technology that was more devastating than nuclear weaponry, a nanodevice capable of destroying organic material while leaving the infrastructure intact with no way to combat it. Israel was now within the crosshairs.

Other segments appeared scattered, the messages themselves needing to be determined as to what Levine was trying to express. Apparently, the man was in a rush.

Inside the facility next to the lab lies the true Ark of the Covenant. What it was meant to be used for wasn't quite clear, the codes indecipherable. But it was apparent that it had meaning in the scheme of things to come. What that was, however, would remain a mystery since some of the data was corrupted.

"It's not uniform," said Benyamin.

Paled had to agree. "That means Aryeh was pressed for time. Not a good sign, I'm afraid. As much as I want to hope for his safety, I believe that I may be hoping for too much."

"The Alborz is rather cold this time of year—too cold for any man to survive."

"But he did what was required of him," said Paled. The man bent over the console, the light of the monitor glowing against the sharp features of his face. He scrutinized the screen, the messages, and read into them. "Nanotechnology," he said. "There's a name attached to this: A Doctor Leonid Sakharov." He turned to Benyamin. "Find out what you can about this man and get back to me. If Aryeh has requested an immediate and illegal incursion to these coordinates, then it is with good reason that we must take it seriously."

"Of course, there will be fallout from the international community."

"When the life of Israel is at stake, then the voice of the international community means little . . . Doctor Leonid Sakharov. Find out what you can about this man while we consider a strike against Iran. And quickly, Benyamin, time may be limited, so a decision will have to be made soon."

"Yes, Yitzhak, I'll do so right away." The large man was gone, leaving Yitzhak Paled to gnaw unknowingly on his lower lip in concentration as his mind formulated the beginnings of a strike mission.

Of course, he would have to contact the proper authorities by moving up the chain of command, which ended with Prime Minister Netanyahu. But Israel's previous strikes and assassinations against Iran's nuclear scientists to retard their so-called facilities that "produce the peaceful means of nuclear power" drew the ire of the international community, as Benyamin had said. But here was confirmation from a stellar operative sending a transmission from a covert facility hidden away from the scrupulous eyes of Mossad and the CIA. Such an operation was meant to be concealed. And when an operation is meant to be concealed, then that operation is normally classified as the creation of a WMD, which, in this case, is nanotechnology, a weapon geared to destroy organic matter while leaving the infrastructure unmolested.

"You did well, my friend," he whispered. He then drew the tips of his fingers over the monitor screen, over the data. "You got your message across."


**In less than** an hour, Benyamin returned with a dossier on Leonid J. Sakharov, and sat at a table with Yitzhak Paled and held counsel.

Benyamin opened the file. "Doctor Leonid J. Sakharov was a leading scientist in Russia during the Cold War and a short time thereafter. His primary field of study was in the field of nanotechnology from the mid- to the late eighties. According to our data, the man was years beyond other scientists in his field with this type of technology. And it appears, even as the Wall fell, that the Russian government continued to fund his program into the nineties." He slid a black-and-white glossy photo of a much younger Sakharov to Paled, who examined the man in the picture with a keen eye, studying everything about the man's hardened features, his mind to never forget the man's face.

"There was a purported accident in one of the labs, the data not quite clear. But it appears that Dr. Sakharov initiated a test of his findings prematurely, causing the deaths of his technicians. With Russia being the way it was at the time, they saw this as a step forward and allowed him to go on, the deaths of the techs serving as an example of what his experiments can do, rather than to see the tragedy of their demise. Apparently, Sakharov sobered to the idea of what his research was capable of and destroyed the data, earning him a long stint in Vladimir Central Prison."

"So, he's incarcerated?"

Benyamin shook his head. "Not anymore. He was released after the principals running Vladimir were allegedly in negotiations with this man to release him." He slid another photo across the table. It was a photo of a Middle Eastern man wearing an elegant outfit. "Several months ago, Sakharov was visited by this man. His name is Adham al-Ghazi. And we believe him to be a high-ranking member of al-Qaeda. Information on this guy is limited. But we're trying to learn as much as we can about him."

"This doesn't make sense."

"It gets better," added Benyamin. "Sakharov was living on a small government stipend in Moscow until a few weeks ago."

"And?"

Another photo slid across the table, one that was appropriated from the memory files of a digital security camera near the Kremlin. "This is al-Ghazi a day or two before Sakharov disappeared," he continued. "We believe that al-Ghazi was there for Sakharov. And ironically, after this picture was taken, Doctor Sakharov was on a flight to Tehran within days. So, tell me, Yitzhak, why would a man of age, a man like Sakharov, whose only roots lie within Russia, go to Tehran?"

Paled nodded. "Because, my friend, sometimes when a man grows old and begins to feel left behind and forgotten, he needs to feel useful.

In this case, I believe Doctor Sakharov was allowed to feel useful once again, a second chance at life rather than to sit back, exist, then die without anyone knowing your name."

"So, he's in Tehran."

"No," he answered. "He's in this covert facility at Mount Damavand. Otherwise, Aryeh never would have known him. Doctor Sakharov, nanotechnology, it all fits. Sakharov has completed what he started years ago in Russia. And somehow al-Ghazi and the Iranian government have colluded to benefit by sharing a common goal, despite their suspicion of one another. It's no secret that Ahmadinejad has been recruiting these factions over those past few years to carry out their deeds, so they can sit back and deny culpability by pointing the accusing finger at a scapegoat."

He leaned back in his chair and gazed into Benyamin's eyes. "They have perfected a weapon to take out Israel," he told him. "Aryeh got enough across to tell us that. He also told us that they had the true Ark of the Covenant. By telling us the exact location and the purpose of this facility, I see no choice but to destroy it in its entirety."

"We'll need to contact the Prime Minister."

"Who will then inform our allies of our findings. The CIA will then use their satellites to zone in on the position and confirm this facility as we did. On the ridgeline are numerous fuel cells maintaining the power of the complex—a target that should aid in its fall."

"The United States may want further proof than just a few encryptions."

"It's not their choice. The United States needs to think less about how they can profit from this and make their economy swing better. Because if they allow this to continue, if Iran and al-Qaeda go forward with this technology, then Israel, the United States, and their allies may not have an economy withstanding at all."

"And the Ark?"

Paled's eyes went soft. "It will be lost forever, I'm afraid."

"Such a treasure for the world to behold."

"If we don't do this, Benyamin, then there will be no world to treasure."

# CHAPTER THIRTY

*Rome, Italy*

Leviticus was sitting at his desk wearing slacks, a white shirt, and a black tie, which was far from the uniform he was accustomed to as a Vatican Knight. For the past six months, he'd been working as a security analyst working for an Italian investment firm with interests abroad.

Although Leviticus was not his proper name, it was the moniker he bore as a Vatican Knight. His true name was Danny Keaton, a man who was born, bred, and raised in Brooklyn, New York.

While carefully perusing over documents regarding the recent hacking attempts against a billion-dollar investment firm in Belize, a country with a company tie, came a light tapping against the door.

He looked up and laid the papers aside on the desktop. "Come in."

An unattractive woman with dishwater-brown hair tied up into a bun opened the door. Her smile, however, was quite becoming and electric. "Mr. Keaton, there's a priest here to see you."

*A priest?*

"You can send him in. Thank you."

She stepped back and allowed the priest to enter the office, then closed the door softly behind him. For a long moment, the priest stood there looking through glasses that magnified his eyes, the man suffering from some clinical form of visual degeneration. On the pocket of his clerical shirt was the symbol of the SIV. In his hand an aluminum suitcase. "Mr. Keaton," he said, coming forward and offering his free hand. "I'm Father Domicelli of the *Servicio de Inteligencia del Vaticano.*"

"The SIV. I know. I saw the emblem on your shirt." Leviticus gestured to the seat in front of his desk as an invitation for the Jesuit to sit. "How can I help you?"

"You can help us," he said, "by servicing the needs of the Church."

"You knew my place within the Church?"

"I do. It is within the scope of our knowledge under the exclusive sponsorship of the pope to know so." Then with cool evenness and little hesitation, he said, "You were a Vatican Knight."

Leviticus fell back into his seat. "Again: How can I help you?"

The Jesuit's smile never left him. "Of course, you know the result of the conclave."

He nodded. "The good Cardinal Vessucci has taken the papal throne. A good man in a deserving position."

"And in turn, the pontiff has requested your assistance," he returned. Father Domicelli then raised the aluminum suitcase for show and pointed to the desktop. "May I?"

Leviticus swept the papers aside. "Yes, of course."

The Jesuit laid the suitcase on the desktop, undid the clasps, and lifted the lid. Inside were crisp, clean clerical shirts and clerical collars as pristine as snow, the shirts neatly folded. Beneath them were military-style pants with cargo pockets and freshly glossed military boots. On the shirt pocket was the logo of the Vatican Knights, a blue and gray shield with a Pattée cross as its center point, and two Heraldic lions standing on their hind legs holding the shield stable with their forepaws. Upon seeing this Leviticus worked his lip into a minor tic, a micro-expression of pride over the embroidery that meant so much.

In slow reaction, he reached for one of the shirts and held it within his hands as if the fabric was as fragile as threadbare silk. And with either caution or homage or perhaps even both, he brushed his fingertips over the embroidered shield. "I remember," he simply said.

"The shirt is set to specifics," he told him. "Pope Pius the Fourteenth has decided to reinstate the Vatican Knights, and he needs your efforts, should you accept his proposal, to serve the Church once again."

Leviticus never took his eyes off the shirt. "I still have my old uniforms," he said in a dreamy, almost distant tone. "I have all of them."

"Would you be interested in reprising the role as the second lieutenant of the Vatican Knights?"

He looked at the priest and nodded. "It would be my absolute honor."

Father Domicelli extended his hand. "Welcome back, Leviticus."

*The Temapache Orphanage, Mexico*

The Mexican desert was arid at the site of the mission where Isaiah had been adopted from by Cardinal Vessucci all those years ago and then taken to Vatican City. The structural body of the orphanage hardly changed—although the cracks were wider, longer, and the surrounding adobe walls bleached lighter than what he recalled. The rooms, the hallways, the lighted core of its essence remained the same, however. Even after all these years.

Though his moniker was Isaiah, his given name was Christian Placentia, a child orphaned at an early age who wound up half-dead at the missionary doors. Summarily taken in and nourished by a kindly nun, Christian soon caught the eye of the missionary priest who noted the child's exemplary physical skills, high intelligence, and good character. Word soon reached across the ocean to the ear of a cardinal in Vatican City—a world away—who saw in Christian the potentials required of a Vatican Knight. For years, the young man trained diligently, if not fanatically, learning the skills of an elite fighter, as well as the philosophies regarding the differences between right and wrong, and how to employ 'just' reasoning to awkward states of affairs. Philosophies, teachings, and classical readings were a must. Martial arts became a discipline of self-defense not only to protect himself but for those who could not protect themselves. Not only did the Church turn children like him into men with a particular set of combat skills, but also compounded their development by fashioning unfaltering character by embedding the mantra *Loyalty above all else, except Honor*, as a code of unwavering principle.

It was a credo he lived by as a Vatican Knight. It was also a credo he lived by as a missionary who now served the orphanage that he had grown up in.

Dressed in a cleric's shirt and Roman Catholic collar, wearing faded dungarees and work boots, Christian worked the garden tilling the soil with a hoe, the muscles of his arms becoming ropy and sinewy with every strike that drove the implement's blade into the ground.

After mopping his brow with his forearm and leaving a greasy smudge, he rested against the hoe's handle for a brief moment.

"Christian Placentia?"

The former Knight turned toward the voice. Beneath the bullet-shaped entryway leading into the garden stood two priests, one a near facsimile of the other in appearance with the exception that one was slightly taller. While one stood idle with his hands crossed before him, the other remained just as idle with an aluminum suitcase in his grasp.

"Yes."

"May we have a word with you?"

Isaiah nodded and gestured them forward with a beckoning of a dirty hand. "Please," he said, "come in. The garden is for all to share."

They pressed forward and took a seat upon a decorative bench bearing the faces of smiling cherubs. On the pockets of their robes were the emblems of the SIV.

"You're from the Vatican," Christian stated rhetorically.

The man with the suitcase nodded. "We are."

"What can I do you for?"

"As you know a new pontiff was elected."

"The venerable Cardinal Vessucci—a good man."

"That's correct. And since we are SIV, we come under the rule of the pope regarding undisclosed matters that must remain unknown to the clerical population of the Vatican."

Christian waited.

"We know that you were a Vatican Knight," the Jesuit finally said.

"And you came all the way from the Vatican to tell me this?"

The priest with the suitcase laid it against the ground, undid the clasps, and opened the lid. Inside was a pristine uniform of a Vatican Knight. "The pope has requested, should you approve and accept, that you return to the Vatican as a Knight. The unit is being reinstated."

At first, Christian appeared unemotional until the Jesuits saw that the Knight's eyes insisted otherwise. They were bright and dazzling and filled with undeniable joy.

"Pope Pius the Fourteenth has respectfully requested that you rejoin as a Second Lieutenant—the same position you held six months ago before the unit was disbanded by Pope Gregory. Others are returning to the Vatican as we speak."

Christian got on a bended knee and lifted the shirt from the case, noted the emblem on the pocket, and drew it close.

"Do you accept the pontiff's invitation to reunite?"

He looked at them, his eyes saying it all. "Of course," he said. "Yes."

The priest then nudged the aluminum case closer to Christian with his foot. "Welcome aboard, *Isaiah*," he said, emphasizing his callsign. "The pontiff will be pleased by your decision."

"When am I to return?'

"After you conduct your first mission," he quickly answered.

"And that would be?"

"To Las Vegas," the Jesuit answered, standing.

The other Jesuit followed his partner's lead and took to his feet as well.

"Las Vegas?"

The taller of the two Jesuits answered with sadness. "There's someone there who needs your help, Isaiah—a friend who may be losing his way."

"And who would that be?"

"Kimball," said the other. "We're talking about Kimball Hayden."

# CHAPTER THIRTY-ONE

*Las Vegas, Nevada, The Following Day*

It was night in downtown Las Vegas and the canopy of the Experience was in full cartoonish display with brightly lit images playing across the awning, as a vintage Rolling Stones song served as the musical soundtrack.

Kimball stood beneath the canopy eating shrimp from his parfait glass. Tonight, he had chosen to work the swing shift. The bruise above his eye drew inquisitive questions, which he deflected with untruths, saying for the most part that he walked into a wall, or a cabinet, or an open door with no two answers alike.

When the show ended and the overhead canopy winked off, Kimball made his way home walking the seedy avenue of Freemont Street. The whores, the pimps, the homeless, and drug dealers staked their territorial claims—living within the same dark corners and the same dark recesses with their faces obscured by a mixture of both shadow and light.

Kimball ignored the calls of the bartering pimps, refused their offers, and dismissed the pleas of hardened meth whores looking for their next fix without so much as acknowledging their existence when they shared the same sidewalk.

Sirens and lights of two police cruisers passed him, stopping at a nearby motel advertised as a daily, weekly, or monthly rental when, in fact, they served as places of ill repute.

Taking the steps to his apartment, Kimball suddenly felt a glaring shift in awareness the same way the hackle of an animal rises after sensing great danger. The windows were blacked out, the place looking as he left it, untouched. But he had learned to trust his senses long ago.

He tested the knob with a slow turn, locked.

Nor did he carry his weapon of choice, a commando blade. It was inside, hidden.

With careful prudence, he inserted the key, turned with the click audible to his ear, and swung the door open with ease.

The apartment was dark, a mistake on his part. By working the swing shift he had forgotten to turn on the lights before he left, the sun still shining at that time.

As he took a step inside shadows pooled around him, his eyes trying to adjust, to focus, to see if the darkness within was taking on a life of its own and edging closer with the intent to kill.

He saw nothing.

But there was definitely a presence.

He then stepped back onto the landing before the doorway, a slow exit, the animal instinct in him telling him to take flight rather than fight, to come back to live another day.

And then a light went on from inside, the lamp on the nightstand casting a feeble glow.

Kimball stood at the fringe of the light's cast and noted the man who sat in a chair with his legs crossed in leisure, a smile on his face. For a moment he thought his heart would misfire.

Isaiah sat wearing the full Vatican Knight regalia including the beret, the Roman Catholic collar, and mixed military array. On the pocket of his shirt was the embroidery of the Vatican Knights, the shield, and silver Cross Pattée. Beside him sat an aluminum suitcase.

If Kimball was happy to see his old friend, he didn't show it. "It's a little early for Halloween, isn't it?" he asked, stepping inside and closing the door behind him.

"You knew I was here."

"I knew somebody was here."

"That's good," Isaiah said evenly. "Your senses are still sharp."

"You're lucky I didn't kill you."

The moment Isaiah gained his feet Kimball crossed the floor and the two men embraced each other. As they backed off Kimball took appraisal of his former second lieutenant, taking in the man's dress, saw the whiteness of the clerical collar and the memories it suddenly wrought.

"Why are you dressed like this?" he asked. "I thought you were going back to the orphanage."

Isaiah returned to the seat. "I did," he answered. "Up until yesterday, I was tilling the soil in the garden. Now . . ." He let his words fall away as he held his arms out in an act that said it all: *Now I'm here.*

There was a momentary pause between them. But it wasn't awkward by any means. It was more of an intake of a cherished friendship, an umbilical tie between brothers reconnecting. "As good as it is to see you," he finally said, "I need to know why you're here, Isaiah?" He looked at the suitcase. "Are you planning to move in or something?"

"No, Kimball. Or would you prefer to be called J.J. Doetsch?"

Kimball smiled. "You've been keeping tabs on me."

"Actually, no, I haven't. But the Vatican has. And as for this," he said, sliding the suitcase forward. "It's for you."

Kimball stepped forward. "Well, I have to admit," he told him, "that I like a man who bears gifts."

"Then you'll like this one."

Kimball studied the suitcase.

"Go ahead," said Isaiah, "open it." He then slid the suitcase across the floor until it rested at Kimball's feet.

Kimball gave him a suspicious, sidelong glance.

"Open it," he pressed.

Kimball bent down, laid the suitcase on the floor, undid the clasps, and opened the lid. A black clerical shirt with the Roman Catholic collar already fitted around the loop of the shirt's neckline lay neatly folded. The emblem of the Vatican Knights stood brightly against the shirt's pocket.

Kimball just stared at it. Whether he was transfixed, confused, or in simple awe, Isaiah couldn't quite decipher Kimball's reaction. "It's your uniform," he finally said. "Bonasero is calling us home to serve the Church once again."

Kimball knelt beside the case with the stillness of a mannequin for a long and silent moment before closing the lid with mechanical slowness. He then locked it shut. "I can't," he said softly.

Isaiah tilted his head questioningly. "What?"

Kimball looked him squarely in the eye, gained his feet, then went to the refrigerator where he grabbed his bottle of Jack and took the seat opposite Isaiah. "I said . . . I can't."

Isaiah fell back in defeat, his face drawing amazement and shock, his mouth wanting to say something, anything, but words were lost to him.

Kimball opened the cap and took a long swig before coming up for air. And then: "Do you remember the day when Ezekiel tried to kill me?" he said. "When Ezekiel betrayed us all?"

Isaiah accepted this as rhetorical, so he remained silent and waited as Kimball drew a second pull from the half-empty bottle before setting the container on the armrest.

"It was then that I realized something about myself," he continued. "When I served as a Vatican Knight, I believed that I was serving the Church to maintain the integrity of the Vatican by protecting its sovereignty, its interests, and its citizenry. I killed only as a last option because I believed that even God recognizes the fact that good people have the right to protect themselves or to protect the lives of good people who can't defend themselves. I believed that. And then I realized that it was nothing more than a feeble justification for killing another man. I led myself to believe that I killed because I *had* to, not because I *wanted* to. But after Ezekiel killed my old team of the Force Elite, when he murdered members of the Vatican Knights to cover his deeds, it was then that I realized who I truly was." He turned and stared at the bottle, the muscles in the back of his jaw working furiously as if containing his rage. "I learned that I wanted to kill Ezekiel so badly that I could taste it. I didn't want to kill him because I *had* to. I wanted to kill him because I *wanted* to." He never took his gaze off the bottle. "It's just the way I am, Isaiah. The difference between me and you and the other Knights is that I *want* to kill." He then looked at the hard shell of the suitcase, thought of the uniform inside, what it used to mean to him as he sought his salvation. "I don't deserve to wear this," he finally said, then kicked the suitcase back to Isaiah. "Take it back."

Kimball tipped the bottle back and took another swig, the liquor going fast.

"Kimball," Isaiah's voice was beseechingly calm. "Ezekiel did what he did because he was filled with anger that had festered over time."

"And I was the one who fostered that anger because *I* was the one who killed his grandfather. Tell Bonasero that I love him and that I'm sorry. But it is what it is. And the truth is, Isaiah, is that I kill because I want to. Not because I have to."

"You're selling yourself short and letting your emotions warp your sense of reasoning."

Kimball snapped the bottle away from his lips angrily. "Really, Isaiah? Is that what you think?"

"Kimball, you tried to save Ezekiel, not hurt him. He was the one who lost his way. Not you."

Kimball stared at him, his face betraying nothing. And then: "I still plan to kill him," he said lightly, "when I find him."

"You plan to find him at the bottom of that bottle?"

Kimball took another long pull before setting the bottle aside. "Maybe," he answered.

"I so looked forward to being your second lieutenant once again." Isaiah appeared dour, his face hanging with incredible sadness within the cast of feeble lighting. "And so was Leviticus."

"He's returning to the fold as well?"

"We all are," he said.

"No. Not everyone."

Isaiah sighed. "I wanted to return to the Vatican with you as a team member. Perhaps we could talk tomorrow when you have had a little bit less to drink?"

"Don't count on it." He sipped from the bottle again.

Isaiah stood.

"Don't forget the suitcase," Kimball said coolly.

Isaiah declined. "I'm leaving it here," he told him. "Maybe you'll change your mind when you sober up."

"I'm not drunk yet." He held the bottle out to him. "But I'm working on it."

Isaiah was deeply saddened. Kimball could see it on his face. He didn't intend to hurt his friend by driving a wedge of disappointment to the very core of his soul. But Kimball knew in his heart that he was not fit to don the uniform with a mindset that would offend God, the Church, or Bonasero Vessucci.

*I kill because I want to . . . Not because I have to.*

*I kill people . . . It's what I do . . . It's what I'm good at.*

"All I ask is that you think about it. That's all I'm asking. Try on the uniform. Get the feel of it. And remember all the lives you saved while wearing the collar. Remember the good, Kimball. All you have to do is remember the good. If you do that, then the rest will take care of itself." With that he nudged the suitcase back to Kimball's direction with the toe-end of his boot, the aluminum case sliding next to Kimball's chair.

Kimball refused to acknowledge it.

After tipping his head in a gesture meaning goodbye Isaiah left the apartment, leaving Kimball to stew alone with his bottle of Jack.


**Once Isaiah left** Kimball did not drink. In fact, the bottle remained untouched beside the chair. He sat with a detached daze looking straight ahead. The activity playing out across his mind's eye, however, was clear and crisp. He visualized old memories—saw the battles he partook while in the Philippines and in third world countries where innocent people such as children, women, and old men who could not protect themselves had looked upon him with impossibly large eyes, imploring eyes that were slick with the glassy onset of tears begging him to become their champion, to save them.

They were good people who wanted to till the soil and to raise their children under a friendly sky, to embed values of goodness to pass on to subsequent generations to create a better standard of living, a better place to live.

But there were hard-line factions, there were always hard-line factions, who yielded to personal hatreds and prejudices warped by the interpretations of religious texts or the hardcore ramblings of religious extremists. The subversives tended to lean toward annihilation, the cost of a human life insignificant.

And Kimball relished these moments by laying down his law as a Vatican Knight to save those who could not save themselves and fighting until his adrenaline caused his heart to palpitate with raw excitement. In the end, he was fulfilled by the dark cravings of battle that served as sustenance. Not by the plight of salvation he so badly sought.

And here was the problem: He was by nature a killer and resigned himself to that fact. Therefore, he was not fit to wear the uniform of a Vatican Knight.

He sat with his eyes cast forward.

. . . *I kill people* . . .

. . . *It's what I do* . . .

. . . *It's what I'm good at* . . .

The aluminum case lay beside his chair, ultimately drawing his eye.

Despite what he had come to believe of himself, he could not deny the goodness the uniform provided him either. He had saved lives and felt good about it. He could remember the numerous times when the bony hands of those he had saved reached out and grabbed his hand, only to speak by drawing it close and kissing the backside with eternal gratefulness. And then in summation they would draw the backside of his hand to their cheek and look up at him wallow-eyed, the message clear: *You saved my life. And by doing so, you have saved the lives of future generations. My children will be good people. As will their children.*

*. . . But I kill people . . .*

*. . . It's what I do . . .*

*. . . It's what I'm good at . . .*

He closed his eyes.

Then in a voice that was not his: *You saved my life. And by doing so, you have saved the lives of future generations. My children will be good people. As will their children.*

He opened his eyes and looked at the suitcase once again, noting its dull silver coat. In a fluid motion, he exited from the chair, got on bended knees, and lowered the case so that it sat flat against the floor. For a long moment, he stared at it with his mind growing blank, and was unsure of his next move until his hand finally reached out and undid the clasps, with the clicks sounding louder than they should have, he thought.

Tipping back the lid he saw the shirt, the Roman Catholic collar, the insignia, all driving the memories harder, stronger, recalling the faces of those he had saved. Men. Women. Children. Faces by the hundreds shot through his mind like the files of a Rolodex turning over with blinding speed, revealing every single card with every card a face.

So many lives.

He reached down and grabbed the shirt, tracing the insignia of the Vatican Knights with the back of his thumb.

He pressed the shirt close to him, could smell the indescribable cleanliness to it, and closed his eyes.

After a moment, he then reached into the case and grabbed the beret, noting the same emblem on the hat, and smiled, the man feeling the pride of serving.

Gingerly laying the shirt in the suitcase as though he was paying homage to the fabric, Kimball went to the bathroom and fixed the beret on his head, turning his head from left to right to appraise his appearance beneath the dim cast of light over the bathroom mirror.

After a minute, perhaps two, he returned to his seat.

He sat idle for several more hours as his mind vacillated between his individuality regarding the powers between his good and evil, and wondered if he still had any hope of seeing the light of salvation. Or more importantly, he wondered if the God of the Vatican was willing to proffer him the spark of a new beginning.

He sat.

And he wondered.

# CHAPTER THIRTY-TWO

*Vatican City*

Inside the papal chamber, Pope Pius XIV sat at his desk while Leviticus stood to the side wearing the uniform of Vatican Security rather than that of a Vatican Knight. It was all a ruse, however, to keep Cardinal Angullo from making further inquiries as to the alien dress of a Vatican Knight —the beret, the military attire, the insignia. He did not want Leviticus to become the catalyst of Angullo's inquisitive nature, no doubt pressing from the cardinal a curious investigation into Leviticus' wear, as to who he represented under the Vatican banner.

When Cardinal Angullo entered the chamber, he did so with humility. He was slightly bent at the waist, giving his lean figure a slight curvature. Although his eyes were cast to the floor, they were there for only a short moment before shifting his gaze to Leviticus, then back to Pope Pius. "You requested my presence, Your Holiness?"

"Please," he said pointing to the chair before him, "have a seat."

Angullo lifted the hem of his garment and sat down, his eyes settling once more on the large man who stood sentinel beyond the pope with calculating appraisal. "You have security?" he asked. "Is there a problem, Your Holiness?"

Bonasero Vessucci ignored him by veering off into a tangent. "I've asked you here for a reason," he told him.

"That's quite obvious."

"Giuseppe, I'm going to make this quite clear," he said. "You're being reassigned."

Cardinal Angullo smiled humorlessly. "I figured as much," he said. "I assume it's in retaliation for being assigned your position when Pope Gregory took the papal throne?"

"Retaliation? No."

"Then why? I believe my actions as second-in-command have spoken for themselves over the past several months, yes?"

"Your action, Giuseppe, as to the way you achieve your means to attain personal heights rather than through the divine guidance of God, disturbs me greatly. It's all right to aspire. But it's not all right to aspire against the principles of God, which is self over your fellow man."

Angullo's smile widened with sarcasm. "Now because you sit upon the papal throne, it somehow gives you the insight to read what is in the hearts and minds of men?"

"Hardly. I have watched your slow decline over years, Giuseppe. I sadly watched a man who was a giant in the College lose himself to his growing ambitions. I watched you slowly gravitate away from the true nature of God."

"I see," he said simply. "But your appraisal, Your Holiness, is without merit. I can guarantee that there are men within the College who see me with the same subjective eye; that I am a just man who keeps God close to his heart." He fell back into his seat. "No, no," he said, waving his hand in dismissal. "There is no true justification other than retaliation. And we both know it."

"Believe what you will," he returned. "But my intentions are whole when I say that I'm trying to save you."

"Save me? And how will you do that? Will you send me to Boston to fill the vacancy you left behind?"

"You will be sent to a venue that I believe will do you good," he stated firmly. "I need you to rediscover the man who was once essential to this Church. I need you to find yourself, Giuseppe. And by this, I will send you somewhere where you can best serve man *and* yourself."

"I see." He looked at Leviticus glaringly, but the large man held his gaze with an unblinking stare. "Were you afraid, Your Holiness, that I would come to some kind of violent means by this news, given your suspicion of me regarding the good Pope Gregory? Is that why you've called upon security?"

Bonasero did not want to provide the man with anything further. He simply cast off the cardinal's question as something unremarkable and undeserving of a merited response. Instead, he deflected his question with direction. "Within a few days, you will be notified of my decision," he said evenly. "Until then you will continue in the capacity of secretary of state until I find a suitable replacement."

Cardinal Angullo gazed at the man for a long and unabashed moment before laboring to his feet. "As you wish, Your Holiness."

When Bonasero reached his hand out, Cardinal Angullo accepted it and brought the pope's hand to his lips, kissing the Fisherman's Ring.

When everything was said and done, Cardinal Angullo left the papal chamber closing the door behind him.

As the bolt snickered into place, only then did the pope drops his shoulders to ease the tension. "He's completely lost," he whispered to himself.

Leviticus took the seat the cardinal just vacated. It was still warm. "So, what happens now?"

Bonasero Vessucci continued to stare at the door, his eyes fixed. "We wait," he said. "Should the good cardinal feel threatened, then he may act accordingly to his nature. If he feels that the throne is well out of his reach, then I believe he will act in a manner of desperation."

"You truly believe he had something to do with Gregory's death?"

"I can't prove it," he answered. "But Cardinal Angullo is not the same man. I believe he positioned himself to usurp the throne after he engineered my expulsion from Vatican City. But he didn't count—or perhaps didn't believe—on my rebounding back to the good graces of the College. I was his only true threat in the *Preferiti*."

"So now you think he plans to retaliate?"

"I don't know. But that's why I need you here, Leviticus. I need your protection."

"You'll be safe, Bonasero. You have my word."

"I know that. But there are other ways to get to me," he said. "Poisons, ways that only a lost mind filled with dark ambitions could think of."

"Then we'll have the Knights watch the staff and kitchen crew, we'll put eyes everywhere."

"The value of the Vatican Knights is abroad," he reminded him, "to protect the interests of the Church and the citizenry of its people, not security. We have people for that."

"Then what?"

"I want you to shadow the good cardinal," he told him. "I want you to watch his every move. If Cardinal Angullo is feeling the insecurities of his position, he may likely falter in his maneuverings knowing that time is limited and will need to act quickly. But with that being said, he will also be very careful not to draw suspicion with the death of one pope arriving so quickly after the death of another. After all, John Paul I was in office for one month until his untimely death with no questions asked. My death would only serve under the same scenario."

"Understood."

Pope Pius faced the Vatican Knight with obvious sadness lining his hanging features. "Leviticus, I need you by my side until the good cardinal is reassigned to a place where the Vatican is well beyond his tentacle reach."

"There's no need to worry, Bonasero."

But the pontiff did worry.

Cardinal Angullo was a man of incredible cunning and calculation and not to be underestimated. And with that thought on his mind, Pope Pius the Fourteenth looked out beyond the open doors leading to the balcony and noted the dark clouds of a tempest moving quickly towards the Vatican.

*Las Vegas*

The morning sun had crested the horizon, shining a light upon the smog that was already beginning to settle close to the valley floor.

Isaiah stood in front of Kimball's apartment wearing plain clothes, so as not to draw attention to himself by wearing the incongruous wear of clerical attire mixed with military garb. Last night was one thing. It was dark and late. But now, the day was young and bright.

He stood there, waiting. But for what, he didn't know. What he did know was that he was stunned by Kimball's decision to reject the very uniform he once revered. More so, he was taken aback by the man's indifferent attitude.

Taking the steps slowly to the front door, and then noting that the door had faded and chipped from the constant bombardment of the hot sun, he wrapped his knuckles lightly on the panel.

"Come in."

Isaiah opened the door. The smell of stale air and musk greeted him, as well as a wave of intense heat.

Kimball sat in the same chair that Isaiah left him in the night before. Only this time the man was wearing his clerical shirt, military pants, boots, and beret. Most striking was the whiteness of the Roman Catholic collar, which shone brilliantly in contrast against his shirt.

Kimball did not smile, nor did not betray any emotion or offer words of greeting. He simply sat with his eyes fixed on Isaiah.

Isaiah closed the door behind him. The room was stifling, dry, and in desperate need to be aired out.

"It looks good on you," he finally told him, taking a seat opposite Kimball. "Really good."

Kimball sighed. "When I came here," he stated, "I had a dream. I was going to make some quick cash and buy a little place and start my own business, to be independent. Then I got involved with cage fighting." He grazed his fingertips over the bump above his eye. "As you can probably see." He lowered his hand and set it on the armrest. "The money was coming in fast—lots of it. And my dreams a little more within reach. I was gonna take that money, get out of the business, and start over. Just get rid of the man that used to be Kimball Hayden and become someone else and forget my past. I told myself to become someone new, to be someone good. And when I made enough, then I was going to run and leave everyone behind without saying goodbye. I was just gonna go."

"And now?"

Kimball hesitated before answering. "Then I realized that no matter what, all the money in the world isn't going to matter. I am what I am and that's not going to change. Money isn't the panacea to change the man I truly am." He looked at Isaiah squarely in the eyes. "And then I remembered what you said about the uniform, looked at it, and remembered things that I had forgotten. I remembered my humanity. The lives I had saved." His gaze never departed. "I also remembered the darkness of my life—the times I murdered people, sometimes good people, at the colossal whims of corrupt government officials who told me that what I was doing I was doing for the good of the government entity when the truth was that I was only serving their reprehensible needs to promote black agendas. I became their machine who enjoyed doing what I did. I enjoyed it, Isaiah. I enjoyed killing those without impunity, as well as holding the power to decide whether or not they lived or died by my hand."

"You haven't been that way for a while, Kimball."

Kimball removed the beret and stared at it. "Deep down I wonder," he told him flatly. "So, I did a little soul searching. And with it, I found the faces of those I had saved. I remembered them taking my hand in gratitude and kissing it. I remembered the faces of the children, the incredible fears they held in their eyes, and the subsequent smiles of relief when I got them to safety. And then I told myself that I enjoyed that more than killing without impunity." He placed the beret back on his head and formed it to specs. "Last night," he began, "after you left, I took into consideration what you said—about thinking it over."

"And?"

Kimball smiled, but lightly. "It's time to go home," he said. "It's time to go back home."

"It's where you belong," said Isaiah. "The Vatican Knights would not be the Vatican Knights without its leader. You know that."

Kimball took in a long breath of stale air, looked around the apartment one last time, and realized that he was not going to miss this place or Las Vegas at all.

"There's one last thing I have to do," he told him. "Just one." He turned toward Isaiah, a faint smile still showing. "Once done, then we can go home."

**There was this** little church on Casino Center Drive right next to the Court House and CCDC, the Clark County Detention Center. It was a building made of cinderblocks with a small bell tower and token religious statues standing sentinel by the front door. When Kimball tried the door, it was locked, so he went around the back, which was an alleyway, and stood before the gate leading into the garden area. Standing by clumps of brightly lit shrubbery stood a priest and a nun, conversing.

"Excuse me!"

When the priest and the nun turned, Kimball beckoned them forward. Only the priest answered the call and walked toward the gate. "Can I help you?"

Kimball was not wearing the uniform of a Vatican Knight, but plain clothes. "I was hoping to get into the church," he told him.

"I'm afraid the church is closed. But if you come back this evening between six and seven, that is when we open for confessional."

"I've nothing to confess, Father. God knows what I did."

"I see."

"I've come for another matter. Perhaps you can help me out?"

"I can try."

Kimball removed a wad of hundred-dollar bills from his shirt pocket, the money earned from his fights, the money he was putting aside toward the pursuit of his dreams, and then he forwarded the money through the bars of the gate. "It's for the poor," he told him.

The priest took the money, his mouth slowly falling into a perfect O.

"There's over six thousand dollars there," Kimball told him. "Put it to good use."

Kimball turned and began to walk away.

"Wait!"

Kimball halted and turned to face the priest but didn't say a word.

It was obvious the clergyman was stunned. "Are you sure? This is a lot of money."

Kimball was positive and gave a nod to that effect. "Put to good use, Father. Some people need it more than I do," he said.

Without saying another word Kimball was gone, surrendering his dream for the pursuit of another: His salvation.


**That night they** took an immediate departure from Terminal Two at McCarran Airport. Kimball took the window seat, wanting to see the lights of Las Vegas pass beneath him for the last time. He didn't appear apprehensive or excited, he just remained impassively quiet. Nor did Isaiah do anything to change Kimball's current state or try to curb his lack of enthusiasm. Instead, Isaiah let the man sit alone with his thoughts, while he took the aisle seat and read the current aeronautical magazine.

As the plane taxied and took off, the dazzling lights of Las Vegas were in full display, the Strip no doubt capable of rivaling the lights of Paris.

As the plane banked, Kimball realized that he held no regrets for surrendering the money to the church. Although ill-gotten, it would certainly do a lot of good in the right hands.

Kimball was at peace.

When the plane began its long journey eastbound, he settled back and looked to the overhead bin above him.

Inside the bin was the aluminum suitcase. And inside the suitcase was his only possession, the only thing of importance, and that was the uniform of a Vatican Knight.

Kimball then closed his eyes and settled back for the long flight.
He was at rest.
And he was at peace.

# CHAPTER THIRTY-THREE

*Mount Damavand. The Alborz Region, The Facility*

Aryeh Levine was in obvious agony. He had been placed inside a vacuum chamber with his feet dangling downward in stomach-churning angles. His skin was badly swollen and mottled with gangrenous colors.

Al-Sherrod stood behind the partition. To his left was al-Ghazi. Both men stood with totally different aspects. Whereas al-Sherrod looked on with indifference, al-Ghazi appeared as wounded as a man could be under such circumstances. He had trusted Umar, which was unlikely his real name, with brotherly reverence. Only to be violated in the worst imaginable way.

Al-Sherrod stepped closer to the glass with the marginal interest of examining a strange-looking insect beneath the lens of a glass a moment before angling it in such a way that the rays of the sun would cremate it. And that's how he saw Levine, like an insect. "The transmission traces back to Tel Aviv," he finally said. And then he turned to al-Ghazi whose eyes remained focused on Levine, the muscles in the back of his jaw twitching. "And we both know what exclusive fraternity resides in Tel Aviv, don't we Adham?"

He could see al-Ghazi reaching a boiling point.

"He is Mossad."

Al-Ghazi went to the glass partition and placed his palm against the glass. "Can you hear me?" he asked.

Levine answered with a pain-riddled grimace, teeth clenching, his eyes rolling up into slivers of white and on the cusp of passing out before coming back.

"Can you hear me?" he repeated.

"I . . . hear you," he said.

Al-Ghazi sighed and pressed his forehead against the glass. It was cool to the touch. "Why?"

Levine shook his head. The agony was too much to bear.

"I treated you like a brother, loved you as one. I trusted you with my darkest secrets."

Levine gripped the armrests, his knuckles going white.

"Are you Mossad?"

"What do you think?"

Al-Ghazi stepped away, angry and saddened at the same time.

"Do you usually incorporate the enemy into your leagues?" asked al-Sherrod. But al-Ghazi could tell that he was being sarcastic and ignored him. "Perhaps you should apply better methods of recruitment, so as not to bring aboard anyone who can compromise our position."

Al-Ghazi closed his eyes and fought for calm. Al-Sherrod was pushing his buttons. He would rather have the man curse him out and be done with it, rather than his constant needling.

"You are a traitor to the cause," al-Ghazi said through the glass. "You are a Zionist, you are Mossad, and there can be no other outcome other than death." *And you have broken my heart, Umar.*

Al-Ghazi stepped back and forced upon him the features of indifference, which al-Sherrod immediately saw through.

"Do what you must," he told al-Sherrod. "Be done with him."

Al-Sherrod nodded. And then over his shoulder: "Bring in the good professor," he ordered. Then more softly to al-Ghazi: "I think it's time to see the true nature of the beast, don't you? I'm curious to see the demons that Doctor Sakharov created at work." He turned to al-Ghazi who kept his focus on Levine. "As I'm sure you are," he added with a grin of malicious amusement that was almost as disturbing as his needling, thought al-Ghazi, if not more so.

Sakharov was roughly escorted to an open seat before a console granting an open view of the chamber, a premiere accommodation for the upcoming event.

"My good Doctor," said al-Sherrod, approaching him with his hands placed securely behind the small of his back. "Comfortable?"

"Those apes of yours hurt me. I'm an old man. I can only move so fast."

The man bowed in feigned apology. "Then let me be the first to apologize on their behalf," he said. "But I thought it would be important that you see the fruits of your labor."

Sakharov saw Levine inside the chamber; saw the man's badly broken and swollen ankles. When he was incarcerated in Vladimir Central, he had seen the same thing. Often guards would take their truncheons to the kneecaps and ankles, breaking them until the bones became free-floating. Nevertheless, the unnatural angles always made him turn away, as he did now.

"Don't worry, Doctor," said al-Sherrod. "We're going to fix his ailment permanently."

Al-Sherrod walked away and took up the area next to al-Ghazi. "Is there anything more you wish to ask the Jew?"

Al-Ghazi could only stare, not understanding in his heart why he cared so much for this man. He cared for him deeply, even now as Levine sat riding out unimaginable pain. It didn't matter to him that Levine—or Umar—was a Jew or that he was Mossad. All he knew was that his heart ached deeply for the man whom he had come to care for as a brother and will probably grieve for as well.

"Do what you must," he finally answered. "I've said all I had to say."

Al-Sherrod smiled. "Good, good. Then perhaps you would like to engage the button then. After all, it might do your soul good to be rid of the man who compromised your position. Certainly, this wouldn't look good in the eyes of al-Zawahiri should this man go unpunished by your hand. Perhaps this will be the first step of redemption in the old warrior's eyes, yes?"

Al-Ghazi faced him, his eyes and face lit up with anger. Did al-Sherrod have the insight to see what he was thinking or feeling regarding Aryeh Levine? Or was his malice simply a part of his makeup in which it was mere sustenance that moved him forward?

"You will push the button, won't you?" al-Sherrod pressed.

"He is a traitor, what do you think?"

The diminutive man's smile flourished. "Then let's see what the good doctor's discoveries have brought us, shall we?" He turned to Sakharov; his enthusiasm unbridled. "Good Doctor," he said, pointing to Levine. "I want you to take a good long look at the beginning of the end."

With a quick flick of his hand, a technician began to type in the required codes. When he was done, he fell back in his seat and rolled his chair away from the console. In al-Ghazi's eyes the ENTER button was starkly larger than all the rest when, in fact, the button was no larger than any other on the keyboard.

"Go ahead," said al-Sherrod, placing a hand on al-Ghazi's shoulder and directing toward the console. "Seek revenge against the Zionist. Make yourself whole in the eyes of al-Zawahiri."

Al-Ghazi stood over the panel and stared at the ENTER button.

His heart thrummed. Never had he hesitated when granted such an opportunity.

"Adham, the good doctor is waiting."

Al-Ghazi faced Sakharov and saw that the man appeared as lost as he was, perhaps realizing that his ambitions had taken him beyond something he could live with on a moral level, with the pain of his guilt growing exponentially. Al-Ghazi, on the other hand, despite his extremist position and Zionist prejudices, felt the same climatic guilt for what he was about to do. In their pinning gaze, they saw one man sensing the wrongful deed of the other but had no choice in the matter. It was what it was.

"I'm not getting younger, Adham."

Al-Ghazi turned away from Sakharov and faced Levine. The man was in such agony that al-Ghazi prayed that he would lose consciousness. But he didn't. The fault to maintain his awareness was a noble trait, but also a foolish one.

He pressed the button.

Within fifteen seconds a waspy hum sounded out over the loudspeakers, the press of the button activating the sound waves to stimulate the nanobots.

Levine's eyes opened to the size of saucers, his body going erect and statuesque as the bots, creatures so small that a hundred thousand could fit on the head of a pin, began to dissolve the man by the inches. Levine screamed, his hands going to his face that dissolved and liquefied under the onslaught; his eyes popping, then sliding within his orbital sockets, disappearing; the flesh around his mouth paring back before disappearing, showing the horrific smile of a skeletal grin. The fabric of his clothes began to turn red, his blood from gaping wounds beneath his shirt and garments ripping apart as flesh was rented and torn asunder, the imprint of his ribs now showing through his shirt. His legs seemed to dissolve beneath his pants, the material of his camouflage suit deflating until his legs appeared no thicker than broomsticks. And then he was gone, leaving skeletal remains draped in bloody fabric.

Al-Ghazi looked at the remains and noted that the skull was turned right at him, its smile a grim reflection that would haunt him for the rest of his life. Oddly enough, Levine had the presence of mind to point a bony finger in al-Ghazi's direction, as well. Or perhaps, he thought, it was by mere coincidence that the accusing talon was directed his way during the throes of writhing agony.

"Outstanding," said al-Sherrod, moving closer to the window. "Absolutely amazing."

The waspy hum decreased over time, the nano mass deteriorating by the half-life code embedded into them by Sakharov, making them less critical. Within fifteen minutes their lifespan was diluted to the point where their existence had zero effect. More so, they only attacked organic matter. Everything had been a resounding success.

"Do you see, Doctor, what you've brought us? The ultimate solution in changing the world," said al-Sherrod. His happiness could hardly be contained. "A controlled weapon of mass destruction."

Whereas al-Sherrod saw it as a way for Iran to bully their way into a position as a world power, al-Ghazi saw it as a device to rid the world of Zionists and infidels, two totally separate agendas. Sakharov, however, with his scientific mind saw this as End Times. Such a weapon in the minds of corrupted officials tend to lose reason and foresight as their ambitions become too great to control, thereby creating the eventual aftermath of complete and total destruction.

Sakharov knew that Russia would have exercised the same set of ambitions to recertify their egotistic and divine power over the United States, even with the Cold War over. Number one was everything. Number two was insignificant.

"So now I must express to you, my good Doctor, the gratitude of my countryman, the gratitude of President Ahmadinejad, and, of course, my appreciation, for what you have given us."

Sakharov sat back in his seat. And when he spoke, he didn't speak in his usual hardened manner. It was a side of him he never revealed to any of them before, the side of a man possessed with calm intellect. "In the pursuit of progress," he said, "I have abandoned my humanity. And should there be a Devil, then I have surely nailed my soul to the Devil's Altar."

Al-Sherrod stared at him.

"Now I know how J. Robert Oppenheimer felt after he developed the bomb," he added, "after he realized its horrific potential."

"Regrets, Doctor?"

"You just heard what I said, didn't you? Anything of this magnitude can be controlled for so long before human nature finally takes over by someone who thinks he can manage the power. Ultimately, that war is lost and so will all of humanity . . . eventually."

"You're wrong, Doctor. In the right hands, under the right minds, nothing can go wrong."

The old Doctor Sakharov returned. "Then you're as ignorant as you look."

The smile washed away from al-Sherrod's face. "See the good doctor back to his chamber," he said. "And do be as rough with him as you were getting him here."

Two Quds soldiers hoisted Sakharov roughly to his feet and escorted him away.

"Hey! Careful! I'm an old man!"

He then turned to al-Ghazi, who appeared mesmerized by the remains of Levine. "He deserved what he got, yes?"

Al-Ghazi remained quiet.

"If I didn't know better, Adham, I'd say you were mourning the loss of the Zionist. Surely this isn't so?"

He flashed the man a hard gaze. "I'm tired of your little innuendos, al-Sherrod. If you've got something to say, then say it."

"I'm merely proposing my thoughts of what I believe to see."

"Then you're blind," he returned.

"Am I?"

AL-Sherrod confronted al-Ghazi by standing between him and the body of Levine, their eyes steely and intent. "We do have another pressing issue at hand here," he said.

Al-Ghazi nodded in agreement.

"The operative which you solely placed into our facility has compromised the very location of this facility to Mossad; therefore, we must consider the probability of a possible strike. If that is the case, then we must abandon this area immediately. We are now put into a position of denying culpability when we were never in such a position before."

"Then we have no other choice," he said. "We wipe away all prints that this facility ever existed."

Al-Sherrod lifted a hand to al-Ghazi's shoulder. "None of this will matter anyway," he told him. "We have what we want, so this facility has become irrelevant. We are now in a position to fear no one."

"No doubt Mossad is deciding what to do."

"No doubt. We were able to decipher some of the encrypted contents sent. They know the location and specific agenda of Sakharov's findings. So I assume they'll send their concerns up the Zionist chain of command to justify a prompt strike. And, of course, they'll notify the United States and its allies of their intentions. And, of course, the United States will try to stall them, which will aid us with the necessary time to move our assets."

"How long?"

"Two, maybe three days," he answered. "Ahmadinejad is being notified as we speak."

Al-Ghazi had his data files locked away in his satellite office in Tehran, so he was safe. What happened to the facility, its wares, or its people was beyond his concern. In fact, he didn't care what happened to them, as long as he was in Tehran. But he did have a singular concern regarding the timeline of their conspiracy against the Vatican. "Does that give us enough time to get things in motion?"

"It'll be tight," he said. "But doable."

"And Doctor Sakharov?"

Al-Sherrod shot off another one of his malicious and annoying smiles. "Now that, Ahmad, is another matter. His mind is too valuable an asset, wouldn't you agree?"

"Which means that he's staying with your organization?"

Al-Sherrod did little to hide his zeal, his smile widening to a Cheshire grin. "Did you believe otherwise?"


**Doctor Leonid J.** Sakharov sat alone in his residence, his sight stretching out for a long moment into the darkness, his eyes unwavering. But his mind churned with the bombarding madness of nonstop memories.

When he was in Vladimir Central prison he subsisted on his memories, which drove in him the compassion to live, to survive, to keep moving no matter how much the guards broke his body down. With random beatings by their truncheons, and then to see those around him die with their eyes staring at nothing in particular as the spark of life left them when their souls departed, he kept going, afraid to die.

While in Vladimir Central he dreamed of buckyballs, of his science, the molecular chains becoming the driving sustenance that kept him alive during those wintery nights beneath threadbare blankets and lived by the power of prayer, his science his God.

Now, with his dreams finally coming to fruition, he realized that his God was a dark one.

He had seen its intention, to kill without impunity or conscience or remorse. And he was the one to helm and unleash its ferocity into the hands of extremists who bore no intent of purity in its application.

*What have I done?*

His ambitions had corrupted him, he knew that. And he had no justification for what he did because he knew their intent all along. He simply chose to turn a blind eye knowing the power of his creation.

In the darkness, the old man brought his hands up and cradled his head.

*What have I done?*

With his aging eyes, he watched his discovery tear a man apart, saw the acid bite of his creation destroy flesh and sinew with quick and ravenous hunger.

Feeling contrite to the point where his soul had paid a horrible price, though not a religious man, old man Sakharov got to his feet. He was no longer afraid.

When the door of his residential capsule opened, he was greeted by a harsh light coming from the hallway, causing his eyes to squint until they adjusted.

The hallway was empty.

He sauntered into the corridor in a gait that spoke volumes—that he was not a threat by any physical means, could hardly raise a hand in defiance let alone in retaliation. But it wasn't his body they had to worry about. It was his mind.

Old Man Sakharov made his way to the lab and silently watched a tech at the console typing a program related to his nanotechnology, the data transmitting as scientific cuneiform on the monitor. In a slow curdle deep within the pit of his stomach; Sakharov could feel a slow boil.

Quietly he made his way behind the tech, and in doing so picked up a metal clipboard on his way. After hefting it he realized that it was too light to cause any real damage. Perhaps striking the man at the temple, a well-placed blow, he considered.

Taking careful aim, the man's head stationary, a firm and unmoving target, Sakharov swung the clipboard as hard as he could, the corner catching the tech at the thinnest point of his temple, cutting deep, the head wound bleeding out as the tech fell to the side with his hand clutching at the deep incision.

Sakharov hit the man repeatedly as though he was a guard at Vladimir Central, the man never relenting with blow after blow, adding more cuts, more wounds, more blood.

The tech tried to crawl away.

As the tech lay dazed with the collar of his lab coat saturated with blood, Sakharov labored into the seat and attempted to wipe away the data. But the characters were in Farsi. He looked over the console, a quick perusal. The keyboard he used for his experiments, the one with Russian characters, was gone.

The data continued to download on the screen before him.

He tapped the buttons in random.

Nothing.

And then he became desperate, almost feral.

He looked at the tech that had crawled his way to another terminal, saw the blood track he left in his wake on the floor and the bloody handprint on the silent alarm, which he pressed before passing out.

Sakharov got to his feet and found an inner strength. He was no longer afraid, but angry, his mind closing out all forms of impending punishments, not caring, his will to succeed in the dismantling of his findings far greater than the retribution he was about to receive.

He picked up the chair, though his arms found it difficult, and swung it against the console, then against the monitor, causing a star-shaped crack in the glass. Another strike, the blow futile and causing no damage, his arms weakening in the process, the muscles starting to turn to gel.

And then he heard the sound of coming footsteps, the Quds approaching.

After another feeble blow, Sakharov turned, only to be met with the stock end of a rifle.

Lights out.

# CHAPTER THIRTY-FOUR

The ceiling.

The walls.

The lights.

The glass partition.

When Sakharov came to, he saw that he was inside a vacuum chamber. Immediately, he conceded to his fate.

"Good morning, Doctor," said Al-Sherrod, his voice coming through the mike system. His face appeared humorless with no lines of his ugly Cheshire teeth showing. Beside him stood al-Ghazi, who shared the same flat appearance, the same emotionless expression. "You've been out for most of the day. Welcome back."

Sakharov measured his surroundings. *Did he expect anything less?*

"I hardly thought that you'd make such an attempt, Doctor. My mistake for letting my guard down. I didn't believe you had it in you."

Sakharov looked at the diminutive man and at al-Ghazi, who stood much taller. "So now you're going to kill me the same way you killed Umar?"

"Umar was not his real name. He was a Zionist."

"Does it matter?

Al-Sherrod deflected him with another direction of answering. "I had plans for you, Doctor Sakharov. Huge plans."

"Not interested."

"I gathered that since your little escapade early this morning. But there's good news, I suppose. The only damage you inflicted was a broken monitor, nothing more. So, you failed in your attempt to annihilate your findings, which I assume was the purpose of your action?"

When Sakharov didn't answer, al-Sherrod paced back and forth in front of the glass like a caged feline, to and fro, looking and studying

Sakharov who watched his every move.

"Big plans," he finally commented. "President Ahmadinejad presumed to move you and your findings to a different locale so that you could further your studies."

*Studies? Is that what you call it?*

"I have resigned to my fate," he answered. "I will not lift another finger to help you or your regime. I was foolish to do so in the first place."

"So, you said, Doctor. I believe the term you used was 'In the pursuit of my own progress, I have abandoned my humanity.'"

"And should there be a Devil," he added, "then I have surely nailed my soul to the Devil's Altar."

"Foolishly poetic," said al-Sherrod, "but your so-called lack of humanity is actually a state in which 'true' evil will be eradicated, and the infidels laden impotent once and for all." Then, as if imploring his line of thought: "Don't you see, Doctor, your technology will evolve the world into a much better place."

"My technology will destroy this planet because of people like you who do not bear the insight or foresight of its true capacity. You only see what you want to see without realizing the destructive potential of what I created. You are misled to believe that a simple program can put you in a position of control when, in fact, you fail to see your own short fallings in the same way I was unable to foresee my own . . . And in the end, I lost. The same will happen to you."

"Hardly," was his response. "You are a foolish old man who could not control his passions. But your ideas will live on, Doctor. And they will do so under the Iranian banner."

Sakharov's jaw clenched.

"Unfortunately for you, Doctor, I presume that your action early this morning means that you refuse to further the program with extensive studies to add, or perhaps modify, your findings?"

"Piss off," he said.

Al-Sherrod turned to al-Ghazi for clarification. "Piss off?"

"It's a derogatory remark telling you to back off. It's a crude expression."

"I see." He turned back to Sakharov. "Is that your final answer, Doctor? To tell me to 'piss off'?"

Sakharov did not respond, the man resigning himself.

"Then you leave me no choice," said al-Sherrod. With a motion of his hand, al-Sherrod proffered an order to the tech manning the console.

The tech that Sakharov had beaten with the clipboard tapped a command into the keyboard, then waited for further instructions from al-Sherrod, who stretched the moment out as long as he could as the gazes between, he and Sakharov remained steady.

And then: "Do it."

The tech pressed the ENTER button, initiating the sound waves.

Sakharov then closed his eyes and braced himself, his hands clutching at the armrests of his chair as the waspy hum began to advance on him.

Within less than two minutes it was over.

And Leonid Sakharov, a man with a brilliant mind, had succumbed to the creations of his ambitions.


**As al-Ghazi and** al-Sherrod watched the Quds soldiers remove the remains of Sakharov from the chamber, al-Ghazi turned to the diminutive man with pressing questions.

"It won't be long until the Zionists retaliate," he said simply.

"The Americans will stall them," he returned. "So we have time."

"We don't know this for sure."

"The Americans are intent to keep their economy in check. Such a violation against Iranian sovereignty only provokes to cripple an already hurting economy by escalating gas prices, which is a major concern for the Americans. He who holds the oil, my friend, also holds the scepter of rule. And the Americans know this. They will talk the Zionists to stave off their attack and let the sanctions work."

"But Israel will not hold off forever."

"Of course not," he said. "Past history has shown that. But past history has also shown that they will wait long enough to placate the United States, as well." Then: "We still have time. We simply need to be careful with our applications and not rush into this with any chance of failure."

"How long?"

Al-Sherrod mused over this for a long moment before answering. "A week," he finally answered. "Perhaps two."

"Two weeks may be too long," he replied.

"Your impatience is showing, Adham. I thought it was a conviction of your people to exhibit the virtue of patience."

"We are not without reality, either," he told him. "The gamble is too great should the Israeli's decide to strike. The optimum thing to do is to act accordingly to the situation. And the situation dictates that the location of the facility has been compromised and the nature of our findings made clear to the enemy."

Al-Sherrod considered this.

"We have the technology," said al-Ghazi. "We have the capability to manufacture enough nanobots to achieve the means of an initial strike against the Vatican. We cannot wait on the assumptions of what the United States and Israel might do."

Al-Sherrod looked at al-Ghazi squarely in the eyes and noted his fiery determination. "One week," he finally said. "I believe we can produce enough of the quantity necessary to achieve the means. But will that give you enough time to set everything in motion?"

"I have replaced Umar with others," he told him. "They have decided to martyr themselves."

"Are they capable?"

"They are skilled to initiate the program," he said. "It's just a matter of introducing the Ark in a timely fashion."

"And how will you do this?"

"I will contact a leading religious principal with the condition that the true Ark will be an offering to be shared by all religions, with its opening to be commenced at the Vatican with all leading principals and political states of head present. When the lid is opened to reveal the tablets, then the canisters inside will be activated. Everything made of organic matter within Vatican City will be destroyed within minutes."

Al-Sherrod suppressed his smile. The leading political principals, as well as leading religious leaders and other spiritual dignitaries who pray to false gods, will be neutralized. But his goal was not borne of religious extremism, but out of political radicalism.

"Should this succeed," he told al-Ghazi, "then we will plant such canisters in New York, Washington D.C., Tel Aviv, London, to whatever locations that will propel Iran as an international power."

"You do whatever your agenda requires," said al-Ghazi. "If yours is strictly political, so be it. Ours is for religious purposes only. We do this for the sake of Allah."

"I see."

"We need to commence this while we have the advantage."

Al-Sherrod nodded. "Then the Ark is yours," he said. "Do with it what you will and set forth the precedence of changing the balance."

Al-Ghazi, at least for the moment, shared his enthusiasm. "Then with the will of Allah," he said, "let us set forth Pandora's Ark."

# CHAPTER THIRTY-FIVE

*Vatican City*

When the plane finally landed in Rome, Kimball felt something he hadn't felt in an exceptionally long time: elation, purpose, and true belonging.

When he arrived at the Vatican he was shelled with old memories. The wonderful imagery when he was a Vatican Knight when things were at their worst, but he was at his best, making a difference in the lives of others rather than taking them away.

He had finally come home.

When he entered the dormitory housing of the Vatican Knights, he felt an indescribable belonging. Above the door to his quarters was the acid-etched stencil of the Knights' coat of arms, the symbol of faith, loyalty, honor, courage, and strength. Reaching up, he brushed his fingers over the engraving.

Opening the door, he found the room the way he left it six months before. To the left were his bed and nightstand. To the right the small votive rack, kneeling rail, and podium which held a Bible, with its cover dust-laden. His first action was to go to the Bible where he drew a breath and blew the dust away in a plume. He did not open the book. Instead, he put the aluminum case beside the nightstand and headed for the mirror.

In the past six months, he had aged little. In fact, the only process he noted was that his crow's feet had deepened, the lines stretching closer toward the temples. Other than that, there was nothing to show that he had become hardened over the past six months with constant drink and the feeling of self-loathing and failure.

Although he wanted to smile, he did not.

After donning his uniform as a Vatican Knight, he returned to the mirror and contorted the beret to specs, the embroidered symbol of the team, the powder blue shield and silver Pattée, stood front and center. His clerical collar was pristine, his shirt and pants pressed.

Kimball was now in his element.

After cleaning his quarters, a knock came at the door, a few sharp raps.

It was Leviticus. And the two men embraced.

"The pontiff wishes to speak with you," Leviticus finally told him.

"Our first mission?"

"In a manner of speaking, yes. But it's not what you think, Kimball."

"How so?"

"Bonasero's life may be in jeopardy."


**Kimball sat before** the papal desk with Leviticus sitting beside him. Bonasero Vessucci could not have been happier, his expression a genuine model that this gathering was an overwhelmingly joyous affair.

"You have no idea how good it is to see you again," he said. "To see the both of you together."

Kimball nodded. "And you, Your Holiness."

"Kimball," he spoke to him in a rare but subtle tone nearing admonishment, almost childlike in its inflection. "To you I'm Bonasero. We have been through too much together to bandy about titles, yes?"

Kimball smiled. "Then it's Bonasero."

"Good." The pontiff sat back in his chair. "But the issues I propose to you both will be hard to accept, I'm afraid. Leviticus already knows, but I believe that an attempt on my life will be committed very shortly."

"By whom?"

Bonasero sighed. "I believe by the good Cardinal Angullo."

"Angullo?" Kimball sounded incredulous. He knew the man and envisioned him as someone incapable of lifting a hand against somebody, let alone as someone capable of driving a stake through another man's heart. Again, he said: "Angullo?"

"He is not the same man, Kimball. He's been a man driven by his ambitions rather than seeking the true nature of God. He's lost his way and I believe that he murdered Pope Gregory."

An awkward moment fell between them as Kimball digested this, hearing for the first time that Pope Gregory's death was no accident as the press had indicated. *Murdered?* "You think Cardinal Angullo killed Gregory?"

"I've no proof, but yes."

"And why would you think that?"

"Cardinal Angullo knew that I was part of the *Preferiti* and engineered my removal as Vatican secretary of state as soon as Pope Gregory entered office. Promises were made to ensure Gregory's station as the pope with certain favors granted to Angullo should his camp join Gregory's to ascertain the votes necessary. Once I was removed, then he set himself up in a position to succeed the throne upon Gregory's passing."

"And because of that, you think he murdered the pope?"

"I say that because I know it's true in my heart, Kimball. Cardinal Angullo has conspired to the papal throne for some time, often making deals for favors to promote his best interests, which is not the way of God or the Church."

"Yeah, but, Bonasero . . ." He let his words falter. For one supreme clergyman to take the life of another, it was incomprehensible.

"Despite what you may think, Kimball, murder has always been an unfortunate undermining within the Church. Satan has his reaches everywhere by turning good souls into dispassionate ones by corrupting them with power."

Kimball was still having a hard time buying it.

So, when the pope saw this, he continued on. "Cardinal Angullo has already been told that he is being reassigned, which means that his power within the Church is crumbling as we speak. With the limited time he has left, I believe he will make a well, thought-out attempt on my life."

Kimball looked at Leviticus and saw that he was a believer. And though he had no reason to disbelieve the man whom he had grown to love as a father, he still found it difficult to swallow. "Angullo couldn't fight off a fly," he finally said.

"The man has guile and ambition, the two tools necessary for an assault." The pope leaned forward in his chair, placing his arms and tenting his fingers on the desktop before him. "Kimball, maybe I'm wrong, but I don't think so. I set the gears in motion. If Angullo is going to strike, then it will be soon. I need the two of you to keep this from happening."

"Of course," he said. "When is he being transferred?"

"I've put the word out that he is to leave within the next three days."

"So, you think he may act by when? Tomorrow?"

The pontiff hesitated before answering. "If he is a man of true desperation," he began, "then I believe that he may act as early as tonight."

Kimball sat while gnawing on his lower lip and wondered how he was supposed to raise a hand against a leading clergyman. *Nothing like coming back to the Vatican and walking into a dilemma,* he thought.

He continued to nibble on his lower lip.

# CHAPTER THIRTY-SIX

*Tel Aviv, Israel, Mossad Headquarters*

Yitzhak Paled moved up the chain of command as required. First beginning with the Israeli Defense Minister, and then ending up with Prime Minister Benjamin Netanyahu. Talk was plentiful, to say the least, the inevitable outcome being that Israel's sovereignty must be protected at all costs regardless of the United States' input, which would be to stand by with guarded patience and let the sanctions take hold, crippling Iran further. Israel's stance on the matter was that Iran's sanctioned position was pushing the Arab state into a corner, forcing them to fight their way back into contention.

Now, with the United States taking the position of playing both sides of the fence by supporting Israel, but not entirely, left Israel to act accordingly to the situation growing at hand. Iran was in possession of a WMD in an unchartered facility in the Alborz region, the coordinates given to the US command so that they could hone their satellites to the targeted position. Secondly, Aryeh Levine was off the grid, the man presumed dead, which means that the Iranian political constituency knew that they had been compromised and was most likely forming a plan of evacuation.

If Israel needed to act, then the time was now, before the WMD was removed from the facility.

There was a three-way conversation going on through the speakerphone. A live feed was also being dispatched on wall monitors so that all three men—the Defense Minister, the Prime Minister, and Yitzhak Paled—could see each other in high-definition quality.

In a small conference room that was paneled with light wood tones, Yitzhak Paled sat at the end of the table, facing the wall screens. On the left was Netanyahu. On the right screen was Defense Minister

Ehud Barak.

"What is your final analysis?" asked Netanyahu.

Yitzhak spoke freely. "I believe, Mr. Prime Minister, that if we follow the advice of the United States, then it will be too late," he said. "I further believe that our man has been dispatched since he has fallen off the grid. And it appears that a trace has been placed on the encrypted message sent to us from the same coordinates it originated from."

"From the Alborz facility?" asked Barak.

Paled nodded. "They now know it went to Headquarters, which means that they also know that their position has been compromised. And as we sit here, gentlemen, they are getting into position to respond accordingly."

"And this weapon," began Netanyahu, his face registering deep concern, "what do you know about it?"

"We believe that it was engineered by Doctor Leonid Sakharov, a one-time leading scientist in Russia. His technology was quite advanced in its time, years ahead of other nations studying the same science of nanotechnology. A few weeks ago, we believe he met with a known terrorist, Ahmad al-Ghazi, and then he subsequently left for Tehran." Yitzhak leaned forward, his elbows fanning out across the tabletop, his fingers interlocking. "From what we gathered; Sakharov's technology is devastating. We believe that he has created, fashioned, and programmed a science that is capable of destroying anything organic—flesh, bone, sinew, anything that was once alive, while leaving the infrastructure intact."

"Such technology exists?"

"It's been around since the eighties," he said. "It's just been perfected by Sakharov."

"And how is this implemented," asked the Prime Minister.

"We're not sure," he told him. "But there has to be a source to stimulate these bots into action."

"Stimulate? You mean these things are alive?"

"Yes, sir. They're living molecular chains programmed to perform accordingly. It's like designing a DNA link directly into their system to perform according to the desire of its programming. A driving instinct, as you will."

"Yitzhak, do we know how far along they are with this technology?"

206

"Unfortunately, no. Our man on the inside did not expound on that issue. But the fact remains the same, gentlemen. Regardless of the advancement, of whether or not the technology has been completed or near completion, I believe we need to act accordingly despite the wishes of our allies."

The Prime Minister mulled this over. "They know they have been compromised," he finally said. "So, of course, they'll act on their end by denying culpability and, most likely, move their resources elsewhere."

"And that's why, Mr. Prime Minister, we need to act as quickly as possible."

"Your thoughts, Ehud."

The Defense Minister piped up. "Whether or not they have completed the program, are close to completing the program, or nowhere near completing the program, is immaterial. The fact is that they are devising a weapon of mass destruction with no other intention but to destroy—plain and simple. They can manage a leg to stand on by claiming that their nuclear program is geared toward energy needs. But if we attack this facility based on a single encrypted message, and if it doesn't pan out to be true, then we put Israel in a very precarious position."

"But if it is true?" asked the Prime Minister.

"Then we act accordingly. We take out this facility with a sortie. We attack the fuel cells, which will implode the facility, and take out its resources. It's a simple resolution to the problem. But in retaliation Iran will rattle its saber, condemn the state of Israel by declaring war, and then call upon its Arab brothers." On the monitor the Defense Minister leaned forward, his image looming large. "Yitzhak, based on this encryption, how sure are you regarding this technology?"

"Aryeh Levine was one of our supreme assets," he told him. "The message was a quick feed, so we believe that his time was limited, so he got off enough hoping that we could decipher the materials he presented to us."

"And if you deciphered wrongly?"

"I strongly believe that Levine got enough of the message across to state the purpose of the facility's intent. They are building a weapon of mass destruction. And given how they feel about Israel, they will use it against us."

The Defense Minister fell back into his seat. "The president of the

United States is not on board for a full-on strike, even though their CIA has verified the location of the facility in the Alborz. This proposes another problem."

"With all due respect, Mr. Prime Minister, if we should strike then oil prices will rise, putting America's economy at risk. This is not about the American economy, which is their sole concern. This is about Israeli sovereignty."

The Prime Minister had to concur.

And then: "I believe a strike is warranted," said Netanyahu. "I will contact the U.S. and inform them of our intentions. Ehud, alert the command center and inform the *Ramatkal* at the IDF to prepare for a strike. Tell them to remain on alert status waiting for the go."

"Yes, sir."

"And, Yitzhak."

"Yes, Mr. Prime Minister."

"Your man better be right. If not, then we may be on the verge of a World War once this is said and done."

"I understand."

"Then let's make this work."

# CHAPTER THIRTY-SEVEN

*Vatican City*

Cardinal Angullo had received word that he was being reassigned within a three-day window, even though a venue had yet to be set or a new secretary of state chosen to succeed his position.

He stood before the window of his residence looking out at the forming clouds that were sliding closer to the Vatican, dark ominous clouds, storm clouds, the type of clouds that brought torrential rains and celestial staircases of lightning that were bright and angry in their staccato flashes.

He felt the same type of seething, the anger building within the pit of his soul. He had positioned himself perfectly to usurp the papal throne, only to fall short by a thin margin within the conclave.

With his hand he grabbed the fabric of his garment and balled it within his fist, turning, twisting, like his soul. It was as if his anger was something alive and writhing, something working its way to the surface.

Within three days. That's all he had: three days.

But Angullo knew that he couldn't wait until the last day or risk drawing undue intention. He had to act quickly, intelligently, and with great prudence.

He would go undetected, like last time; on the night he pushed Gregory over the balcony's edge by slipping through the hallways where there were no cameras, no spying eyes. He would enter the chamber like last time, quietly, like a wraith, unheard and undetected until it was too late. But how to achieve the means was left up in the air.

No poisons. No sense of duplicating the last scenario with a simple shove to the pavement below—too risky a scenario coming so close on the heels of Gregory. *No, mix it up, change the stage with a dazzling performance by adding a sense of mystery.*

Angullo's mind toiled for hours, the clouds moving in until the sky was black, the rain coming down in sheets, the lightning strikes as brilliant as the sun.

It was two o'clock in the morning, the weather abating little, the possibility of the lightning posing a problem, which may give up his position within the papal chamber before he could finish his attempt upon the pontiff's life.

He had no choice—none whatsoever. Not only was the window closing, but it was slamming shut.

But how to do the deed? That was the question. No knives or blunt weapons, nothing that would leave a mark or cause suspicion that would draw investigators to the scene like flies to honey.

That left the pillow, hardly a weapon of choice but weapon enough. He would take the pillow and apply it to the pontiff's face, smothering him, then set the stage that Pius had died in his sleep. This he could manage, having the vantage point of standing over the weaker man and pressing down until he extinguished his life.

But there was a problem even with this application, the act leaving telltale signs of a murder. When a person is smothered by this method the capillaries in the whites of the victim's eyes burst from the pressure, leaving the whites mottled with patches of red.

The window was lowering, and quickly.

And he could feel the rush of blood course through his veins, the surge of adrenaline fueling him, prompting him to make the move, which was now, before the sun rose.

He took the same route to the papal chamber as he did on the night of Gregory's passing by taking the tunnels beneath the Basilica, the ancient hallways that had been abandoned for years as the musty, old-time smells assaulted him. He carried a lamp with him, the fringe of light barely strong enough to direct his way to the ancient doorways leading to the levels above. The ceilings of the corridors were low, causing him to stoop as he walked, and the surrounding bricks of the walls were made of stone the color of desert sand. The earth beneath his feet was as fine as moon dust as he kicked up small plumes with his footfalls, leaving clear and precise prints in his wake.

Once he reached the stairwell he lifted the lamp, the light casting a feeble glow that revealed an uneven rise of steps. Lifting the hem of his garment, Cardinal Angullo began his climb to the upper level.

Since he had bypassed all the cameras, he would not be seen by any security guards watching the monitors. He was a ghost.

Feeling slightly winded at the top of the stairwell, he came upon a wooden door that was held together by black steel bands and rivets, something from medieval lore, and used a key to open it. It was the only way to open the passage from his side, the side of the ancient hallway.

The door opened, the hinges protesting lightly, and used the light as a wedge to keep the door open for his escape back to the sanctuary of the *Domus Sanctæ Marthæ*.

He moved quietly down the hallway, which was a dead-end except for the door that was presumed locked and inaccessible. At the mouth of the hallway, at the opposite end where Angullo entered, stood a Swiss Guard. Not a problem for the cardinal since the guard stood thirty meters away and had his attention focused elsewhere.

The cardinal moved cautiously, silently, his movement fluid and fleeting. If the man was seen through the lens of a camera, those watching would have sworn that the cleric was gliding on air like something phantasmal, eerie, or supernatural.

When he reached the pontiff's door, he placed an ear against the panel and listened.

Like on the night of Gregory's death he heard nothing but the stillness of the night, a good omen, and entered the chamber with not even the sound of a whisper of wind.

He stood there, listening. And then he moved closer to the walls where the shadows pooled, becoming a part of them. He moved slowly, gracefully, using the darkness as his ally.

And then a flash of lightning, giving light and pushing back the darkness, exposing him. But it also granted him the necessary vision to see that the pontiff was lying in bed with the blanket drawn to his chin and halfway across his face.

There was another quick flash that proposed enough light to see the man shift beneath the covers and turned his back to him.

Angullo smiled because God presenting him with the opportune moment to strike. He saw an unused pillow next to the pontiff's head, the means and necessity within reach. It was as if God was sending his divine light to show him the way. He quietly moved closer with unheard footfalls.

And then he stood still, his senses suddenly kicking in.

Something was wrong. The air suddenly seemed oppressive and heavy, a viable threat lingering close by. In reaction the cardinal assessed the situation, feeling an unease that drove him away from the bed and back into the shadows.

As he glided back towards the darkness, a black mass shot up from the bed. In the cardinal's eyes, it appeared impossibly large, the shadow rising, the blanket flaring upward and outward like a frill, the thing beneath it reaching for him, grabbing him, the strength of its grip clutching his throat in a choking embrace, crushing his windpipe, and forcing him against the wall.

The cardinal's heart raced with uncontrollable panic. The thing before him was massive, large, and in the subsequent pulse of lightning, he witnessed the murderous rage in the man's eyes, saw the hateful intent and the willingness to gladly snuff out his life with a twist of his hand and snapping his neck where he stood.

Only it was not the pontiff.

This man was large and bulky with broad shoulders and thick arms. His face was angular and sharp. And his teeth gritted as he pressed his hand across the cardinal's throat as though he was trying to force the man's neck through the wall.

The cardinal grunted, then gasped, his world starting to go black as pinpricks of light started to shoot off in his field of vision.

Suddenly the light came on. In the background stood Bonasero Vessucci wearing a sleeping garment that covered him from neck to toe. Beside him stood the man he had seen earlier, the security guard. But this time he was wearing different garb. He wore a cleric's shirt and Roman Catholic collar. His pants were of military fashion, as were the boots—a weird display of uniform. And then he focused on the man who pressed him tightly against the wall, noting the same outfit.

"Ease up, Kimball," said the pontiff.

But Kimball held tight, fighting off the urge to push the man through the marble wall if that was possible.

"Kimball, enough."

The Vatican Knight eased off and let the cardinal regain his breath, but stood close by to engineer another thorough choking, if necessary.

Bonasero Vessucci advanced slowly, his saddened eyes set on Angullo. "You truly are a lost soul, Giuseppe; can't you see that by your attempt tonight?"

Angullo stared up at Kimball for a brief moment before sidestepping him. "Attempt?"

"Why are you here at so early an hour?"

"To try to talk you out of my reassignment," he answered.

"It couldn't wait until tomorrow?"

"My apologies," he said. "But the idea of such an assignment has been eating away at me. I was hoping to conclude the matter as quickly as possible. I have to admit, Your Holiness, that my actions were not thought out and premature, allowing my impulse to react rather than my patience."

The pontiff sighed. "Do you think I believe that, Giuseppe?"

"It is the truth."

Vessucci stared at him for a brief moment before a rebuttal. "No, Giuseppe, it's not. I gave specific orders to the guard not to allow anyone in this hallway. No one. Yet here you are." He cocked his head questioningly to the side. "So, tell me, how did you get here?"

Angullo remained quiet, the microexpression of his eyes flaring with animalistic fear.

"How did you get here?" he repeated.

Silence.

"Did you use the same route the night you visited Pope Gregory?"

The walls were closing in on Angullo and he knew it, feeling dangerously oppressed.

"If I view the security cameras, will I see you? Or did you use a route that was not within the scope of the cameras' eyes?"

"Is there such a passageway?" asked Kimball.

"An ancient one," said Bonasero. He took a step closer to the cardinal. "Did you take the ancient tunnels, Giuseppe? Did you purposely use the tunnels to avoid the cameras?"

Angullo closed in on himself, drawing his shoulders inward as if imploding, making him smaller.

Kimball reached out and grabbed the man by the collar, setting him straight. "The pontiff asked you a question. Don't you think you better answer him?"

Angullo held his hands out imploringly. "Please, Bonasero, my intentions were sincere."

"Then why take the old passageway? It only confirms what I thought," he said, "since we could not locate you on the cameras on the night of Gregory's death. And now you come into my chamber using the same course with perhaps the same intent in your heart? Does the power of supreme leadership mean so much to you that you're willing to kill for it?"

"Your Holiness, my intent was to plea for your forgiveness and to entreat you to maintain my position here at the Vatican since a secretary of state has yet to be chosen."

"In the eyes of God, Giuseppe, you lie . . . In the eyes of God. Do you think when it's your time of Judgment that God will roll out the red carpet for you?"

Angullo swallowed.

"I feel sorry for you, Giuseppe. I'm not sure that your soul can be saved. I pray it can. But I doubt it."

"What I say is true."

"Stop it!" yelled the pontiff. "Every time you tell a lie, you take one step closer to Hell. Lying is not the way of absolution, Giuseppe, but the truth is."

The cardinal measured the Knights, turning his gaze to Kimball, to Leviticus, then back to Bonasero Vessucci. "I see," he said. "I see that you reinstated the Vatican Knights, yes? Your personal army of killers, correct?"

Kimball's grip tightened on the cardinal's collar, causing the cleric to gasp.

And then, with an uplifting and sardonic grin, the cardinal went on. "How easy it is to justify your needs, assembling murderers to achieve the means. Tell me, Bonasero, do *you* think that God will roll out the red carpet for *you* on the Day of Judgment?" His smile widened. "It's a stop we all have to make someday."

"My intentions are good, Giuseppe. What is in my heart, what is in the hearts of these men, bear nothing but good intentions. These killers, as you call them, work abroad saving the lives of those who cannot protect themselves. Women, children, those who are feeble-minded or incapable of raising a voice in fear of fatal reprisals, such as having a knife driven across their throat, or perhaps a child tries to run away from someone who wants to incorporate them into their dark legions by placing a gun in their hands and tells them to kill or be killed, like in Uganda or Burma."

"And you really think that these men can alter destiny?"

"These men provide salvation when salvation is all but lost. In your case, Giuseppe, these men can do nothing for you." And then:

214

"Kimball."

It was Kimball's cue to release the man, which he did, with the cardinal's collar settling as bunched fabric along his left shoulder.

"So now what?" asked the cardinal. "Obviously, you do not intend to hear my pleas or take into consideration my request to remain here at the Vatican."

"You're right. I don't." Bonasero took a step closer, intent on driving his point home. "You're lucky, Giuseppe, that I don't take further action against you. Your blatant trespass into the papal chamber is criminal enough. But let it be known that you will be watched. These men will maintain a constant vigil over you. No matter where you are. No matter what you do. Believe me when I say that your every move is being watched. You won't see them. But trust me, they will see you."

"And if I divulge your little secret society?"

Kimball placed his hand on the cardinal's shoulder, twisting the fabric until the collar tightened.

"I see," said the cardinal. "You will keep me in line with physical threats. How holy of you to allow this, Bonasero. How holy, indeed."

"You're a man of dark means, Giuseppe. And you don't deserve to wear the shrouds you don. I will not judge you. That's not my right. That right belongs to the Lord. And I pray that He can somehow forgive you for what you have done." Bonasero held out his hand. "Now give me the key," he ordered. "Return to the dormitory and never use the ancient corridors again. You will be assigned soon, Giuseppe, very soon. And may God have mercy on your soul." The pontiff then flexed his fingers quickly, a gesture that he was ready to accept the key.

Giuseppe stared a long moment and could feel his power slipping. He could also sense that everything he worked for was forever lost to him. Begrudgingly, he reached his hand into his pocket, grabbed the key, and handed it to Bonasero by dropping it into his palm.

"I assume that you used light to get here. The ancient tunnels, after all, are dark."

"I left the light at the ancient doorway."

"These men will escort you back to the way you entered. Once gone, Giuseppe, I want you to know that the door will be forever sealed." And then: "Have a good night."

Giuseppe could feel himself cave. He had lost everything. His drives, his ambition, his dream, perhaps even his soul.

After Kimball and Leviticus ushered him to the ancient doorway, Cardinal Angullo grabbed the light, turned it on, and stepped onto the top stair leading down into the corridor. When the door closed behind him, it was as if the hollow click was more than just a sound. It was a climactic end to his rise with the closing door a metaphorical suggestion that his time was truly up.

Taking the steps with his shoulders lowered in defeat, Cardinal Giuseppe Angullo made his way back through the corridors that looked so much like an artist's rendition of Hell, that of complete and utter darkness with no hope of seeing the light.

# CHAPTER THIRTY-EIGHT

*Vatican City, Inside the SIV Command Center*

Bonasero Vessucci and Kimball were inside the SIV Command Center alongside Fathers Essex and Auciello. They sat before the console in front of multiple screens watching the world play out before them from live satellite feeds. They watched the skirmishes in the southern Philippines, the multiple atrocities going on in Africa, and the rampaging crusades in the Middle East and Syria. The world was a mess, and the messes were piling high.

Father Auciello toyed with a dial, zooming in on a location in the Alborz region. On the master screen, he singled in on the coordinates given by a Mossad agent who was able to send an encrypted message to Tel Aviv regarding an unchartered facility dealing with the manufacturing of a WMD. From their overhead vantage point, they could spy down and zoom in to the point where they could see the two gunnery nests and the fuel cells lining the ridgeline. They also spotted a helipad and a lot with two canvas-covered transport vehicles to carry mobile units.

"We've been staying on top of Mossad since their mention of the Ark of the Covenant," said Auciello, playing the dial until the screen came into sharp focus. "It appears that the operative got a message out regarding the facility's clandestine operations."

"Creating weapons of mass destruction," Kimball commented.

"Exactly. Furthermore, he's confirming the location of the Ark." He took his hand away from the dial. "It's there, gentlemen, inside that facility. The question is: why place the Ark of the Covenant inside a manufacturing center that is constructing a weapon of mass destruction? Why take the Ark from the grounds of the Temple Mount and send it to the Alborz region? What's their purpose? Or do they have a purpose? What's their agenda?"

They were solid inquiries that nobody had answers to, the questions serving as ill-fitting pieces to a vague puzzle.

Kimball shifted in his seat and studied the screen, his eyes squinting in the quasi-darkness. He absorbed the makeup of the land, the surrounding paths, and the serpentine road that led to the facility. He marked the gunnery nests in his mind and noted the helipad at the ridgeline close to the fenced-in fuel cells. He was tracing a map in his mind.

"We also intercepted messages from Prime Minister Netanyahu and his Defense Minister," added Essex, "to the president of the United States conveying Israel's concern that the facility poses a major threat to Israel's sovereignty; therefore, they are in the planning stages of committing to a preemptive strike against the facility in the near future should they decide to act, even though it's against the wishes of the United States for fear of rising fuel costs, as well as placing Israel on the verge of war with Iran, which may incite other Arab nations to join in the skirmish. Right now, Israel is on the fence leaning towards attack, but the United States is stalling them."

"If they strike, then the Ark will be lost forever," said Bonasero.

"If they should strike," said Essex. "Israel hasn't fully committed yet."

"It is never the Church's intent to get involved with political events or the involvements of warring government factions, but the Ark is a sacred relic and an interest of the Church," he said. "In this case, we know where the Ark of the Covenant is. We also know that this facility is in the process of creating a weapon of mass destruction that may undermine the stability of the Middle East, should Israel commit to an airstrike. Should that be the case, then the Ark will be forever lost."

Kimball knew where this was going.

The pope faced the Vatican Knight. "Good could be borne from evil," he said to him evenly. "We know where the Ark is, we know the intent of this facility. We send in a team to extract the Ark and destroy the facility before Israel commits to battle. That way, Israel cannot be held responsible, though an accusing finger will most certainly be pointed their way." Bonasero stood, laboring to a stance, then moved closer to the screen. "We get the Ark, take out the facility, and place Israel in a position to avert war."

"Bonasero, this won't be an easy task," said Kimball. "We're talking about breaching a highly-secured facility manned by Quds, an elite force. Not an easy task." Kimball pointed to the screen. "The landscape is elevated, giving them the advantage of the high point. There's one road leading in and out of the area—not good for escape should factions come up on the rear and box us in. The facility itself is secured with gunnery nests overlooking the entryway. Combat space is minimal. The only positive is the helipad, which could be a viable method of escape should a helicopter be stationed there. Even then we would be in Iranian air space and the chopper too slow to outrun their jets."

"You have to have faith, Kimball. There's a solution for everything."

"Bonasero, you're asking me to place my men into a situation that's impossible."

The pontiff returned to his seat. "You're a Vatican Knight," he said softly. "And, of course, your skills and insight are invaluable, and your insight to combat far greater than mine. But we're not talking just about the Ark of the Covenant here. We're talking about a weapon that could destroy countless lives, perhaps even initiate a war between nations where untold scores of innocent people die. We are in a position to do something about this. You and your team have the skills to pull this off."

Kimball held back for a moment, contemplating. He had performed missions in the past hinging on the thought that they were impossible to pull off, the risks too high, the outcome deemed too low to be successful. But he had come to learn over time that the word 'impossible' didn't mean that something couldn't be done; it only measured the degree of difficulty.

"It'll have to be quick," he finally said. "How long before Israel commits to a strike, you think?"

Father Essex shrugged, hazarding a guess. "Two, maybe three days at the most. I can't speak for the Israeli Defense agency. I can only give you what I have, which is that Israel is non-committal at this time. But I don't think they'll hang in that balance too much longer. Sooner or later, they'll decide. And I believe that decision will be to commit to a strike, whether they have the approval of the United States or not."

Kimball asked Auciello to zoom out to give him a much more overhead view and spread of the layout. The area was mountainous, one ridgeline higher than the other heading to the west. Obviously, the road was out, not a good strategy to take since it would be highly manned with security. They would have to get to the facility another way. And then deal with the gunnery nests and the Quds. They would have to breach the complex, exit with the Ark, destroy the fuel cells, and escape. His head was spinning. No matter how he looked at it, no matter from what angle or vantage point, he saw nothing positive, the requirements too much to overcome.

"How are we going to get the Ark out of there?" he asked softly. "We could commandeer one of the trucks; put the Ark in the back. But then we'd be running a gauntlet to get away since there's only one road leading to the lower elevation where I'm sure the opposition will be waiting."

"There's the helipad," said Essex. "Once you engage and clear the area, then we can land a chopper big enough to carry the Ark and the Knights. Run your combat mission, grab the Ark, set the charges at the fuel cells, and then off we go. We can fly low enough to escape radar detection. But if we fly too low, and given that we have to run at night, poses a problem since we'd be flying at low altitudes in a mountain range. We'll have to go in with NVG capability and fly northwest to Turkey."

"And the pilot?"

"We have operatives with exceptional ability," said Auciello. "We employ a select few who are pilots in service with the Vatican through the *Aeronautica Milatare*. Their mission is to serve the Church with no questions asked."

"So, we have the means of escape," said Kimball. "We can set off an explosive at the fuel cells from a cell phone inside the chopper once we're airborne, leveling the facility if the fuel cells are volatile enough. All that remains is how are we going to get to the facility without drawing the opposition's fire." He studied the map further. And then: "Father Essex, that ridge to the west, what's its elevation point compared to the ridgeline of the facility?"

Essex went to a keyboard and typed in commands, the image going from sky view to ground view. From there he was able to calculate the differences. The ridgeline Kimball inquired about was approximately 2,200 feet higher than the facility. There was his vantage point. "And how far away is it?" he asked. Essex drew a computerized ruler from point A to point B. The distance was two clicks, approximately one point two miles.

Perfect! Now he had his entry point.

"And how do you plan to do that?" asked Bonasero.

"We can't risk choppers for entry," said Father Essex. "It would be too risky. You'd have to go in silent."

"Going in by chopper was the furthest thing from my mind," he answered.

"Then how do you plan to breach the compound?" ask Bonasero. "Do you plan to fly in on the wings of eagles?"

Kimball smiled slyly and nodded. "Close," he said. "Very close."

No one knew what he was talking about.

And then, after getting to his feet, Kimball said, "We need to move."

*Tel Aviv, Israel, Mossad Headquarters*

"The United States does not approve of our stance," said Yitzhak Paled. He sat behind his desk with his hands clasped together in an attitude of prayer. The top button of his shirt was undone, the knob of his tie lowered. On the mini screen on his desk was the Defense Minister, Ehud Barak. "They feel that Iran will retaliate and press us into war. What they fail to see is that Iran has already made that decision."

Barak appeared somber. The inevitable had finally come to Israel's doorstep. "Then we will act accordingly," he said. "The IDF is on alert. However, the prime minister is not without political etiquette. He is informing the United States that there is no other alternative as we speak. War may be inevitable, Yitzhak. Hopefully, should their president lend his support, it might be enough to deter other Arab nations from uniting with Iran with military efforts."

From his end, Yitzhak could hear Barak's line drone. On-screen, he watched Barak wave his hand at him as a gesture to be excused and picked up the phone.

"I see," he said into the phone, nodding. "Yes . . . I understand." He hung up and stared at the phone as if expecting it to ring again. It didn't. So, he faced Yitzhak through the monitor. "That was the *Ramatkal* at the IDF," he said.

*And?*

Barak leaned closer to the screen. "The command was given. We attack the facility within the next twenty-four hours without the support of the United States."

# CHAPTER THIRTY-NINE

*The Alborz Mountain Range, Ten Hours Later*

It was night. And the air surrounding Mount Damavand was glacially cold.

Kimball Hayden stood at the edge of the precipice that overlooked the valley that separated his team of twelve from the ridgeline of the facility, a distance of two clicks of open-air space between them.

He immediately assembled his team and briefed them on their journey through Turkey. Then from there, they took a Chinook to the neighboring mount where they disembarked at its base and hiked to their current position.

The Chinook remained at the debarkation point, the pilot waiting on Kimball's order once the Quds were neutralized and the Ark firmly under his jurisdiction. Once the Semtex was mounted against the fuel cells, the chopper would then be dispatched to the extraction point where the Ark would then be loaded, and the charges set off in calibration. The fuel cells going off like dominoes from left to right, the chopper lifting and veering north toward Turkey as the facility imploded into a ruin of gravel and dust and smoke. At least that was the plan.

Kimball stood at the edge looking through an NVG monocular and calculated the downward distance of a thirty-percent grade until they reached their landing position by the fuel cells, which were located above the machine gun nests.

Through the lens of the monocular Kimball could clearly see the MG nests, two Quds to a nest. And then he calibrated the lens to zoom in on the terrain. He noted the fuel cells, the helipad, the lot for the trucks, scanning and sighting two Quds soldiers standing by the fuel cells conversing, the men rubbing their gloved hands together to stay warm. The problem was that they stood at the breach point, posing as a possible threat to compromise their approach. So he had little choice but to take them out during the fly run by gauging his targets through his gun sights and firing off quick taps to their heads. Not an easy task but doable.

He lowered the monocular and tucked it away in a side pocket of his glide suit. "Two clicks," he said to Leviticus, "at thirty degrees on a downward slope. The breach points are north and south of the fuel cells, above the MG nests. Team A will head for the nest above the facility's entrance and neutralize that post. Team B will work their way to the second nest located at the lower base and defuse the unit there. There are two guards posted by the fuel cells. I'll approach them on the fly run and take them out systematically with kill shots. Should I miss during my run, then I'll need you to follow up with their neutralization. So stay close."

"Understood."

Kimball pulled back from the edge and headed for his team. They stood as silhouettes against the brilliantly lit feature of the gibbous moon, waiting, a band of brothers who were at peace knowing that not all of them would return home alive on this night.

Kimball informed them of their mission, the locales of the MG nests, and the importance of a quick strike and an even quicker exit.

Once the team was apprised of their duties, once every man knew his place in the scheme of personal commitment, they geared for action.

Each man took his position along the edge of the rim, the sudden drop before them straight down and seemingly endless in the dark. They were wearing special jumpsuits called wingsuits, a garment which added surface area to the body to enable a significant increase in their lift by adding fabric between the legs and under the arms like the expansive wings of a flying squirrel, the ensuing flight a horizontal one from points A to B, the shortest distance being a straight line. At the flight's end, a parachute will deploy at a planned altitude and unzips the arm wings so that the person flying can reach up to the control toggles and fly to a normal parachute landing.

Kimball stood overlooking the ledge, then dropped his NVG goggles for his flight over the valley, the world suddenly becoming phosphorous green. He'd be gliding at more than sixty miles per hour, only to pull up during his deployment and drop silently into the compound. He would then take measure, and summarily dispatched the guards with calculated aim.

He checked his suppressor-fitted Heckler and Koch MP-5, which was attached to a belt festooning across his chest, and then charged his firearm, a Glock Smith & Wesson. After making an initial check that his combat fighting blades were securely fastened to his shin guards, he took a leap of faith and jumped from the ledge, spreading his arms and legs, his flight taking him toward the compound of the facility in a horizontal plane.

Leviticus soon followed. And then one by one the Vatican Knights jumped, each man leaping into open space until the wings of their suits caught a level plane of flight and glided closer to battle at speeds nearing seventy miles per hour.

In less than two minutes Kimball had to peel back to slow his speed, the fabric fanning out and acting as aeronautical brakes, and deployed his chute. His descent was slow and quiet. And in the sights of his MP5, he took careful aim with the Quds totally unaware of his advancement and pulled the trigger in quick succession.

*Tap! . . . Tap!*

The Quds went limp, their bodies falling boneless to the ground, apparently dead before their brains even registered the end of their lives.

Kimball landed evenly on the terrain, followed by Leviticus.

"Nice shooting," Leviticus said as he pulled his chute closed before disengaging it.

But Kimball didn't comment. The man was focused, intent, and in warrior mode. With Leviticus by his side, they got down on a bended knee with their weapons held close and watched the rest of the Vatican Knights drift lazily from the sky.


**They hit the** MG nest situated above the facility door first.

The team moved in quiet and catlike. The Quds soldier manning the Browning with his arms draped casually over the weapon while the other sat on top of the sandbags, speaking in Farsi in what seemed to be banter, the other man laughing as if he had just heard something humorous. Their complacency was their downfall; both men were taken down and rendered unconscious, their wrists bound with flex cuffs.

The second team at the second MG nest was not as lucky. The Quds team was alert and responsive with their eyes cast forward with the point of the Browning poised to kill. Since the Knights had little opportunity to approach their position, they had no choice but to extinguish them with well-placed shots to neutralize the situation.

Within three minutes both nests were cleared, and the landing secured. All that remained was to breach the facility and acquire the Ark. And they had to do it while fending off an elite force.

Kimball stood by the massive vault door leading into the facility and placed the flat of his palm against the cold steel.

His pulse began to race.

The firefight was about to begin.

*Negev Desert on the Western Outskirts of Beersheba, Hatzerim Israeli Air Force Base*

At 1930 hours an order was mandated by the Prime Minister to initiate a sortie against an unchartered facility located in the Alborz Mountain region, most notably Mount Damavand. The precise coordinates were given, and an aerial raid was to begin and end with the complete destruction of the facility.

No reason was given for the strike. And no questions were asked.

A dozen F-16I Israeli fighter jets were loaded with heavy payloads, the pilots instructed to terminate the target with such precision that it would take years for the dust to settle.

Lining up on the tarmac the planes took off in timed succession, approximately thirty seconds apart until all the jets were airborne and heading toward Mount Damavand.

In the Prime Minister's office, as Netanyahu watched his monitor and saw the planes take off, he could sense the heaviness of an oncoming war settling over him like a pall.

*Turkey/Iranian Border, Vatican Base Command*

The SIV, in collusion with the Turkish government, had set up a post on the Turkey side of the border that was less than five miles from the Iranian boundary line.

Father Essex was manning the Comm Center, a makeshift camp erected with canvas tents and expensive electronic equipment. The flaps blew wildly with the course of a brutal wind, the heat lamps doing little to abate the chill from his bones, as he monitored feeds coming from the SIV Center at the Vatican, which was helmed by Father Auciello.

Other SIV officials milled about, monitoring radar display screens and intercepted radio chats from the Ukraine to Iran to Israel to the United States, compiling detailed information as world events pressed on. One event, in particular, emerged from Israel. Apparently, the powers that be had ordered an illegal incursion into Iran with the objective to take out a target located at the base of Mount Damavand.

Father Essex knew exactly what Israel's intent was. Nor did he hesitate to act. He inquired another SIV operative as to the current location of the strike team in flight. The news was not good. When the coordinates were finally given, Father Essex put on his headgear, typed in a command to initiate communication, and spoke into his lip mike. "Romeo-One, this is Base Command. Do you copy?"

**The pilot of** the Chinook sat idle in the valley below, waiting until he received word from Father Essex at the Vatican Base Command which was posted at the Turkey/Iranian border.

"*Romeo-One, this is Base Command. Do you copy?*"

The pilot spoke into his lip mike. "This is Romeo-One. Go ahead."

"*Romeo-One, you need to contact Team Leader Bravo and inform him that IDF has launched their eagles and are heading toward the precision point with an ETA of thirty minutes. Do you copy?*"

The pilot looked at his synchronized watch. *Thirty minutes?* There wasn't enough time for Kimball to pull off the mission, he considered. Not nearly enough.

"Base Command, do you want me to abort the mission and pull the team?"

"*That's negative, Romeo-One. You need to contact Team Leader Bravo and apprise him of the situation.*"

"Copy that, Base Command. . . Out."

The pilot shook his head. Those men, he knew, and if they didn't get out now, were as good as dead.

He tapped a button on his headgear. "Romeo-One to Team Leader Bravo. Come in, Team Leader Bravo . . ."

**Kimball stood back** from the vault when his earbud went off. *"Romeo-One to Team Leader Bravo. Come in, Team Leader Bravo . . ."*

"This is Team Leader Bravo. Go ahead."

*"I just got word from Base Command that IDF has launched eagles and are bearing down with an ETA of thirty."*

*Thirty minutes?*

"Copy that, Romeo-One."

*"You want me to start the evacuation process?"*

"Negative. Stand by and wait for my command."

*"Copy that."*

Kimball appeared worried—something Leviticus never thought he'd see on the Vatican Knight's face. So, he had to ask. "What's the matter?"

Kimball turned to him. "It appears that Israel is committing to a preemptive strike quicker than we planned."

"You're telling me that they're in flight?"

"That's exactly what I'm telling you."

"How long?"

"Thirty minutes."

"That's cutting it close, Kimball."

"I agree." Kimball then walked toward Ezra—whose exclusive skill and purpose were setting explosive charges for maximum effect—with urgency to his gait. "Ezra, we need to get inside ASAP."

Ezra sized up the door. "I can place explosives against the wall, which is approximately three feet thick, the same as the door. It'll take three, maybe four discharges before we breach the facility."

"How long to set them off?"

"Ten minutes."

"You have five. Get us in there."

"Yes, sir."

Kimball fell back to access the situation only to be met by Leviticus, who grabbed him by the crook of the elbow and pulled him into close counsel. "We're cutting it close, Kimball. I say we cut our losses and blow the facility before their jets rain down on us. At least we can keep Israel from committing themselves to a situation with serious ramifications."

"We have thirty minutes," he told him. "We can be well on our way to Turkey in twenty."

Leviticus released him. "You do realize that the Quds aren't exactly going to let us walk right in and take the Ark, right? You know that, don't you?"

"Leviticus, this is what we're all about. Is it not? Is this not why we are Vatican Knights?"

Leviticus stood motionless, considering, and then he nodded. "Twenty minutes," he said.

"That's all I ask. If we're not in possession of the Ark by then, then we'll bug out and destroy the facility."

"Agreed."

Both men turned toward Ezra who placed a packet of Semtex to the right of the door and against the stone wall. It was Ezra's thought that blowing through concrete was the more expedient way than trying to breach the steel of the vault door.

"All right, boys," he said, activating the detonator. "It's time to make some noise." And then: "*Cover!*"

Kimball looked at his watch: twenty-seven minutes to go. *Do it!*

Ezra pressed the command, setting off the Semtex. The explosion was massive as rock and debris went everywhere. When the dust settled a gaping hole the size of a small entryway was situated beside the vault door, the door itself was blackened and charred but held nary a dent.

The team examined the break and saw that it blew inwards of nearly two feet. As far as Kimball could tell it was a great mining tool, but they were still outside the facility, and time was running short.

*Twenty-five minutes.*

"One, maybe two more charges," said Ezra. "But I'll get us in."

Kimball looked skyward, could almost hear the approaching jets.

No doubt the explosion alerted the Quds inside, causing them to side up in defense formation.

"How much Semtex you got left?" he asked.

"Two bundles."

"Use them both as one discharge," he told him.

"That's a lot of power, sir."

"Ezra, I'm not asking you, I'm telling you. Use them both. We're running out of time."

"Yes, sir."

Ezra worked quickly, piecing the explosives as a unit of one. Since

Semtex was one of the most volatile explosives ever created, the blowout would be massive. After setting the charges, Ezra cautioned the team to fall way back.

*Twenty-two minutes.*

"*Cover!*" He pressed the button. The stone wall, the world, the ground beneath them, all shook with apocalyptic reverberations that seemed never-ending as cloying dust as thick as a London fog circled in lazy eddies, refusing to settle.

But through that haze, they could see the light within the complex. The center had been breached.

"MOVE! MOVE! MOVE!"

Kimball led the way with his MP-5 directed front and center, the mouth of the weapon's barrel poised to kill. He easily breached the hole, which was massive, the force of the explosion blowing hot chunks of rock throughout the center with scalpel-like intensity, the energy of the blast causing the stones to act as shrapnel that destroyed everything in its path perforating the walls with numerous holes. If Quds forces had been standing at the end of the corridor waiting in defense, then they would have been cut down to pieces, their bodies' most likely ending up as tangled masses of freshly sliced meat.

But no one was there.

The lab was empty.

The complex was completely evacuated.

Whatever machines that once filled the center were now gone.

Kimball lowered his weapon, slowly, as if dismayed by his surroundings.

The entire facility had bugged out, leaving a minimal force behind for cosmetics. Most likely as an excuse to use their deaths against the sortie that was coming. Iran was bracing itself for war. And Israel was falling right into the spider's web.

*Eighteen minutes.*

"There's nothing here!" yelled Leviticus. "We have to go!"

"Check the facility for the Ark," yelled Kimball. "We still have time. Just keep your head on a swivel, just in case!"

The Vatican Knights branched out, their weapons at eye level as they moved along the corridors clearing the way.

Except for a single broken monitor that was lying on its side, the lab was completely hollow. The only telltale sign that anything existed at all was the scuff marks along the tiled floor indicating that something of volume had once stood in its place. To the left was another chamber. And when Kimball entered, he knew immediately that this was the chamber that housed the Ark of the Covenant.

And like everything else, it was gone.

"That's it," he finally said. "We're done! Everybody out!"

The Knights quickly banded together, exited the facility, and raced for the high ground of the helipad.

Kimball spoke into his mike. "Romeo-One, this is Team Leader Bravo! Do you copy?"

"*Copy, Team Leader Bravo.*"

"Get that chopper to the extraction point now!"

"*Copy!*"


**The jets were** zeroing in on their target and less than fifteen minutes out.

In Tehran, as expected, they were picked up on the radar, which was a blatant and illegal incursion into Iranian airspace which drew immediate condemnation from Iranian officials. In response Iran immediately sent their jets to retaliate, knowing full well that they were too far away to engage the enemy. But the retaliatory action was for cosmetics to show the world that Iran was well within its rights to protect itself as a sovereign country against the Zionist state of Israel.

Of course, they demanded that the Israeli's turn back.

And of course, the demand went unheeded.

When the sortie team was less than ten minutes away from their strike point, the world once again erupted in a fiery blast that sent a mushroom flame high above Mount Damavand.


**The two men** at the MG nest were quickly gathered by Kimball's team and ushered to the helipad. By the time they got there, the Chinook was landing, the rotors kicking up a wash of dust. As the door opened, the Quds were tossed inside.

"What are you going to do with them?" asked the pilot.

"If we leave them here, they'll die. We'll let them go at the border," said Kimball.

"And the Ark?"

Kimball nodded.

Once the rest of the team boarded, Kimball signaled to the pilot to get the bird going.

The rotors quickened, and then the chopper lifted, hovering, then banked, and headed north toward Turkey.

"All right, Ezra!" Kimball had to yell over the thrumming of the blades. "Light her up!"

Ezra typed his fingers furiously against the touch screen of an iPhone, the last tap having emphasis. A signal was sent through cyberspace and the charges on the fuel cells went off in synchronized succession starting from left to right, the cells bursting like dominoes and sending a fiery plume skyward, the cavern collapsing upon itself. A concussion wave then moved through the air at a rate of speed faster than the chopper could travel and tossed it violently from side to side in seesaw fashion before the pilot was able to regain control. Once the Chinook was stabilized, they then headed for Turkey.

**At the moment** of the explosion, two things happened: First, the Israeli sortie was ordered to return to base—the precision point of attack, for whatever reason, had been terminated for reasons unknown. Secondly, the Iranian leadership could not figure out why the facility destructed prematurely when the sortie was ten minutes out. So, when the Israeli's headed back, the Iranian government saved face by puffing out their chest and sent forth a declaration remarking that the sortie retreated due to the advancement of their own intercepting forces. Therefore, the Israeli's did not want to confront a superior power.

Israel, of course, scoffed at this.

But in the end, war was averted.

**When the Chinook** landed on the Turkish side of the border, and as the two Quds were ushered to an unknown point within the Comm Center camp, Kimball entered the tent where Father Essex sat behind the Comm console watching high-definition monitors.

Kimball grabbed his beret and tossed it roughly against the console in disappointment. "They bugged out," he said. "They knew they were compromised, so they set up a neat little package to draw the fly to the honey," he said tersely. "But they were expecting Israel to make a strike, not us."

"It would have been the catalyst necessary to justify war," said Father Essex casually. "Israel would have made accusations regarding weapons of mass destruction. And Ahmadinejad would have denied everything. So, the mission wasn't without its merits . . . Even if the Ark is still missing."

Kimball took a seat as his anger rushed through him as quickly as the beat of his pulse, hard and fast. In his heart, he knew he was within reach, perhaps by hours, only for the Ark to slip through his fingers, most likely under the cover of darkness when the satellites were at their weakest point of visual perception.

Kimball then leaned his head back, closed his eyes, and tried to relax. But he would not find the comfort necessary to pacify him until he returned to the Vatican on the following day.

# CHAPTER FORTY

*Tehran, Iran, Warehouse District, Two Days After the Assault on The Facility*

In the Warehouse District in southern Tehran, al-Ghazi stood alongside al-Sherrod and other personnel who milled about a stockroom the size of a football field. The massive area was vacant, the surrounding floor, for the most part, littered with debris and rubble, the building having been abandoned long ago. Pigeons alighting on the overhead beams continued to pass their droppings to the floor. And the windows, which lined the top tier just below the roofline, were oxidized, cracked, or broken. In the center of the warehouse was a raised platform surrounded by lights powered by generators. On the center of that platform lay the Ark of the Covenant, its lid off and to the side, a gold aura fanning out from its shell against the cast of the reflecting light.

Al-Ghazi stood back with his hands clasped behind the small of his back and watched his team rig the Ark with a false bottom.

Before leaving the facility at Mount Damavand, Sakharov's techs had engineered a flat box made of a composite not detectable by x-ray and then infused it with nanobots. The flat box, approximately covering the entire floorboard of the Ark and an inch high, would be undetectable once the false bottom was set in place. Pinprick holes unseen by the naked eye would perforate the false flooring. The holes appearing like gaping chasms to the bots since a hundred thousand could fit on the head of a pin, thereby providing numerous escape routes once the sound waves stimulated the bots into action.

They would then take flight and devour anything organic within fifteen-minutes, and killing without impunity, conscience, and simply by design.

Al-Ghazi watched as his engineers carefully laid the flat box containing the nanobots along the floor of the Ark, then fitted the false bottom over it so that the interior appeared uniform and untouched. In further examination, they passed scopes and wands capable of detecting alien composites not existing at the time the Ark was created. This was done so as not to draw suspicion from scholars examining the Ark, and then warranting further scrutiny should they detect anomalous blends not historically existing at that time, such as the composite structure of the flat box, which was the last thing al-Ghazi wanted. X-rays were then taken from every angle, the nano container and false bottom going undetected, the bots all but invisible.

Al-Ghazi was pleased.

"Should the initial run succeed, Ahmad, then you will be cast in history as a savior." Al-Sherrod smiled with his little, yellow teeth.

But it wasn't about punctuating his place in history, he thought. It was about shining in the eyes of his God.

In silence they watched the tablets of the Ten Commandments returned, the lid resettled. The Ark was now ready as it sat within its nimbus of light, its glow moving, living, writhing, taking on a life of its own.

"So how will you introduce it to the infidels?" asked al-Sherrod. "Now that Umar is no longer the instrument to perform such duties."

"I have contacted an Islamic cleric respected by all religious and political authorities," he answered. "He is a man who believes that Islamic teachings should be taught by way of peace rather than jihad— a true pacifist. I told him that the true Ark of the Covenant was a negotiable item and will be granted as a relic to be shared and cherished by all, should he follow certain guidelines."

"And how will that benefit us? We agreed that Vatican City would serve as Ground Zero. Placing it within the authority of Muslim cleric will serve us no purpose."

Al-Ghazi raised a hand and patted the air, the gesture telling al-Sherrod to 'hold on.' "The Ark is also symbolic to the Jews regarding their Exodus from Egypt under Pharaoh's rule and Moses' journey to Mount Sinai, where the commandments were created by the 'finger' of God. This segues into the interest of the Catholics, who use these commandments as the governing laws of their religion."

Al-Sherrod waited.

"Should the good cleric want to lay his eyes upon the Ark,"

continued al-Ghazi, "then he is bound to share the Ark in good faith with all denominations that hold a related interest and share in its opening. The Jews. The Muslims. The Catholics—everyone."

"And he is in full agreement?"

"He is a pacifist who is naïve and believes that such a venture is warranted in promoting goodwill between the faiths. He sees this as an opportunity to show the world that the Muslim approach to religion is truly the path of goodness and peace." Al-Ghazi walked to the Ark and placed a palm against its gold shell, his face a blend of yellow and gold within its glow. "I have set the parameters," he went on dispassionately, "by telling him that if this was truly his goal, then he needs to display the Ark at a site for all to share with religious and political dignitaries in attendance."

Al-Sherrod continued to remain silent as al-Ghazi stepped away from the Ark.

Al-Ghazi faced him. "This cleric doesn't even know that I'm setting him up as the vehicle to achieve the means," he said. "By offering the Ark to promote goodwill on his behalf, he is duty-bound to adhere to my negotiations without the dignitaries knowing that I am the one calling the shots. The cleric is merely voicing my demands through his proxy."

"And he complies with this?"

Al-Ghazi nodded. "Unwittingly for him, yes. He is negotiating with the Zionist and Catholic factions as we speak. The terms are as follows: The Ark of the Covenant will be shared by all under mutual authority for the opening to be held at Vatican City, and then summarily thereafter transported to a neutral site, which we're indicating to be Switzerland. He will receive the Ark by way of Jordan so that it will not be traced back to us."

"And these factions readily agreed for the viewing to be held at Vatican City?"

"Not by the Muslim and Jewish constituency, of course. But the supporting argument was that there were no neutral grounds in Israel for Muslims and no neutral lands in the Arab states for Jews. Vatican City, however, provided neutrality for all religions without fear of retaliation."

Al-Sherrod smiled; the man was impressed. "This cleric, he is esteemed, yes?"

"Very. He is known to be a gentle soul of great faith who is unwilling to raise a hand in the name of jihad. Everybody knows this. But he will get the job done by my direction not knowing that he is partaking in jihad, nonetheless."

They looked at the Ark, realizing that Sakharov's demons were ready to be released.

"You know they will open the Ark and examine it to make sure there is nothing amiss," said al-Sherrod.

"They will find nothing," returned al-Ghazi. "The composite of the flat box is undetectable, as is the false bottom. Their dogs, their Geiger counters, their electromagnetic meters, or biological detection systems will detect nothing until it's too late." For the first time, al-Ghazi smiled.

Sakharov's technology in its whole was the perfect killing machine.

And in his mind's eye, he could see himself pump his fist in victory. *Allahu Akbar*!


**When the set** up of the Ark was completed, once the gears were set in motion, al-Ghazi chose his team wisely.

He had chosen a team of four; all committed to the service of Allah, all claiming to be equally at peace with surrendering their lives without further consideration. They had been warriors in past skirmishes—whether it was on the front lines during the Iranian war, or later finding service with al-Qaeda after freelance fighting. Either way, they were highly skilled in combat techniques.

Inside his office which overlooked the dust-laden air of busy Tehran streets, al-Ghazi briefed his team, who were sitting wherever a seat was available.

"You are al-Qaeda," he told them. It was the way he started every briefing, always reminding those as to who and what they were, soldiers of war. "You have been given a wonderful opportunity for martyrdom," he said. "A wonderful opportunity."

And then al-Ghazi assigned them their duties in explicit detail from their arrival in Vatican City to the final moment of their lives. Sayyid, the most experienced in computer technology, was assigned to be the trigger man to initiate the program that stimulated the bots. The other three would act as buffers keeping anyone from getting close.

They would go in silently, set up a station where the frequency from Sayyid's could be engaged, and set the nanobots alight. All he needed was thirty seconds.

*Thirty . . . seconds.*

Should security attempt to stop them, then they would come up against the buffers.

Reaching into the drawer of his desk, al-Ghazi removed a brand-new laptop and slid it across the desk toward Sayyid. "There's a program embedded in that computer as an encrypted cipher," he told him. "It's encrypted to ensure that the data on board will not be appropriated from outside sources, should you be compromised. You will commit to memory a series of commands that will enable you to decipher and initiate the process. On the final command, a series of speakers within the flat box will set off sound waves that will stimulate the bots. Only you will have this information, Sayyid, and no one else. Not even your team." He fell back into his seat, looking casual. "Do you have any questions?"

"None, al-Ghazi." Sayyid took the laptop and ran his fingertips over the smooth cover, a seemingly loving caress.

"Then Allah will favor you all and Paradise will be yours," he said. And then: "*Allahu Akbar!*"

In unison from his team: "*Allahu Akbar!*"

# CHAPTER FORTY-ONE

*Vatican City, Inside the Papal Chamber*

Father Auciello slid the dossier of Imam Qusim Abul, a Muslim leader who was respected and revered by the Islamic community.

Pope Pius opened the folder. The picture that stared back at him was an aged man who could have been anywhere from his early seventies to late eighties, given the deep-set wrinkles that lined his face, the vestiges of hard living. His beard was long, tapered, and fashioned from minute loops of curly hair.

"Qusim Abul," said Auciello. "He's a respected leader of the Islamic faith who just happens to be in the alleged possession of the Ark of the Covenant. But he's not saying how he came into its possession. But that he's amenable to sharing in its glory with all faiths as a promotion of goodwill."

Bonasero mulled this over as he stared at the photo. Carefully, he placed the photo down on the desktop. "He has no explanation at all?"

"None that he's willing to offer," he returned. "He's deflecting. But he's standing firm about the Ark being shared by all at the moment of its opening."

"Can he be trusted?"

"Absolutely," he said. "He's a true imam who is frustrated with extremists and abhors violence or anything regarding a jihad."

Bonasero nodded. "True Muslims are pacifists," he said. "Violence is not even a consideration with them."

"He's reached out to all political and religious leaders for a Summit to be held at Vatican City," said Auciello.

"Which raises suspicions," returned Bonasero. "But he is a respected imam."

"He's claiming valid points as to why it should be held here."

"Namely?"

"He wants to maintain a safe haven for Jews and Muslims," he answered. "His points are that there are no real sites of neutrality in any of the Arab or Israeli states since prejudices continue to run high and guarantees for safety cannot be assured. Right now, the Vatican appears to be the likeliest location where multiple denominations can gather in relative safety. For this to happen, however, the imam is requesting that the Ark be placed at a neutral site after the Summit, so that everybody can share in its wealth without one religion maintaining dominion over the relic. Right now, Switzerland is being bandied about as the state of neutrality."

"It would be a masterful showing of goodwill between the religions," he said. "Perhaps this is the beginning of true healing."

"The imam bears no ill will."

The pontiff thought this over. "Of course, we'll have to open the Ark," he said. "At least to make sure that it bears nothing of ill-intent—that being germ, biological, or radioactive. Everything needs to be thoroughly examined."

"We have scholars, scientists, and historians waiting in the wings," Auciello told him.

"Then make it happen," he said firmly. "I'll contact Kimball and advise him to set up an elite security line surrounding the dignitaries. In the meantime, contact the imam and set up delivery in Rome per my instructions. The Ark will be sent to the lab and examined in a controlled environment to ensure that it's sanitized. It should take about a week. During that time, I want the bishops of the Holy See to extend a hand to all clerics of the Islamic, Hebrew, and Catholic faiths. And to formally invite all the political principals willing to attend the Ark's revealing. Such a promotion between the denominations will only serve as a message that the religions may not be so different after all."

After Father Auciello left the pontiff's chamber, Bonasero sat alone, musing over the fact that everything looked fine on the surface but not so in his heart. True, the imam was a man of devout faith whose conviction was geared toward sanctity and peace. But on the flip side, Bonasero referred to his instincts and sensed that something was slightly amiss, perhaps an inborn caution.

Though the display of the Ark was too good to pass up, Bonasero would maintain prudence by having it thoroughly examined, at least giving him some control over its introduction. He would then request that the Ark be sealed and placed within a controlled environment prior to transport, and then sequestered upon its arrival in Rome where it would be scientifically examined.

Being in such an advantageous position, Bonasero Vessucci saw the glory of the Summit. But he also saw a side that could become the critical mass of pure darkness in which the intentional good behind the unveiling held nothing but the absence of light.

Picking up the phone, Pope Pius called Kimball Hayden.

# CHAPTER FORTY-TWO

*Vatican City, Two Days Later*

Upon the clandestine arrival of the Ark in Rome by way of Jordan, a massive security detail made up of the Italian Polizia Municipale and Vatican Security—who in essence were Vatican Knights in security dress—arrived with a hermetically sealed container. The crate was boarded up so that the Polizia Municipale could not see the relic within. They only knew that the item was to be guarded during its transport to the Micron Environmental Laboratory in Rome, where it was to undergo the most advanced technological examination.

The Micron Laboratory was a building that was glass with concrete walkways and manicured landscaping. In the lower tiers below ground, laboratories with state-of-the-art equipment filled a particular chamber where the platform rose approximately a foot off the floor. The surface of the platform was entirely constructed of solid glass that served as the lens of an x-ray machine. Its purpose was to scan the entire object from underneath. There were also diagnostic imaging machines with robotic arms that moved swiftly from one spot to another on command, snapping photos as it circled the Ark. Imaging scanners were used, emitting doses of radiation to clarify certain aspects of the artifact. Viral scans, infrared technology, and bio checks looking for biochemical fingerprints were also utilized. Geiger counters measuring radioactive traces other than the doses proffered by the imaging scanners were sought for. Swabs of the Ark's shell were taken, looking for biological or chemical attachments.

Over the past few days, tests were conducted repeatedly in search of anomalous readings. But the findings were consistent and nothing out of the ordinary was found.

The Ark was completely sanitized.

The only anomaly, at least according to scripture, was that the Ark appeared to contain the tablets of the Ten Commandments and nothing more. Missing was the staff of Aaron and the golden bowl of manna.

After the fifth day of continuous testing with negative results, the Vatican was informed of its findings.

Bonasero Vessucci had set his reservations aside and invited the Ark to be transported to the Basilica, where it would be displayed behind cordoned-off partitions until its unveiling before the congregation of VIPs in front of the Papal Altar.

On the sixth day, it was crated and transported to the Basilica, where it was placed in the *Cathedra Petri* behind partitioned walls. The security was immense.

Inside the *Cathedra Petri*, Bonasero stood before the Ark in paralytic awe, realizing that what he felt was novel. The Ark held something wonderfully golden in its existence, something tangible and intangible at the same time. It was the feeling of true serenity, the feeling of seeing the advent of His true Light. In homage he placed his hands on the Ark and closed his eyes, almost expecting to see or feel something spectacular.

Kimball stood behind him, watching, seeing the Ark as nothing but a container encrusted with gold.

"Isn't it wonderful, Kimball? Can you feel it?"

"Feel what?"

Bonasero stood back with eyes filled with adoration. "It's realness," he said. Kimball laid a hand on the Ark but couldn't sense or feel what it was that Bonasero was experiencing. "Uh, well, not really," he said.

Bonasero smiled. In his heart, he knew it to be real. And for his hands to touch the Ark, he considered, was a gift from God.

"Tomorrow," said Bonasero, "world dignitaries will arrive. Are we prepared to ensure their safety for the unveiling on the day after?"

Kimball nodded. "The Polizia Municipale will be posted at the outskirts of Vatican City," he told him. "The Swiss Guard will be positioned at all entrances, and Vatican Security will float around the city in plain clothes looking for anyone on the grid who may appear suspicious. The Vatican Knights will remain ready to be dispatched to problem spots, should they arise."

Bonasero nodded.

Everything appeared to be in place.

**The very moment** Kimball and Bonasero Vessucci stood inside the Papal Altar and the *Baldacchino*, Sayyid and his team entered Rome and took residence in one of the hotels. The four men shared a two-bedroom suite that overlooked the ruins of Augustus's palace.

Sayyid sat on the balcony, a beautiful day with a clear blue sky, his laptop on the table before him, tapping away. He pulled up the rune-like encryptions, deciphered the instructions, and committed them to memory. Without running the actual program, he used the instructions to run facsimiles and engaged in false scenarios that enabled the bots to initiate. He did this several times until the process became a habit, with his fingers and mind exercising the procedure so that the real program could be set off through muscle and finger memory within seconds. It was like a pianist perfecting the craft of learning a musical score until every chord was perfected.

After painstaking hours, after the once blue sky began to evolve into sunset blends of reds and yellows and oranges, he closed the lid.

He was ready.

And in less than twenty-four hours he and his team would be in Paradise while the infidels burned in the pits of Hell.

*Allahu Akbar*!

# CHAPTER FORTY-THREE

*Vatican City, The Day Before the Unveiling*

Sayyid left the hotel with two of his guards and the laptop, which always seemed affixed to his hand, and headed to a café less than a quarter of a mile from their stay. They maintained an upbeat tempo, their voyage to Allah getting closer with every passing moment, which caught the attention of two Polizia Municipale, who were informed to profile anyone of Mid-East origin within earshot of the Vatican.

Pictures were taken and questions were asked at the hotel's front desk.

One officer learned that there were four registrants in total, all arriving the day before and paying for the suite with euros, a red flag. The clerk was then directed by the investigating officer to keep things under wraps without explanation as to why. He simply did what he was told with no questions asked.

Inside the café, where Sayyid and his team had been followed by two plain-clothed members of the Polizia Municipale, photos were taken under covert conditions and then forwarded electronically to Operations, where they were scanned with facial recognition software.

Of the three men under surveillance two were on the Watch List, the third remained unknown, and the fourth had yet to be seen.

And then the joviality stopped, Sayyid's team getting to their feet and quickly exiting the café. The two Polizia Municipale followed, reaching the sidewalk in time to see the men round the bend of an alleyway.

They followed.

As they rounded the corner the men were gone, which was impossible since the stretch of the alley was at least seventy meters in length. They should have been less than halfway down the corridor, the Arabs within sight.

But they weren't.

The two Polizia Municipale picked up their pace into a slow jog to catch up.

Less than halfway down an Arab slid out from behind a Dumpster and slashed his blade across the throat of the first officer, the Polizia Municipale going to his knees with his hands clutching his throat, blood pulsating through the gaps of his fingers, his ever-widening eyes staring disbelievingly into open space, the man surprised at his mortality as his life rushed out of him.

The second officer fumbled for his weapon. But one of Sayyid's teammates came up from behind, crooked a forearm around the man's throat, pulled the officer close, and stabbed him repeatedly, thrust after thrust, the knife mincing the man's innards.

As both officers lay dead Sayyid stood over them, his jaw working.

They had seen the officers inside the café. And Sayyid saw one take a photo with a hidden assemblage, dooming their fate.

Al-Ghazi would not be pleased since they had been ordered to lay low, he knew that. And now they had been compromised.

"We must return to the hotel and get Shareed," said Sayyid. "It appears that Arabs are being profiled."

They raced back to the hotel.


**The two Polizia** Municipale were off the communications grid without explanation until a backup team found their bodies in an alleyway, the lead Polizia Municipale describing their current state as 'butchery.'

This galvanized additional forces to invade the hotel and kick in the door, the elite team of specialty officers holding their weapons forward as they breached the suite, yelling introductions as to who they were and further instructed for whoever was in the suite to 'hit the floor.'

Shareed's response was to return fire with his firearm, which invited a volley of gunshots that chopped and destroyed the wall leading to the bedroom of the suite where Shareed was taking refuge.

When Shared exhausted his clip he closed his eyes, prayed to Allah, ran to the balcony, and launched himself over the side with his arms pinwheeling until he hit the pavement below.

From a distance, Sayyid and his team watched Shareed's descent.

Heard the body hit. They were now a team of three.

Plans would have to be altered.

With the laptop firmly within Sayyid's grasp, the entire team disappeared within the gathering masses.


**Pope Pius had** learned through the SIV that a terrorist faction had checked into a Rome hotel on the previous day. During a Polizia Municipale sweep two officers were killed, but not until they were able to help identify members of the cell.

Why the cell was in Rome was still up for speculation. But Bonasero knew better. The timing was too coincidental, he thought. There was no doubt that the unveiling somehow played a role in their plans.

Leaning forward, Father Auciello slid a series of photos across the papal desk toward Bonasero. Kimball sat next to the Jesuit, taking everything in.

"These were taken by the officers at a café in Rome," he said. "Facial recognition software quickly deciphered as to who these men were."

Bonasero examined the photos. And then he looked at additional pictures of the men taken from the Watch-List Base.

"The main character is Sayyid Bashir," said the Jesuit, "a former militant with ties to extremely violent regimes in the Middle East. The others have minimal history but are linked to al-Qaeda and presumed to have been involved with factions in Afghanistan and Iraq during Iraq's transitional period to a democratic state."

"So, the question begs to be asked: Why are they here?"

"There was nothing in their suite providing any clues or indications. The suite was sterile," he said. "However, in this photo," Auciello flipped through the glossies on the pope's desk and placed his finger on one in particular. It was a photo of Sayyid and his laptop. "You can see that Sayyid is in possession of a laptop. He took the laptop with him but didn't use it. And that leads us to believe that whatever mission they're on is on that computer."

"And do we know the location of Sayyid and his team?"

"They're nowhere to be found."

Bonasero stared at the photos. "Do you believe that the imam is involved in this?"

Auciello nodded. "No, Bonasero, not at all. And that's why we can't afford to make the wrong speculations at this time."

"Two policemen lay a dead and a man deemed to be a terrorist also lies dead—throwing himself off a balcony to protect a secret. There is no other rational explanation."

Auciello had to agree. And so did Kimball.

"The Polizia Municipale have done their job," said Bonasero. "Now we must follow through and do ours since political and religious dignitaries have arrived for tomorrow's unveiling, and we must protect them at all costs. But tell me this Father Auciello, how do we know that there isn't another cell involved in this matter?"

"We don't. But the Polizia Municipale and Italian Intelligence are all over this. So far: nothing."

The pope pushed the photos toward Kimball. "The Ark is sanitized, that much we know," he said. "The unveiling will go on as scheduled since there is no absolute indication as to the intent of this cell. Since they have been compromised, then their mission may have been aborted, if they had a mission devised at all. Nevertheless . . ." His words trailed as he pointed to the pictures. And then to Kimball, who grabbed the glossies. "Commit those faces to memory, just in case," he said. "Make sure every Vatican Knight, every Swiss Guard, and everyone within Vatican Security learns every line on those faces. Should they attempt to cross into Vatican City, then they are to be arrested and held accordingly. Since the unveiling is to be held in the Basilica to a selected few, I want insurances provided that these men will not be within the vicinity of the Church or the dignitaries. Nevertheless, I want all corridors thoroughly inspected for explosive devices or anything anomalous. Search the old tunnels. I want every possible access into Vatican City gone over with a fine-toothed comb. Employ whatever means necessary to protect this city up until the last possible moment."

Kimball was looking at the photos, already committing the faces to memory.

"This event will go on as scheduled," added Bonasero, but his tone seemed to be wilting. "And the doors leading into the Basilica will be locked. We will be protected."

But a thought occurred to him: *Do you honestly believe that, Bonasero?*

The pope labored to his feet and went to the balcony that

overlooked the City. People were there about by the thousands.

And then that thought flashed through his mind once again, adamant for a response: *Do you honestly believe that?*

Bonasero, however, could not bring himself to answer.

**Sayyid prayed with** the laptop beside him. The death of Shareed mattered little. He still had his team intact. But that didn't detract from the situation that his mission had been made more difficult. Obviously, the Italian authorities had been directed to provide security and intel prior to their arrival, which was to be expected. What wasn't expected was to be placed in a position of compromise, for which they now found themselves.

"Nothing has changed," he said out loud and to no one in particular.

Sayyid stood over the rim of a bathtub, the laptop on the toilet seat beside him as he shaved in preparation for Paradise. His team would follow by shaving, and then cleanse themselves with rose water, a form of purification.

Their beards would be gone, and their faces would be different. And by wearing Polizia Municipale uniforms recently purchased through the underground, they had allowed themselves the advantage of hiding in plain sight to those looking for insurgents in plain dress, rather than those wearing official attire.

What was more advantageous was that he wouldn't have to enter Vatican City, as long as he was able to situate himself somewhere along the fringe of the city's border and keep the Basilica within sight. Frequencies, after all, traveled through space. But the laptop's range was limited.

After Shareed's dying plunge, Sayyid and his team did some recon, finding the rooftop of a hotel across from the Vatican Museum a suitable observation post to initiate the nano program. Although the hotel was located within 400 meters of the Basilica, it was still beyond the city's border and beyond Vatican jurisdiction. But with such a clear view of the heart of the Catholic Church, there was no doubt in Sayyid's mind that snipers would be posted there. But his team was adept at killing. And with little or no contest they would take them out quickly, quietly, and with flawless execution.

Yes, he thought, Shareed's death posed no threat to the mission at all. His death proved insignificant in the scheme of things since there was, after all, a solution to everything.

Tomorrow he would enter Paradise along with his teammates. And Vatican City all but destroyed.

Beneath the soft glow of a single light bulb, Sayyid continued to bathe and purify himself with the laptop by his side.

# CHAPTER FORTY-FOUR

*Vatican City, The Day of the Unveiling*

The day was a glorious one with scarce cloud cover and a bright sun. Throngs of people filled St. Peter's Square, a sea of heads bobbing and weaving to get a better look at the doors leading into the Basilica, which were closed.

Wading through the masses looking for suspicious activity wearing plain clothes was the Vatican Security Team, who maintained constant contact with the SIV, who in turn were in contact with Kimball Hayden. The Polizia Municipale maintained the lines at the city's borders. And Italy's elite police squads and sniper units held positional vantage points on rooftops and elevated posts that overlooked the Square.

All teams fell under the same umbrella of communiqué with the SIV Command Post, which was manned by Farther Auciello and his team of Jesuits. Should a team fail to forward their rendezvous code by radio every five minutes, Auciello would then communicate to Kimball of team failure, requiring possible backup from the Vatican Knights.

Before the papal altar inside the Basilica, dignitaries from all over the world—political and religious—ranging from presidents to vice presidents to prime ministers, most notably Vice President John Phippen of the United States and Prime Minister Cameron from Great Britain, along with world leaders from Europe and South America, religious icons ranging from Imam Qusim Abul to the elite rabbi faction of Israel, who sat with the Catholic representative of the pontiff, Pope Pius XIV, with each man each lending a hand of friendship to the other, biases and prejudices forgotten.

Sitting before the altar covered with a scarlet fabric with scalloped hemline draped over it sat the crate containing the Ark of the Covenant.

Voices rose in anticipation.

And Bonasero Vessucci couldn't have been more pleased. Not so much with the unveiling of the Ark, but of the congregation of people from all walks of life with different beliefs and agendas who came together under the banner of friendship and peace. The smiles, the acceptances, and tolerances of one another, were completely genuine.

The pope excused himself and went to the rear of the Basilica where Kimball and his team manned the monitors from the *Baldacchino*, out of sight. They were in full gear, however, wearing the clerics' shirts, Roman Catholic collar, military boots, and pants.

"The unveiling is going to happen in fifteen minutes," the pope told him. "Are there any issues thus far?"

Kimball nodded. "Everything appears copasetic," he told him. "All teams are communicating. Other than a few skirmishes breaking out in the square from people jockeying for position to get a better view of the Basilica, everything looks fine."

"That's what I want to hear."

Kimball shot him a thumbs-up. "Everything's going to be OK, Bonasero. Everything's going to be fine."


**Sayyid and his** two brothers of Jihad stood in front of the Vatican Museum wearing Polizia Municipale uniforms. Across the *Viale Vaticano* was the hotel of their choice to set up shop. From where they stood, they could see a sniper and his teammate, which wasn't surprising since the observation post gave a direct view of the Basilica.

Since they were on the city's border and the masses were inside the square hoping to catch a glimpse of the holy relic, the street was marginally deserted. Yet Sayyid and his team lay low and close to the shadows. More so, they had shaved. And by wearing the uniforms of the Italian police, they appeared less like their photos from the Watch List.

Sayyid turned to his teammates, the laptop in his hand but within a soft case, and said, "You know what to do," he told them. "Make it happen."

The two men walked across the street and entered the hotel.

**The two Arabs** entered the hotel's lobby and were greeted by the clerk, who raised his hands in gesticulation informing them that the upper levels of the hotel were off-limits until after the Ark's unveiling, even to the Polizia Municipale.

One of the Arab's closed in and leaned against the desk. "Is that so?" he said in fluent Italian.

"I'm afraid the upper levels are cordoned off by Special Forces."

"Special Forces? How many?"

"Four."

*Four.* It was more than they had anticipated.

"Thank you," he said. And then he removed a pistol with a suppressor from under his jacket and shot the clerk in the head, a hole magically appearing between the man's eyes as he fell dead behind the counter.

The two men then began to climb the steps.


**Two officers of** Italy's elite NAS police team stood post at the top of the stairwell that led to the roof. As one of Sayyid's teammates took the steps, he was halted by one of the officers who raised a hand to stop the Arab from taking another step.

"Stop right there," he ordered. "I'm afraid the upper levels are off-limits for another hour or two."

"But I am from the Polizia Municipale—"

"I'm afraid the upper levels are off-limits," he repeated sternly. "Even to the Polizia Municipale."

"I see."

The Arab turned and began to descend. And then he stopped on a lower step before facing the officer once again. "You are NAS, yes?"

"Please move along, Officer. I won't ask you again." By this time, the second NAS officer joined his teammate, a small assault weapon in his hands.

*Two on the roof, two in the hallway leading to the roof, for a total of four,* considered the Arab. The entire NAS team was accounted for.

The Arab smiled. Neither officer held the point of his weapon at him, but downward, an act of complacency.

"For elite soldiers," the Arab said, still smiling, "you never would have made my team."

The Arab stepped aside, allowing the second Arab to round the bend of the stairwell, his pistol already drawn, the point of the laser light finding its mark of the first officer. *Tap! Tap!* Two shots to the man's throat, throwing wads of meat and gristle into the background, the officer falling backward to the floor, eyes already at half-mast, his life extinguished as he landed hard on the floor.

The second target was bringing up his weapon, fast, the mouth of the barrel rising, rising. *Tap! Tap!* Two more shots, loud spits in quick succession through the suppressor as the bullets scored, shearing off the left side of the officer's head as blood, gore, and gray matter marked the wall next to him in a macabre Pollock design.

The Arabs raced up the stairs, their guns ready.


**Sayyid checked his** watch. There were thirteen minutes left for the unveiling, give another five to lift the lid from the Ark, a total of eighteen minutes.

He checked his watch. His team had already been in the hotel for two minutes and the sniper team was still manning their posts.

*What's taking them so long?*

There were twelve minutes left.


**The NAS sniper** examined the grounds surrounding the Basilica through the lens of his Leupold scope, the crosshairs bouncing from person to person in St. Peters Square. Everything appeared fine.

His NAS partner stood looking through binoculars. In his ear was a communication bud. Every five minutes he reported his call sign, which was 'Kill Shot One-O-One.' He checked his watch. He had two minutes to go before calling in his sign to SIV.


**The two Arabs** were quiet when they opened the door leading to the roof, the sunlight slanting into the stairwell as the door slowly opened, the beam getting wider.

They moved softly and quietly, their guns holding steady.

Footfall after footfall, with the gravel beneath their feet failing to yield a noise, they neared the NAS team.

The Arab on the left aimed his weapon, the red dot finding the base of the skull of the sniper and pulled the trigger. The officer snapped backward with his spine arching and the point of his rifle aiming upward. And then he fell back onto the roof, and hard, with the rifle skating freely across the gravel.

The second NAS officer stood in awe, his mind not appearing to register the moment or the reality of his partner's death. He was unarmed, the binocular in his hands a useless weapon.

"Come here," said the Arab, beckoning the man closer with his free hand, the pistol in the other. "I won't hurt you."

The NAS officer maintained a nonplussed look, noting their uniforms. And then a revelation that was horribly dark and ugly struck him like a hammer blow. "Please," he said, raising his hands slowly, "I have three children."

Once the NAS officer moved away from the edge, the Arab shot him in the forehead.

They then went to the rail overlooking the Vatican Museum. Sayyid was still standing where they left him and then waved him up.

After looking both ways along the *Vaile Vaticano*, Sayyid crossed the street.


**Two minutes passed** and Father Auciello did not hear from 'Kill Shot One-O-One.' He allowed another minute to lapse before calling the team.

"Kill Shot One-O-One, this is Command Center. Do you read me?"

Silence.

Then: "Kill Shot One-O-One, this is Command Center. Do you read me?"

Still no answer other than the white noise that continued to sound over the speakers, an obvious red flag since NAS was impeccably anal about communication protocol.

"Kill Shot One-O-One, this is Command Center. Are you reading me? Come in, Kill Shot One-O-One"

When there was no answer Father Auciello contacted Kimball inside the Basilica. "Kimball."

"*Yeah.*"

"We're not getting a response from Kill Shot One-O-One."

"*What's their twenty?*"

"The rooftop of the hotel across the street from the Vatican

255

Museum."

*"Copy that. Any teams in the area?"*

"Negative. They're 400 meters out and on the borderline of VC. They're looking for suspicious activity of vehicles, such as vans and trucks taking the *Vaile Vaticano* when the street has been restricted."

"Copy that."

"I hope everything's Code Five."

*"I'm sure it is. Out."*


**Sayyid stood at** the rail overlooking the street and the front of the museum across the way and then stared at the magnificent structure of the Basilica's dome. He saw the people standing about the square, noted that the doors leading to the Basilica were closed and locked, a force of Swiss Guards maintaining vigilance at the gates.

The good thing about nanotechnology, he thought, was that it did not possess any smell or emit radiation, hold any biological or chemical traces, or tip its hand that it even existed at all until it was too late. It was the perfect weapon of non-detection. And it didn't matter if they were behind closed doors. Frequencies were capable of passing through walls and windows, at least enough to stimulate the bots into action. So, by locking the doors of the Basilica, they have all but sealed their own fate.

And the fate of those within the plaza was just as bleak, the openings beneath the locked doors of the Basilica causeways for the bots to enter the open forum of St. Peters Square.

Sayyid removed the laptop from his padded case and placed it on the flat part of the railing. He then lifted the lid and booted up, the laptop whirring to life.

"I want one downstairs manning the lobby," he told them. "I don't care which one. You decide. The other I want to man the top of the stairway and to make sure that no one gets by, should the man in the lobby fail to hold back the infidels."

One of the Arabs stepped forward, waving the point of his weapon at the Basilica. "It's quite a way," he commented. "Perhaps we're too far from the bots when they escape, yes? Perhaps we have a chance?"

Sayyid nodded. "They will last long enough to enter parts of Rome. Still, we will be too close."

The Arab seemed disappointed in this, which was indicated by his weapon hand falling to his side.

"You are disappointed?" asked Sayyid.

"I was just wondering," he answered.

"Then wonder no more," he told him harshly. "You have chosen to martyr yourself. Do you think Allah will favor a man who is second-guessing his decision?"

"No, Sayyid."

"Then get below and prepare yourself for Glory," he said. He looked at his watch. "In less than fifteen minutes you will be in Paradise."

"Yes, Sayyid."

The terrorist was gone.


**Moments before the** unveiling Kimball called upon a bishop to have Bonasero Vessucci return to the *Baldacchino*.

"I got a call from SIV," he told the pope; there was a slight urgency in his tone. "It appears that a NAS team has not responded according to protocol, so I'm heading to their position with Leviticus and Isaiah."

"We're moments away from the unveiling, Kimball."

"I know that. But I'd rather be safe than sorry."

"Where?"

"They're on a rooftop directly across from the Vatican Museum."

"That's quite a way off."

"But still within sniper range."

"But the dignitaries are inside."

"Who's to say that they're the targets? If someone is there, perhaps they have another agenda."

"Please be careful," he returned.

"I plan to." Kimball removed his earbuds and motioned to Leviticus and Isaiah to follow. The good thing about Kill Shot's position was that it was opposite the square and through Vatican grounds, where the public was not allowed. It was nothing but open fields, gardens, and walkways a straight and unimpeded path. They would be there within minutes.


**When Pius returned** to the dignitaries he did so as the emcee. He stood next to the guarded crate, a hand on the fabric.


257

Looking over the audience and seeing the almost child-like anticipation they harbored, he waited no longer. With the aid of accompanying bishops, he removed the fabric and pulled it away from a Plexiglas enclosure.

The Ark of the Covenant, even in its casing, glowed with such radiance it was almost too much to believe or comprehend that gold could cast such light. It was astounding, the ethereal glow reaching outward as if trying to touch the audience, to accept them within the warmth of its magnificent aura.

The dignitaries stood in paralytic awe with their mouths extended. From some, tears slipped from the corners of their eyes with the moment overwhelming.

"What I show you," began Bonasero, "is more than the true Ark of the Covenant. What I offer you is the beginning of the healing process where all religions, all faiths, and all denominations can share and enjoy the true meaning this relic provides to all of us."

The Plexiglas was then removed with great effort, allowing the Ark to stand alone before the Basilica's altar. Dignitaries and religious leaders bandied around, touching it, bathing in its glory, its aura, swearing upon their souls that they could feel an indescribable elation. More people wept, including political principals suddenly enlightened by their misguided values, hoping that God would forgive them for their wayward follies. For some, this was an epiphany. For others, it was an awakening that the power of the Ark was real and beyond anything manmade.

There was no doubt that this was the true Ark of the Covenant.

The imam was the first to inquire. "And when can we open the lid, Your Holiness?"

Pope Pius returned the imam's smile with his own. "Now," he said. "We can open the lid now." With a motion of his hand, he gestured for the bishops to carefully lift the lid and set it aside, which they did.

When the seat of the Ark was carefully placed down, the masses crept forward for a view of what lies within.

The first word that was spoken: *Amazing.*


**Kimball, Leviticus, and** Isaiah hastened across the grounds and sighted the back of the museum. When they reached the *Viale Vaticano*, they remained hidden behind the concrete columns until they could verify Kill Shot's team and move forward.

The street was quiet. Even from this distance, they could hear the cheers of the crowd.

The team could see a single man standing at the edge of the hotel's railing working a laptop. No one else was in sight.

"Is that NAS?" asked Leviticus.

Kimball held his hand out to Leviticus. "Got a scope?"

"No, but Isaiah does."

Isaiah handed Kimball a long monocular, which Kimball used to zoom in on the man at the railing. It was the man he had seen in the photos. Although he was clean-shaven, he had no doubt that it was Sayyid. He handed the monocular back.

"Kill Shot's dead," he told them lightly. "That's Sayyid, which means his two goons are somewhere close. One in the lobby, for sure. Maybe both." Kimball handed the scope back to Isaiah. "Sayyid's wearing a police uniform," he added, "which is how they got by. I'm sure the others are doing the same, so make positive confirmation before you engage them."

"And the laptop?"

Kimball nodded. It could have been used for anything. "Maybe to set off an explosive somewhere." When he said this, it sounded more like a question than a statement.

"We checked everywhere, Kimball, with bomb-sniffing dogs and tech devices. There's nothing out there."

"What about the nanotechnology?" asked Isaiah.

Kimball shook his head again. "The Ark is clean. The entire city has been swept numerous times."

"Maybe the Ark is a deterrent to throw us off from what they're planning to do. Obviously, they're here for a reason."

Kimball's glanced at his watch. According to the schedule, the lid of the Ark had been removed. And then he returned his gaze to the terrorist. "I'd say we go ask Sayyid and find out. What do you think?"

Both men concurred with 'hoo-rahs.'

"All right then: Ready up."

They were going in cold and without firearms. But they checked their blades. Each man had two combat knives, very sharp, very deadly, and precisely balanced for throw shots.

"Leviticus, Isaiah, go in the back. I'll take the front and draw their fire. And be quick," he added. "I'm not too crazy about going to a gunfight with a knife."

"Don't worry about us," said Isaiah. "You just keep your head down."

They looked up at Sayyid, who seemed to be lost in whatever he was doing.

"Then let's move," said Kimball.

The team began to maneuver into position.


**The man in** the lobby thought he saw movement, a vague shadow passing quickly across the frosted-stain glass of the front door, then gone.

The Arab took position behind the clerk's desk, taking careful aim with his firearm in a two-handed stance. The clerk was lying dead at his feet, staring at the ceiling, his eyes beginning to glaze over with the milky sheen of blindness.

In a fluid motion the door swung open and someone, or something, tumbled into the lobby and took refuge behind a low-level wall that was waist high and topped with vases containing fresh-cut roses.

The Arab fired his weapon in quick succession. The suppressor muting the rapid sounds of fire as the doors shattered into tempered chips of glass, the bullets stitching across the low wall, taking out the vases, rose petals flying everywhere in a riot of colors. Plumes of dust and drywall erupted as the bullets decimated the wall, the assassin hoping to find his mark.

When he emptied the clip, he deftly loaded another, took aim, and waited.

The lobby was quiet.

His target stilled.

The Arab moved away from his post and stepped over the clerk with his pistol drawn in front of him, a keen eye holding steady as to what lies beyond the wall, with his trigger finger applying four of the five pounds of pressure necessary to discharge his weapon.

He stepped forward, cautiously, the point of his gun leading the way, the wall getting closer.

An image appeared.

Kimball lay on his back as the haze of the drywall began to settle, his black uniform becoming laden with dust.

The assassin smiled and raised his weapon. *"Allahu Ak—"*

The Arab's eyes went wide, his mouth opening, and then he fell to his knees, his eyes then rolling upward, and then fell forward, hard, the man taking the teeth-first approach with a knife sticking out at the base of his skull.

Kimball gained his feet and attempted to brush away the dust with futile swipes of his hands. "You were cutting it close," he said. "Too close."

"Had to make sure my aim was true," said Isaiah. He removed the knife from the Arab, the blade extracting wetly, and wiped it clean across the Arab's clothing.

"Eyes peeled," whispered Kimball, pointing to the stairwell. "Now we have to work our way up." And moving up was never easy, the advantage always belonging to those who maintain the high ground.

Kimball, grabbing the assassin's gun, and then extracting the clip and checking to see if it was full, reseated it.

The Knights moved forward.


**There was no** mistaking that the lobby had been breached, thought the Arab who maintained the upper level. With the two NAS officers lying dead at his feet, he stacked one on top of the other to provide a marginal barrier as he hunkered behind them. If his teammate didn't stop the incoming wave, then it was up to him to impede them long enough for Sayyid to complete the mission.

There was an unsettling quiet, a disconcerting hush.

He wanted to call out his comrade's name but didn't want to give his position away.

He held the pistol firmly within his grip, using the bodies of the NAS officers to steady his aim.

The stairway was quiet.

And sweat was beginning to surface on the Arab's brow, causing him to sweep his arm across his forehead.

The air was stifling, and the minutes seemed to drag on for hours, the Arab wondering if Sayyid had tooled the laptop to initiate the program.

He looked at his watch. His heart palpitating. Giving his life to Allah was not as spectacular as he thought it would be. The act of martyrdom was overrated, he considered, the thought of Paradise no longer alluring.

He wanted to run, to live. His mind raced feverishly like a desperate animal trapped against the corner of two walls with nowhere to go, nowhere to hide, his killer edging closer with the intent to kill, emblazoned in his eyes.

Although his killer went unseen, he could sense him coming closer.

He swallowed, looked at his watch. Sweat was coursing profusely along his face. And then self-preservation took over. The Arab stood, yelled, his eyes going feral, and descended the steps shooting blindly at the shadows, at anything that appeared to move, striking nothing but wall, pocking them. When his clip emptied, he fumbled to seat another, the time wasted a fatal one. A bullet found its mark, a shot to the center of body mass, rupturing the man's heart.

The Arab fell like a stone, dead the instant his knees began to buckle and before falling down the stairwell in a tumble.

Leviticus took the man's weapon, grabbed the remaining clip, seated it, and along with Kimball and Isaiah, climbed the last leg of the staircase.


**Sayyid was unaware** of what had taken place inside the hotel since the weapons were geared with suppressors. But he was not totally without the perception that the hotel had been breached since he saw glimpses of shadows attempting to maneuver across the *Viale Vaticano* in a clandestine manner. It was like sighting something at the edge of his periphery vision, but not quite seeing it in its totality.

But it was there no matter how obscure it may have appeared.

He ratcheted up his agenda, his fingers dancing, typing, the encrypted runes becoming letters, the letters becoming commands, the commands initiating the program.

He typed faster, sensing that he was not alone. Something was coming closer—up on his backside.

"Stop right there, Sayyid."

The Arab stared at the monitor. His mission was all but complete. The encryptions were completely deciphered, the program waiting to be initialized with a single push of the ENTER button. His finger hovered over the key and hung there.

"I'm afraid that you are too late," he said. "What will be, will be. And there's nothing you can do to stop this from happening."

"It will if I put a bullet in your brain."

This time the voice sounded nearer, which meant to Sayyid that they were edging closer to his position. So, he slowly lowered his finger, but not touching down.

"If you take another step, I will initiate the program. I may not have eyes in the back of my head, but my hearing is exceptional." The Arab turned to face his attackers. He noted the odd configuration of uniform; saw the black clerics' shirts and Roman Catholic collars, the incongruous combination of military wear, and the attached sheaths with combat knives.

"You are not Swiss Guard or Vatican Security, are you?"

They said nothing, their weapons poised.

"Step away from the computer," said Kimball. "It's not our intention to harm you."

The Arab chortled. "I have already resigned to my fate and gladly offer my life in the name of Allah," he said. The tip of his finger now touched the button. "Should you fire off your weapon, then I will push this button simply by knee-jerk reaction."

Kimball aimed the firearm at the man's head.

And the Arab saw the directed aim. "Headshot or not, my body will react all the same."

Kimball drew in a breath. The Arab was right.

So, in a quick and fluid motion, Kimball directed his aim and shot the computer.

Unfortunately, his aim was not true.


**Sayyid saw the** quickness of Kimball's motion and immediately realized his intention. The Arab quickly shifted his footing, his body acting as a shield as he turned into the bullet's path, taking the strike, the computer untouched as the bullet entered his body and ricocheted until it lodged in his lung, causing considerable damage but not the killing blow.

Before falling to his knees, Sayyid depressed the button.


**Kimball had taken** the gamble and lost.

Stepping to the laptop, he watched the commands on the screen scroll downward.

And then he leaned over Sayyid, grabbed him roughly by the collar, and yanked the man so close that their faces were inches apart. "What have you initiated?" he asked fiercely. "What have you done?"

The Arab laughed. And when he did so blood bubbles formed and burst at the corners of his lips. "You'll find out within minutes," he told him. "Within . . . minutes."

And then his head fell back, slowly, his eyes growing vacant as his life left him.

When Sayyid was dead Kimball released him, and then looked over the railing at the Basilica with grave concern.

*What have I done?*


**The mood inside** the Basilica was a festive one. The Ten Commandments sat inside the Ark, two bullet-shaped tablets with engravings detailing the laws brought down from Mount Sinai by Moses.

People heralded the Ark, the tablets, defining this moment as a great time in history for all of mankind.

People banded about, smiling, Arabs and Jews and Catholics becoming a unit of one. Politicians had their spirits lifted, willing to take back with them what they had seen and felt, the goodness of overwhelming light and indescribable being, and then to share it amongst their constituencies.

And then the joviality came to a resounding halt, smiles withering, ears perking to the sound of something alien.

From the depths of the Ark came the resonance of a hum, low at first, but growing in volume like the nest of agitated wasps ready to take flight.

People backed away.

The waspy hum grew louder.

And then there were cries of pain and fear and the misunderstanding of what was happening.

Their skin begins to itch and turn red, like the beginnings of a rash, their flesh being needled as pinprick bites began to take their toll.

Outside the Basilica doors, no one could hear their screams.


**"Leviticus, do something!"**

Leviticus was a computer expert and hacking his forte. Decoding and deciphering runes, symbols and encryptions was his specialty. His skills were surpassed by a few.

He grabbed the laptop, noted the scrolling symbols, and began to type in his set of commands.

From a distance of 400 meters, they heard something quite odd. Coming from Vatican City was the unmistakable sound of a waspy hum that grew with every passing moment.

"Hurry up, Leviticus. We're running out of time."

He typed furiously. The symbols continued to scroll.

The hum got louder.


**There was nowhere** to run, nowhere to hide. The dignitaries ran to the nearest exits in self-preservation, their flesh now burning as beads of blood began to surface. They battered frantically at something they could not see, slapping their bodies, their faces, rashes now becoming open wounds, bleeding.

And Bonasero was no different. He was human and life to him was precious. More so, he was still a creature and as all creatures do, took flight as his skin began to be eaten away, his mind going into flight syndrome. But his humanity also kicked in, directing others to the rear of the Basilica in a futile attempt to get away.

More cries. More screams. The church filling up with anguished shouts.

And then he gave in to his fate, the pope falling to his knees, his garments becoming bloodied.

And he prayed to God.


**Leviticus typed quickly**, his fingers not missing a required key. And then he hit the ENTER button.

They watched the screen as the symbols stopped scrolling. A moment later the monitor winked off, and then on, a new series of commands taking place, scrolling.

Leviticus had powered down Sayyid's programming with one of his own.

But the hum continued.

And Kimball thought of one thing and one thing only: *We're too late.*

**As Pope Pius** lay there with his skin on fire, he was cognizant enough to realize that the hum was quickly dissipating. And he chalked this up to his soul departing and leaving the corporeal world behind. The sound, the sensations, everything in life was leeching from his body.

But when the sound faded, he opened his eyes and looked at the Papal Altar. People lay about while some belly crawled to nowhere in particular, whereas others struggled to their feet. Everyone was bloodied. And to Bonasero it looked like something apocalyptic, the survivors lost and in ruins, as they wandered about with no aim or direction, just . . . walking.

Reaching down to whatever reserve he had, Bonasero gained his feet, wobbled until the dizziness faded, and began to help others.

What had been a blessing had turned into a nightmare, he thought, turning towards the Ark. Even after all that happened, it continued to maintain its extraordinary luminosity.

He looked upward at the stained glass, at the images, and then looked at the statues of Christ, and then at Michelangelo's *Pieta*. The Church was unharmed.

What happened was inconceivable.

But they were alive.

And for that he was grateful.


**Kimball and his** team did not waste any time. They raced back to the Basilica, went in the back way where they ended up by the *Baldacchino*, and summarily headed into the main area of the Basilica.

The people appeared war-torn and far worse than those in regions where the Vatican Knights performed rescue duties by saving the lives of Third-World refugees. These people looked like they had battled for their lives, their bodies bloodied.

Kimball stepped forward, helping and aiding those in need.

And then seeing Bonasero he went to his aid, making sure that the pontiff took to the floor and rested.

Kimball knelt beside him, a hand on Bonasero's back to keep him in a seated position. "Are you all right?" he asked with concern.

"I'm fine," he answered almost breathlessly. "The others?"

"Battered, bloodied, but nothing life-threatening."

The pontiff forced a smile. "That's good," he said. And then: "What happened?"

"It was Sayyid," he told him. "He and his team were here. They've been neutralized."

The pontiff seemed to understand this and nothing more needed to be said or asked. Kimball had come through, his team of Vatican Knights defusing the situation like so many times before. They upheld the sovereignty of the Church, its interests, and the welfare of its citizenry. They had saved the lives of those who couldn't save their own.

"Please," said the pontiff, pointing to the dignitaries, "help the others."

And Kimball did.

# CHAPTER FORTY-FIVE

*Tehran, Iran*

Al-Ghazi was livid to the point where he smashed valuable items within his office. His team had failed. His reputation in the eyes of his supreme leader all but lost.

He sat at his desk running his fingers through his hair.

At least he had the disc. He could start over. He could revamp a team and create what Sakharov had perfected.

He went to his wall-safe and opened it. Other than a firearm and a few American dollars, which he pocketed, he grabbed the disc and held it up toward the light, watching the iridescent waves cross over the disc's surface. He then placed the disc inside the inner pocket of his sport jacket and turned to leave Tehran for the last time.

Only he was not alone.

Two men stood in the doorway.

"And who may you be?" he demanded.

The men looked impassive and remained unmoving.

This was not good.

Al-Ghazi stood tall, showing an air of defiance and bravado. "Who gave you the right to enter my office unannounced?"

"I did," said the man on the left. The man then produced a weapon with a suppressor as long as the pistol's barrel and aimed it at al-Ghazi.

Al-Ghazi blanched.

In an act of self-preservation, he raised a hand as if to stay the oncoming shots. But it didn't. His fingers took flight as the bullets smashed through his feeble defense and into his face, killing him.

The operatives stood over his body with one man holstering his firearm as al-Sherrod entered the office, the man smiling with his yellow teeth. When he leaned down and reached inside al-Ghazi's jacket, he removed the disc.

Al-Ghazi had served his purpose, he considered. And now the data regarding Sakharov's findings were solely in the hands of Iranian authority.

Ahmadinejad would be pleased.

# CHAPTER FORTY-SIX

*Rome, Italy, Gemelli Polyclinic*

Pope Pius XIV lay in bed at the Gemelli Polyclinic in Rome recuperating. Although he tried to put on an air of good spirits, Kimball knew better as he sat beside the pontiff's bed.

The news media hit the nail on the head and cited the incident as an act of terrorism. Whereas the religious dignitaries wanted to believe in the more mythological aspects that it was an intervention of a spiritual kind, dark or otherwise, the political principals were more down to earth and believed that the Ark was tainted with some kind of bacterial, chemical, or airborne virus that was unleashed.

Al-Qaeda took the blame and proudly, letting the world know that this was the beginning of the end of all infidels, even though they were not apprised of al-Ghazi's death, and therefore without Sakharov's data to move forward. Nevertheless, it was still a scary proclamation. But there was no information by the media regarding the truth behind what happened—that it was nanotechnology and not the chemical, bacterial, or virus scenario that it was made out to be. The truth was far more dangerous. Far more terrifying.

"Nanotechnology," commented the pope. "It can be used for good applications. But it can also be used for wrong purposes as well."

The pontiff looked at Kimball; the man's face was blotchy and scabbed, like a bad case of shingles. The rest of his body didn't fare well either. It was completely bandaged. Nor was he alone. All the dignitaries suffered from the same maladies but were guaranteed that they would be going home shortly since there would be no lingering effects.

Kimball leaned forward. "The SIV has learned that al-Ghazi was assassinated in Tehran," he told him. "They believe by Iranian

270

Intelligence. But nothing is confirmed. Sakharov remains missing but presumed dead, which wipes out any connection or ties to al-Qaeda. We believe that Iran maintains Sakharov's findings, which, in the long run, could prove costly to the safety and welfare of nations across the world."

The pontiff focused his sight on the ceiling. "Not a good scenario," he commented.

Kimball sat in his seat.

And Bonasero sighed. "It was a good notion," he finally said, "to have the Ark serve in a capacity to bring us all together, only to cause doubts in the end. A shame. The imam, the rabbis in attendance, all the political dignitaries wanted to believe that it was something magical when the magic was in their hearts all along. And now it's gone."

"Perhaps not," said Kimball.

But the pontiff knew better as he lay there, staring.

"The new secretary of state," he finally began, "how is he doing during my absence?"

"Cardinal Estanzio is performing quite well," said Kimball. "But he's no Bonasero Vessucci."

This drew a genuine smile from the pontiff's face.

"And please tell me, whatever happened to Cardinal Angullo?"

The pontiff's smile broadened. He just couldn't help himself. "Let's just say that he's probably enjoying a dish of Dim Sum right about now."

Kimball didn't know what he was talking about.

*Beijing, China*

Cardinal Giuseppe Angullo, now Cardinal Bishop Angullo, was given the vacant position to serve as leader of the Beijing Diocese. Although he served a Catholic citizenry of 2.8% of the city's population, it still amounted to more than 30,000 people.

He sat in a spartan office overlooking the city. Some days it was beautiful. On others it was dirty and smog-ridden, the masses of people intolerable. Worse, he found it difficult to learn the language, his mind unwilling to focus or care.

He then came to the bitter conclusion that he had lost his ambition, and with it his faith.

And that Bonasero Vessucci, he considered, was right after all: He

271

had lost his way.

Staring out the window with the city of Beijing in view, with a blanket of smog descending upon the masses, he sighed, resigning himself to his fate of a man who had paved a road closer to Hell than to Heaven.

# EPILOGUE

*Geneva, Switzerland, The Museum of the arts d'Extrême-Orient*

While Kimball stayed behind with the pontiff, Leviticus and Isaiah acted on behalf of the Vatican working as emissaries, making sure that the Ark of the Covenant was properly situated according to the Imam's agreement.

After the debacle inside the Basilica, the Ark was immediately transported back to the Micron Laboratory where the false bottom was located, and the composite removed. The Ark then went through more rigorous examinations, the results negative. But to be accepted by the Museum of the arts d'Extrême-Orient, certain precautions had to be taken.

The Ark was hermetically sealed in a thick Plexiglas container, which meant that oxygen was pumped out and argon gas pumped in. Once the lab gave the clearance that the Ark no longer posed a threat and was thoroughly sealed, only then was it accepted.

The trip was by plane. And the Ark had been placed in a grand-size showroom as the focal point of all the ancient pieces exhibited.

In its casing it showed magnificently, its gold aura expanding in its purest form. And despite what happened in the Basilica, people from all over the world visited the museum and swore that they could feel enlightenment within its presence, an uplifting, and a sense of goodness that overshadowed anything else.

Others felt nothing at all, saying that those who experienced anything at all did so only because they wanted to believe that the Ark was something mythical, and provided solace when solace was nothing more than a state of mind, to begin with.

But Leviticus and Isaiah knew better as they stood there in suit and tie, feeling something over and above solace. It was absolute peace.

Once the Ark was in place, after they had been shown the state-of-the-art security system that was unsurpassable, they left Switzerland and returned to the Vatican, knowing that Kimball would be standing on the tarmac ready to brief them on their next mission.

**THE END**

Printed in Great Britain
by Amazon

21477799R00159